Effra
A Novel

GREG ROUGHAN

GREG ROUGHAN

FOR MY FAMILY

Who encourage me to write (and enjoy a good story).
For Rebecca, my most patient reader.
And to all the others who've guided
me along the way.

CONTENTS

ACKNOWLEDGMENTS

Cover illustrations by Link Choi. Instagram: @tigerbuttercup

The poem, Eurydice, on page 67 is reproduced here with permission
from Sue Hubbard - a freelance, London-based art critic, fiction writer
and award-winning poet. The Poetry Society's only Public Art Poet she
was commissioned to create Eurydice especially for the underpass at Waterloo
by the Arts Council and the BFI in 2000. It was restored
by public subscription in 2011. It has been the subject of two films
and read on BBC Radio 4's Poetry Please and is published in her
collection Ghost Station from Salt publishing. www.suehubbard.com
.

1 AUGUST

You can't look back - that's what I've finally understood. To falter is to break the spell. Look behind you in a moment of doubt, and what you want so desperately will fade before your eyes. You can't look back.

"Finn?"

The wobble in his voice brings me back to the now. How strange to hear Kip so unsure. His face is white and frightened in the glare from the torch. I take a step away from him.

"Will this close the deal?" I call down the long cavern, and my voice echoes back from the sewer's curving roof. Waves are foaming on the surface of the water and there's a fresh smell of rain.

"Is it enough!"

Enough, enough. The current tugs urgently at my waist. Kip is spluttering, struggling to keep his head clear.

"Of course it is!" he brays desperately, as if answering for them both. "Please. *Please* just do it!"

I swing the bolt-cutters.

2 JUNE

"It has always been said that enchantment is bought
in the burying alive of great waters, yet
the purchase may be a perilous one."

- Peter Ackroyd, *London: The Biography*

At five o'clock the air-conditioning shudders to a stop. A sound you've heard all day - a loud sound that you've never registered - is suddenly conspicuous by its absence. People lift their heads from cubicles and look around at the silence. It makes me wonder what else I put up with without noticing. It makes all the others say stupid things:

"Home time!"

"Outta here."

"I'll see YOU chaps Monday."

For once I log off and shut down, flick my coat off the hook and get out before everyone else.

I take the back stairs, hurrying down with feet a blur. It's more controlled fall than safe descent. Partly because I need to get to the mailroom before Brian leaves; partly for the pleasure of it.

Brian's the mail manager. I knock on his door - a half door, one with a top hatch that opens, while the bottom half stays shut - and he eventually shuffles into view. Mail managers are tyrants. They get away with murder, probably really with murder, and hold everyone to ransom. Brian's a surly old git with dirty hair and track pants tucked into work boots. I keep on his good side. I think he likes me because I'm quiet.

"Hey."

"Alright. You want them boxes."

"Thanks Brian."

Brian, bless him, wouldn't have the faintest clue what goes on in my head.

"Wait here."

"Cheers..."

And he shuffles off.

I swear those blue track pants are part of some kind of company uniform. How does our company have a blue track pants uniform?

He gets my boxes, the sum total of my life so far, and stacks them on a trundler. Then he wheels them outside and, without saying a word, stacks them in three piles against the wall - three boxes, two and then one. I must have got him on a good day.

"Thanks Brian."

"Alright."

"Could I use your phone?" He jerks his head back towards his office.

I go in and call a taxi from his desk then head back outside, sit on a box and close my eyes against the afternoon sun.

Just nine months in London and already I guard these moments carefully - the times between time when you're not tied to some task. When you can step out of the churn and rebuild some of the barriers that the city erodes. Sometimes people think I'm cold - I'm sure they do. But really it's the outside world that's cold, and the more I keep it at arm's length, the more I feel whole.

The taxi pulls up.

In the back of the cab I fish a piece of paper from my pocket with my new address and phone number on it. Number nine, Effra mansions, SW2 - with an 0207 number. You've got a lot of codes, London, but these are the simplest. SW for southwest; 0207 for inner city.

We're halfway across the river, on Blackfriars bridge, and I lean across the box that's wedged against my knees to take a look. He's running full - a great thick artery, swollen with refuse from the city's many veins - all being flushed out to sea a few miles further east.

We leave the bridge and weave down a confusing network of roads in South London. Eventually we find Kennington Road with its tall plane trees clattering their leaves in the heat - a reminder of when this was an elegant town, before it was swallowed whole by London's sprawl - then we hit Clapham Road where the traffic seizes up, until fifteen stop-start minutes later I'm hauling my boxes on to the pavement outside my new home.

The driver gets out to pop the boot and retrieve the rest of my gear - there's always that moment with an unlicensed cab where you worry they'll drive off, steal your stuff, and leave you stupid on the side of the road - but of course he unloads it, and I pay his fifteen quid.

He drives away. I turn to look at the green peeling door. A train rumbles by, somewhere near. I lean forward and ring the bell at Effra Mansions.

"Hey hello mate."

My new flatmate is walking up to the door with his keys in hand, looking breezy in a red shirt, and carrying some kind of out-sized designer's satchel.

"Oh hi, um, Heinrich. Good timing."

"National characteristic" he says dryly, a faint hint of German accent coming through. "And Henry's just fine. Come on in," and he unlocks the door with practiced ease. I notice when he swings it open that there are gouge marks from it being crowbarred at some point.

"Would you like a hand with those?"

Ah, thanks Henry. But I'm alright."

"Okay. See you upstairs."

He heads up – and I spend the next ten minutes lugging boxes up the stairwell. Jogging back down after each load, half expecting the remainder to have been nicked off the road. Once they're indoors I find my bare room at the end of the hall and stack the boxes into a pile in the middle. My shirt's damp and my hair's clammy after all the carrying, so I stop for a moment, lean against the wall and take in my room.

There's a tap, tap on the open door – Henry, doing the friendly flatty thing.

"Easy move?"

He leans his shoulder on the jamb, bending his head to look at the room; respecting my space.

"Very. But I'm stalled at the unpacking stage. I could go Spartan for a while. Live from my boxes. What do you think?"

We look at the six pathetic cardboard oblongs on the floor, huddled like abandoned dogs in a pound, and he laughs.

"Listen, we're heading out a bit later - a friend of Jane's is having a party - do you want to have a Friday drink and come with us?

So of course my first reaction is to say no, to stay here in this new room. But I look at Henry in the doorway in his smart red shirt, then back inside. There's a crappy single bed, a square window that looks out through the branches of a tree, a bare bulb, and not much else. Jane and Phil - the house couple - are visible down the hall, sitting in the lounge watching TV.

Unpacking these boxes is suddenly a dreary prospect. And the idea of a beer is appealing.

"Okay" I say, smiling with teeth. "That would be cool".

***

I got kicked out of my last flat because I don't sleep well. It wasn't my finest moment. But I *don't* sleep well. I never have.

It feels too much like giving up. I knew this guy at university, over-muscled freak that he was, who couldn't bring himself to send in papers electronically. What got him was having to click the button on the web page that said "submit". Said his Dad had told him to never submit, and now he couldn't bring himself to do it.

I'm not like that. That guy was a bundle of nerves who couldn't reprogramme his brain for normal life. But there *is* something about letting myself fall into sleep that's creepy. I always feel like a kid who's fallen into a swimming hole and can't make it back up the bank. Sure, maybe if you let go and drift downstream you'll come to a place where you can get out. The problem is you don't know what's out there, so I find myself clinging to the tree roots at the edge for as long as I can.

You have to sleep though. I know what happens if you don't - it doesn't work. So I try to keep my mind occupied while it happens, just so I don't watch myself as I go under. Because I find it a bit creepy, is all.

Usually I spend my evening doing things to avoid thinking about work. If I'm home early, often I'll just cook a meal then hang out in my room, but as the evening gets on I start to develop a slight dread of bed. I'll pace around and do the dishes at 11 o'clock, or watch bad TV until I reach my TV threshold, then watch some more - anything to avoid that moment where you have to lie still, waiting as your brain shuts down. I've never been a good sleeper. Though I found a way to drop off really quickly a while back. I did it for about four months – right up until two weeks ago. I won't be doing it any more.

It started when I was working on a big project. My first big project in my London job and it had gotten to the stage where I realised there was more work than I could do - inside normal hours at least. On the other hand there was no one else who could do it either. Well, maybe there was - the honest truth is I couldn't bear explaining to someone else what needed doing. To get sign-off for help I'd have to go high-up - probably to that old prick Whiting - and he would have sat there looking down his nose at me, pretending to understand what I was on about while I explained how I'd let things slip. Then I'd have to explain it all again to whichever lackey got drafted in from another project to help me - and all that time the work would be building up and up...

Basically I couldn't stand the idea of going for help and tried to do it all myself.

And I guess I started feeling pretty trapped. I was sleeping badly; to the point where it began to snowball. If I had a bad night I couldn't focus during the day, and the work would pile up. So I'd stay late to try to get through it, and get caught up all over again.

So I got home one night, late on a Thursday. I'd finished work just before the off license closed and had bought a sandwich, eating it as I walked home, hunched against the wind - then topped it off with a vitamin pill when I got there. Normally I would sit around with a beer to unwind by the TV, but I didn't feel like it that night. The flatmates weren't in or had gone to bed, and it all seemed too quiet - the wind outside was thrashing the branches of a tree in front of a street light which was sending these queasy patterns lurching around the room, and it didn't feel a nice place to be. Not when I was feeling sorry for myself and all - so I took to my room and lay down on top of the covers. After a while I got up and got my dictaphone and started making notes for myself for work.

I just talked to myself in a low monotone about all the things that were left to do tomorrow and what order to do them in. It was kind of a relief. I started to go into more detail and by the time I'd gone over everything I felt exhausted, sleepy. It could have taken me hours to get to that state, but there I was. So I just shut my eyes and drifted off, the white-noise hiss of the tape like a lullaby.

Then just as I was drifting down, feeling relaxed - at peace and pretty deep - an idea popped into my head. It was a work idea; something startling and original. A solution to some of the grueling, error-prone tasks I'd been stretching myself to focus on - and it seemed so simple. An unusual, upside-down, back-to-front approach for the job I'd been stuck on for weeks. I was too dozy to be excited. I just intoned the idea on to the tape, and that was it: I plummeted into sleep so deep I didn't dream.

When I woke I couldn't believe how refreshed I felt. The tape recorder was lying next to me on the sheet where it had slipped from my hand, but I left it there until I'd gotten up and had a shower and breakfast - a fried one because I was feeling so good, and was up early for once; deliberately leaving the tape for a while, like forcing yourself to be nonchalant about gifts on Christmas morning. Then I made sure I had ten minutes before I needed to leave the house and sat down with the recorder. Played it back. Walked briskly to work, put my idea - *the* idea - into action and made my working life for the next two weeks a much easier thing. I think even Whiting got wind of what I did and was impressed.

Every night from then on, I went to sleep with the recorder, and every morning I played back what I'd mumble as my brain drifted into that free state before sleep took over. Half the time it was pretty useful stuff. Never really any ideas as blinding as the first, but it got to how I wouldn't bother thinking about things at work any more - just got on with putting tasks into action during the day, and trusted myself to work out any issues in the few minutes before bed. I tried not to think about the dead tone in my voice, or how it strange it felt to hear yourself say things you didn't remember saying. But I got a lot of work done. And I slept better than I had for years.

I don't do that now though.

A fortnight ago I woke up feeling pretty good, despite having been out the night before watching football and drinking lager until closing time, and leaned over the edge of the bed to get the dictaphone from where it had fallen on the floor. It was one of those old-style ones with a little cassette inside that I'd had since I was a kid; I'd wrapped it in green electrician's tape a few days back to help it take the knocks when I realised I'd been dropping it out of bed.

I wound the tape to the start and left it on the ground, while I lay face-down and snoozy on the mattress above, drooling a bit on to the sheets. I could hear my voice going over a few things, and I was only half listening - there was nothing spectacular; nothing I couldn't have worked out simply myself in my waking life. My voice mumbled less and less coherently and then stopped. The tape hissed on. I think I drifted off. Until suddenly my voice came through crisp and loud. I woke with a start.

"You think they want you here Finn? You don't belong. They hate you living here! Get out before they make you leave."

The last bit was spat out in defiance and spite. My own voice, but not mine - and louder, clearer, than the tape had ever been before. I felt sick, panicky; it was nothing I'd remembered saying. The tape clicked to an end. I must have been dozing for the last fifteen minutes at least - which means I'd slept that night for quarter of an hour before something in me woke up and said those things.

In retrospect I wasn't as shocked by what the tape had said as I should have been. It was weird and I felt freaked out by the event, but what I didn't do was question what I'd said. I got up, didn't shower, went to work and buried myself.

That night I made myself listen to the tape right through. There was nothing else in the silent fifteen minutes before the end, but when I heard myself again it was horrible. There's something terrible in not recognising your own voice. If anything, I felt worse than I had that morning, and I was still caught up in my head about it as I left my room for the loo and ran straight into my flatmate Shelley as she stepped from the shower, wrapped round in blue fluffy towels.

I was startled. I must have looked it. Something sick was clawing in my stomach and all I could do was stand there like a rabbit in the headlights, blocking the corridor.

"What's up?" she asked, short of anything else to do bar pushing past me. "Are you okay?"

And I snapped. I don't remember what I did. I screamed.

I screamed at her, bug-eyed in the corridor, the veins in my neck straining, yelling "Don't touch me! Don't touch me!" red faced, at the top of my lungs. It was her turn to be shocked. She couldn't get out of the corridor, the bathroom behind her was the only place to go - she must have felt terrible. I don't think she knew what to do. And I just stood there, screaming. I don't know what it was.

The next morning James and Karen told me to come to a flat meeting, and kicked me out. I never saw any of them again.

***

Henry knocks on the door. "Hey mate," he says from outside. "We'll be off in the next ten minutes."

"Alright, cheers" I say, all bright and over-loud. Which means, shit, I've really got to get moving. And get some clothes on - I'm still in my work stuff. Looks like I'm heading out without food inside, too.

The box with my clothes is at the top of the stack. It takes a bit of attacking with my keys before the sticky tape gives way, but I manage to fish out some gears. Crumpled jeans, blue trainers - and if I'm going out to a strange party, then I'm wearing my favourite t-shirt , no questions, and no matter that it's fusty from two wears and being stuffed in a box - what's spray deodorant for, right? It's a shower in a can. Five minutes later no one would know I was an itinerant software engineer come straight from work.

Mind you no-one would tell much about me - I put a lot of effort into being bland. Brown hair and thin, with clothes neither too dull nor too bright. The less curiosity the world has about me, the better.

With a feeling of trepidation I push open the door to introduce myself to the rest of the flat.

Their heads come up in unison when I walk in the room. Already the moment's ritualistic. Jane actually gets out of her seat and Phil, left sitting among three people standing, gets to his feet too.

"Hi!" says Jane with a bright smile. "Welcome to the Effra!"

"Thanks"

She pushes her hands in her pockets and stands to the side, still with a smile. At least she's not going to shake.

Phil's a different story; seems reserved. He leans across with his hand and I stretch forward and shake it. We're like climbers reaching across a crevasse.

"Alright."

"Hi."

"Cheers."

I think I like him.

Hell, I've got low standards in flatmates. I'm hardly the outgoing type. And I've learned that when it comes to house-sharing with strangers, adequate is best. I've seen a decade's worth of flatmates fix an evening meal, mumble a few words, then slink off to their own rooms to eat in front of private televisions. Felt the vague sense of relief as their doors clanked shut.

Phil seems an unapologetic slinker. Yet there's something likeable about him. I hope Jane's not this friendly all the time.

We all stand around with hands in our pockets. German Henry - who I'm seeing now is the flat Dad - lifts his tanned face to ours.

"Shall we get our move on? We can go down to the offie and get some beer. Where do you say this place is Jane?"

And this could be much worse. He clearly knows exactly where the party is, but perhaps Henry's a facilitator, not a dominator. Someone who lets other people make the things happen that he wants done. There's always one person in a household who has the urge to be head ape, but yeah, I reckon you could do a lot worse than this guy.

"Alright, let's boost" says Phil in his drawn-out Northern accent, and:

"... uh-huh, it's just around the corner from the off-license" Jane says. "We can walk from there, to be sure".

Yeah, this could be worse. I think I'll get that beer.

***

It's that time of evening when day makes its slow summer transition into night. The London twilight gathers around the bin bags and the buildings, but the sky is light and the clouds still catch the sun. Jane is up ahead with Henry while Phil and I troop behind. The four of us are wearing scuffed trainers. Surely a sign of something.

"What do you do Phil?"

"I'm a brickie."

"Oh right. Is that interesting?"

"No mate. It's putting bricks together."

"Sure. Okay. So where are you working?"

"Up in Highgate."

"Oh that's nice up there huh. Lots of brick places, there right?"

"Oh shitloads mate. That's the thing about bricks. Everywhere. See that building?"

"Uhh - that one?"

"Yep. Bricks. Hundreds"

"Right. *Right...*"

"Everywhere you look"

"Fair enough. And that guy - check him out."

"Him? The big fella?"

"Yeah - well you know. Built like a brick shithouse."

"Oh yeah. You'd never take him on in a dark alley."

"I'd be shitting bricks..."

"...oh you'd have to be thick as a brick..."

And this is stupid. Phil has a laconic Northern drawl that makes everything he says sound ironic.

"Sorry about banging on about work. It's a bad conversation starter huh."

"Naw mate" - that drawl again - "you're alright."

"Didn't want to brick myself into a corner..."

"Oh very good."

"Thanks."

"Don't know whether to offer you bouquets or brick-bats."

"What the *fuck* are you guys on about?" says Henry with a laugh in his voice. We're outside the off-licence.

"He started it" says Phil. "Talking about work" and he walks in and nods at the Pakistani shop-keeper, who's doing his ever-alert, always-harassed and watching-for-trouble look. Three guys and a girl in his shop, going straight for the lager section: high on the potential trouble radar. But: affable northern bloke with a stoop, followed by grinning computer geek, equals no threat to anyone.

We gather a selection of tins and go to the checkout. I'm tempted to hassle Phil for his choice of northern ales, but I don't want to make a dick of myself. He's alright this guy. For a brickie.

We turn off the high street and wind down a confusing series of same-same roads. Black kids sit on identikit front steps, or wobble on oversized bikes surrounded by shouting brothers and sisters. We cut through quieter and quieter lanes. It's empty here, no shops no nothing, and the dimming light down on the street makes the sky above look luminous and pale. Phil's face is a thumbnail and Jane and Henry's white heels flick up in front. I guess we're in Clapham somewhere. Or Brixton. Or Stockwell - but most likely some no-man's land, lost between them.

And then a relief. Like a rosy firelight in a fairy-tale there's a red light shining up ahead through gauzy curtains, picking out the one landmark for miles: a great thick tree on the other side of the road. Plus the sound of music. And voices - and it's kind of reassuring. I didn't know how empty it was out here 'til the silence was broken.

"Right" says Henry, and he seems relieved too, to have found the place. "Who knows these people?"

"I guess I do" says Jane with a reluctant smile - and hell, it's good to know these people are nervous too; that I'm not the only one here out on a limb - then the door swings open with a noisy spill of light and sound and someone says "...*Dave*" and people come out, and we go in, and the door clicks shut behind us.

The corridor's rammed. The whole place is crammed. The game becomes twisting into gaps and shuffling feet to get anywhere. There's no way anyone's walking directly forward, shoulders wide. Jane turns side-on ahead of me and squeezes between two blokes. Her boobs squash up against some guy. Not precious. She looks back and smiles and says "right!" and pushes on towards the kitchen. I follow, for want of anything else to do.

We pass the stairway on the right. At the top, a tall, thin trendy with an oddball moustache. Sitting on the steps, level with my head, a girl with a dark tumble of hair and gold sandals, drinking wine from a plastic cup. She squeezes to the side without looking up from her conversation, and through the white wood rails I see Henry's trainers as he heads past her and up, looking purposeful. I presume Phil's following us, but can't see him and now I've got a feeling in my gut of anticipation, a looseness in my belly because this is a random party - not a well-managed gathering of people-who-know-people; a controlled, priss affair - it's no rancid squat nonsense either. It's just a perfect scene. A place where you could get lost and talk to nobody, or get trashed; meet people strange and new. Smoke rollies on a garden seat at five in the morning, or spend a whole night trying to pull that one amazing girl and not mind in the slightest that you had no chance. I swallow down my nerves and reach into the bag to crack the top off a can.

Jane's in the kitchen, leaning with her back to the sink. I push through and she reaches into my carrier bag to fish out a beer. I dump the rest of them on the floor between us and suck the first mouthful of cheap lager from the top of my can. "Right" she says again, and I'm like "right" and it's a "here's to random parties and new flatmates" moment, but we never say it, because she's easy to be comfortable around, Jane. So instead she raises her eyebrows and says loudly "house music!" and I say "horrible!" and that gets the guy next to us in on the talk and kicks off a whole round of nonsense - the passionate, flippant talk you can only have in a kitchen when you've just landed among a bunch of drinking randoms and the sink's already full of ice, and bits of plastic bag, and the pull tab tops from cans - and what's up with me tonight?

Normally, here, I would feel so awkward; static amongst a fluid social world, but tonight I feel a flow in me. I yabber about the awful music - feel drunk without drinking - and it turns out the guy I'm talking to is a friend of the DJ and apparently I need an education about the joys of house music, and boy can this dude go on.

Two cans later I smile at Jane, leaving her with the house aficionado and the mess of ice and the bits of sliced lemon.

I head back into the corridor and snoop around. A door to the side opens on to the living room, but it's dull in there, despite the noise. Phil's sidled up to the DJ, chatting and leafing through his records; two girls are dancing badly and the rest of the room is filled with lasses on couches holding court. I stand in the corner for a while, sipping from my can, but there's nothing here for me and I leave.

The stairs are clear now, so I wander up and lo and behold, the next level's just as rammed as the first. This place must be three stories high, with all the levels part of one place. There's cheap orange carpet on the landing and then a second living room opens off the stairs. No sign of moustache man, but others - lots of others - are milling in the room.

It's different music up here, thank God; people are squabbling over the stereo, putting on their favourite tunes. I wander to the other side of the room and push my head between the gap in the drapes. I *thought* this would look out over the garden. The air on the other side of the thick curtains is cool - cold - refreshing on my red face and it's dark enough in the room to see through. I pull the drapes close around my neck to cut off the reflection and crane forward: garden, abandoned chairs, a single pale tree - birch? - then a puff of breath mists the glass and I pull my head back. Must look like an idiot anyway.

And yeah, someone *is* watching me. There's a girl across the way, standing with a loose group of people, but looking straight at me and there's something funny in the way she's disregarding the people next to her to stare openly at the tit with his head in the drapes. She can see me looking back at her. I guess I'm far enough away that it's not uncomfortable. But I look at something else, look down, have a sip of beer - and when I look back she's still gazing over.

Jesus, what am I supposed to do? I know what I'm *supposed* to do - and my face is halfway to being twisted into an abortive smile when she flicks her gaze at something across the room - watches two girls with great balloon glasses of wine for a bit and then flicks back to someone in her group.

There's something I like about her. The way she seems so disconnected from the people she's with, though she's standing just as close as the rest.

And hang on a minute. Look at this. As I loiter, beer in hand, poster child for solo party blokes the world over I notice the person who's joined her group - and who she's spared her attention for, for a few moments - is none other than House Aficionado Number One.

Bollocks. I put up with him for long enough in the kitchen; he can do me a favour back. I cross the room at an angle to him, kind of half slowly, until he looks up in my direction, then I raise my eyebrows just a little - no smile - in a sparse greeting with "I thought you'd be downstairs on the decks mate?" and that twinge of sarcasm certainly wasn't for his benefit.

"Ahh" he says, and falls into my trap by being the gormless smiler that he was born. He pulls a stupid welcome face. It says "I was blabbing at you ten minutes back, I've forgotten your name and now I'm in a minor panic of friendliness". So I help him out.

"It was Richard, yeah?"

"Yeah, that's right" he says, relieved to be let off the hook.

"And, ahh...?"

"Finn."

"...oh yeah of course. Finn: this is Anne."

Which was sudden. Like the lurch in my stomach when, too soon, I have to turn and look.

"Hi", I venture. Conversational genius.

She's small. Kind of small and a bit freckled. But her eyes are the thing you see - light brown and lively. She presses her lips together in a flat smile and says "Hi" in a little amused voice.

"Who are you?"

"Well... I came with Phil and Jane and..." her eyebrows raise in the tiniest 'I know or care about Phil and Jane, how?' look and the smile turns up at the edges. My explanation wafts away in a limp-wristed wave that says 'Phil and

Jane... out there somewhere...' (and where did Henry get to?)

"So what's out the window?"

"Just the garden." Pause. "I just like the way these gardens all join up. You know - there are those little walls, but all the back gardens join together to make a kind of corridor, parallel to the road, like." And what am I on about? But she smiles.

"A road for something. Foxes probably. Maybe it even has a name."

"Ah, but it would be in fox. We couldn't understand it."

"Have you ever heard a fox?" she says, all suddenly serious. I shake my head.

"Fox sex is the most hideous sound."

Her face is so earnest, it's funny. The perfectly composed mouth, lips set in a forthright statement below that freckled nose. I can't believe we're talking like this.

"Honestly." she says "It's awful. The male has a barbed penis and it hurts them both. They can't let go and she makes this awful, awful sound. I used to think it was vampires when I was a kid. The whole neighbourhood would wake up." Finally she smiles.

I'm grinning too when I realise there's silence behind me. An expectant pause - like when the teacher asked you something at school while you were staring out the window, dreaming. Richard's looking at me.

"Sorry?"

"You know - the most London kind of experience. What do you think Finn? Duncan here's just moved in from Cambridge. Reckons he's battling with the big smoke. What sums it up most for you?"

Oh, thanks Richard. Thank-you you interrupting, house-loving, *dick*. And Duncan - check him out - he looks for all the world like a little Boris Johnson and the cloth-headed twat is smiling at me like we've ever met. From nowhere an image of a steel rod lashed across his big open face flares in front of my eyes.

25

"You know?" he says. "Mean streets of London!"

I almost bark. How the hell did this happen? Would you give a guy a chance? And I'm about to say something smarmy and turn away when a memory pops into my head, unbidden. Duncan's sobbing, broken face fades away to be replaced by bitumen shining black with rain: a dark street, strewn with sodden newspapers. From the corner of my eye I see Anne's face tilt to mine.

"Alright *Duncan*. Maybe you'll like this."

I take a breath.

"It was in Brixton. About six months ago. At New Year's Eve. Everyone had gone home, or was indoors, 6am styles. And it was cold - really cold. Been pissing down most of the night and no one was around.

"You guys have all been to the tube in Brixton? You know what it's like round there. It's the central begging district of London - all those scamsters, desperate bearded Portuguese types, hard-boy yardies and the rest. Well at 6am everyone had cleared out. The lot of them. You wouldn't have seen a fox on the street..."

For Anne's benefit

"...it was so miserable. It was still raining. Bits of fried chicken skin were getting washed off the pavement.

"Well, I say there was no one around, but it turned out there *were* a couple of people. The first guy I come across is this miserable looking dude hunched under the ATM. He's out of the rain - just - but he's wrapped up round himself so tight you can tell he's damned cold and that shitty little bit of cardboard he's sitting on looks pretty wet. Fucking guy, hanging out for the last punter to come home for the night, stop for cash, and be so high on pills he goes 'hey - here - take forty quid, and happy New Year!'

"But you know, it ain't happened, and this guy's clung on to the dream too long, and it's not coming true.

"I'm looking at him as I come up - contemplating him a bit, but just really thinking of getting home, because I'm so tired - when his eyes flick up to mine.

"Busted. You know what I mean. You make eye contact with these guys and you know what's coming next. It sounds pretty hard saying it like this. But, hey. I was tired. I wanted home. And you know, maybe I'm just not a nice person.

"So when he opened his eyes and looked at me, I thought, 'No way.'

"He opened his eyes and opened his gob and says 'got a cigarette, mate?'

"I just about laughed. Poor bastard. I don't smoke. And it was just too easy to say, 'Sorry mate. I don't smoke.' Probably opening up my palms in a big generous gesture - and before he could change tack and just ask for some money, I'd walked past, guilt free - didn't even break stride.

"So there I am, walking down the street on the coldest night of the year, smirking about not giving a homeless guy money, when I come across the only other person out on that freezing God damned night.

"It's up the road a bit, near the Peace Gardens - there's a guy standing in the rain.

"He's just there. Bolt upright with his head back, standing in the middle of the footpath on my side of the road.

"Of course I'm pretty nervous right? A bit, anyway. It's way late, I'm exhausted, and there's no one round for miles. You can hear the rain pattering down and a few sodden blackbirds are trying to make like it's morning and sing - but no way. It's dark and it's freezing. I walk towards him, watching as I come up.

"A couple of feet away I slow down a bit and get a good look.

"He's wasted. I guess he's maybe Spanish, maybe Lebanese or something. Quite well dressed with like a brown leather jacket on and big buckled shoes. You know the sort of thing. And it's probably just the shoes that are keeping him up.

"He's got his head back, eyes closed, and he's swaying ever so slightly on those big bucklers. Fat drops of rain are shaking out of the trees and splatting on his face; his hair's all soaked and the miracle of it all is there's a cigarette still in his mouth, with an inch of ash, burning slowly down.

"I get right up in front of him, and stop.

"And okay, this is a bit weird. I guess *I'm* a bit weird. But I look round to check there's really no-one else, then I lean right in to look. You wouldn't want him to open his eyes, if you know what I mean: I'm inches away. But he's toast. Gone. If it wasn't so wet he'd have been mugged long ago - and probably wouldn't have noticed 'til he woke up the next day. He's been caning it on something, alright - and the cigarette? It hasn't even been sucked - which is when I think 'Fuck it. I'm going to give it to the beggar.'"

There's a ripple of laughs from the group. I realise I've been telling the story with my eyes glazed, lost in picturing the scene. Richard and Duncan have smiles on, engrossed - the other people in the circle are listening too - but really, what am I doing? This isn't me; and suddenly it's hard to talk. I don't look at Anne. It's hard to think of the words when you've got an audience.

"So yeah," I stammer. "Well, yeah... I decided to get the fag..."

And Duncan rescues me with his big eager voice.

"Did he wake up?"

Which is a dumb question. But it makes me bolder hearing him make such a hash of the story and I find my voice again.

"Nope. No, I just stand there for a while, to make sure that he's not going to come to. But apart from the slight sway, he doesn't move, right? So I step up close in front again, with my fingers held like this."

I've got my eyes unfocused again, a smile on, and thumb and forefinger held in front of my face. Part of me is clamouring with fear - why am doing this? I hate attention - but another part sees the face of the wasted clubber in my mind, swaying before me, and thrills to this feeling: the grip of the story.

"He sways back... and forward. Back... and forward. Back... and I move my hand right up to his face.

"Ever-so-gently he sways toward me. The cigarette drifts between my fingers. I close my hand. And there: gently, gently, I've gripped the end of the smoke.

"He sways back. And listen: I swear this is true. For a moment the dry paper of the smoke sticks to his wet lip and holds him. He's leaning back and the whole weight of him is held by this tiny stretch of skin from his mouth. For a moment we freeze there. Me holding the cigarette, the cigarette holding his face. And then - woops - it gives way, there's this tiny little sound and Mr Wasted in the Rain rocks gently away.

"I step back and take a breath.

"And that's about it. Sorry if this is a weird story. You know - you did ask. But I got the cigarette out of his mouth and just stood there for a bit, feeling buzzed. I don't know why I did it. But for some reason I felt like I'd just done the most amazing thing. I turned around and walked back up the road.

"The old homeless guy was still there, dozing with his head down in his knees, so I squatted in front of him and put my arm on his shoulder to give him a gentle shake. I wasn't feeling the cold at all.

"'Hey, mate' I said softly. 'Hey'. He woke up and looked at me. 'Hey. This is for you.' And I'm holding the cigarette up to him, right, with the biggest smile on my face.

"He looks at it - then he looks at me, amazed - totally amazed - and his whole face just crumples into the most venomous, repulsed expression.

"'Fuck!' he says, completely disgusted. '*Fuck*.' There's fucking *spit* on that!"

And everyone laughs. They're all laughing - Duncan in big Boris Johnson guffaws. Funny how I've just made his day. It was such a stupid thing to ask about - but it was just the kind of answer that he wanted. I guess everyone needs to tell myths about themselves, and now he's got one: Duncan of London. He'll think about that one for days. But Anne's gone.

The laughter chuckles down, the moment goes. People turn to talk, murmur to each other. Duncan and Richard seem happy as pie. I turn away from the group, suddenly despondent, and put my mouth to the can. You can taste the metallic edge.

So what was the point of that?

And I'm not feeling so hot for some reason. I cross the room and lean against some drawers.

Yeah, things are starting to seem a little strange.

For some reason I don't like looking at the carpet. Something's making me nauseous. It's like there's too much pattern in it, so I look away.

And something's weird with sound. Everything close by is a rumble - but I swear, the dishes in the kitchen downstairs: I can hear them. Mugs clank as someone rummages for something to drink from; a glass thumps as it's put down on the stainless steel bench - and this is mad, but I *know* it's true: I can hear Henry upstairs. He's talking to someone - someone with an excited, pent up voice - and I hear them clear as day.

Now I'm *really* not feeling good. The carpet lurches up suddenly. The pattern seems huge and vivid. My eyes catch wild sudden gestures in the room - arms flicking up, girls tossing hair. And the tight geometry on the far away wallpaper... God, it's making me ill.

There's something behind me. I reel around, horrified, but it's Anne, standing with a glass in each hand, looking at me funny. I feel I can only see her from the sides of my eyes.

"Let's get out of here," she says.

I'm led down the corridor. Must have come down the stairs. Faces and people blur by, but the only thing that's vivid is the cool hand in mine. In all the confusion I feel I can see it in my mind - pale and dry. It's the only thing that's solid and I focus on it. We go outside. Cold air on my face - and that's solid too. It's quiet. I feel better. Anne's stealing someone else's cab. She bundles me in, taking me to hers.

By the time we pull up at a door, I'm back to being me. Dazed, but hanging in there. Anne pushes my hair back with her hand and gets out.

"You doing better there?"

And I try to say something, but I'm too dazed - so I watch her pay the driver, then find her keys. Then she's taking me in and up some stairs.

Upstairs, inside, she's a different person. Owning the place. She shrugs off her bag, dumps it on a table; everything done quickly. She gets me water and I drink it, looking around stupidly.

Already I'm feeling better than I was when we came in, and when we came in, I was better than before. What wakes me up properly, though, is the lurch in my stomach when I see we're in her room. She puts her hand on my shoulder.

I find my mouth pressed against hers. We tumble and gasp, clumsy hands in her hair. She's forward. Calm, but eager. I go along with everything and find myself undressed before I can think what I'm doing. She strips off - body pale, freckled - and my hungry mouth finds the side of her torso, the edge of her breast marked red from her bra. My hands go to her hips, between her legs and into her wetness. And then I'm coming between her legs. Her on top, hands on either side of my face. Gazing at me.

"Sorry" I say, when I stop breathing in shallow gasps. And she dismisses it with a smile, and a shake of her head, and a warm look.

***

I wake. Very slowly.

An orange blackness behind my eyes is telling me that somewhere out there, outside my closed eyelids, the world is filling with light. I become aware of gentle morning sounds – though something else has woken me.

Something small presses into my shoulder. Presses, then pulls away.

I remember one afternoon in my old flat. I had been doing the dishes. It was summer, the weekend, and I'd been quietly working through the sink full of plates at a dreamy pace. Dreaming was what I was doing – and as I stared out the window, lost in my own thoughts, I vaguely became aware of a scratching on my forearm.

I looked down to see soap bubbles crawling slowly down my skin. And my thoughts were so far away – and the sensation of prickling bubbles so ephemeral – that I remember it seemed to be happening to someone else.

It's like that now. The gentle prodding in my shoulder comes again – for all the world like a cat comfortably flexing its claws in your lap – but I'm so distant, detached, so barely awake, it doesn't seem part of me at all.

Slowly, slowly I surface and open my eyes.

Anne's lying in the crook of my arm, head tucked under my chin. Her left arm is draped across my front and with her thumb and then her finger, she's absentmindedly pressing the flesh on my shoulder and watching the white dimple fill slowly again with red. I shift a little and she looks up at me.

Her eyes kindle into an amused little look - a "what have we done, what have we here?" expression - and she smiles a rueful smile. I think my throat is dry.

"Hi" I manage to croak. And: "Morning."

"Good morning you. How are you feeling?"

"Okay -"

She raises her eyebrows.

"I mean, yes - thank you - good" I say with a lopsided grin. "Um, do you have any water? I'm..."

"Sure thing. Hang on." And she levers off me to reach to a bedside table. Her pale breasts are creased from the crumpled sheets. Full and soft-looking; my stomach goes tight.

"Here you go."

"Thanks." And now I really need it.

The water's a morning blessing. God it feels good and it's hard not to gulp the whole glass, but I pass it back to Anne. She finishes it off, puts it back on the board and turns back to me, sitting up now, sheets bundled about her waist.

"We didn't stay long at the party did we?"

"I wasn't feeling so good," I say. And with a frown: "I don't know what it was."

"You're alright now though?"

"I am. Yes, thank you. And thanks for taking me home. I guess just drinking without dinner didn't help. But hey – your place is really nice."

And it is. I look around her light and airy room and feel it's somewhere I could stay forever. It seems so calm and quiet - though maybe that's post-shag bliss.

"Thanks" she says, and curls back tight into my arm. "It's good. I like it. No flatmates either" - and I can feel her smile against my chin.

"So tell me," she says into my neck, her hand wrapping up around me. "Last night. Those guys Richard and Duncan."

"Uh huh..."

She presses my shoulder again. This time hard.

"Did you know them at all?"

"Nope."

The dimple fills up.

"And you're not from London, are you?"

Shake my head.

"Not really."

"But you live here now."

"Well, yeah" I say with a slight stammer - and just like that it's done. I get a sense of her mapping me out, triangulating me with innocent questions as I blab on about things that I'd normally never talk of: my solitude in the city; my parents in Bristol who seem strangers to me and who I never see; my move to the new flat - my new flatmates - and the worry that I left without them knowing where I've gone. Why was I on such a buzz last night? They probably think I'm weird. And I can't let them think that, because I need that place to work...

She's looking at me like she was at the party. A measured look, appraising me to some standard of her own. But she breaks off suddenly – this one never dwells long on anything, I'm starting to see – and skips off the bed to the door. "Loo..." she says, but her fingers brush my arm lightly as she gets up – a tiny reward for my openness. Then she's wrapped in a towel and closing the door behind her.

Something in the silence she leaves behind really wakes me up.

She was hardly doing much talking, but she somehow filled the room – and now, with her outside, the emptiness comes crashing back on in. What have I been doing, sitting in bed with this girl I don't know? Lying here, telling her about my life and my empty flat – when I should be in it, alone; waking up to my first hangover in a new place, and dreading meeting the new housemates by morning light.

Instead I'm here, lazing in the warm with someone who doesn't seem to mind that I'm in her bed. And now my skin goes cold. Really – who is this person? And why the hell has she brought me back? All this time I've been lying here like an idiot - and I've got no idea who this girl is. What the hell would she want from me?

By the time she gets back, I'm sat up in the corner of the bed. She's in a T-shirt now and boxer shorts – which only makes me feel undressed – but she crawls over the bed to sit against me. A little held back, as if she's sensed my unease. Yet even with her here in the room and the hand resting light against my foot, it's like a heater's been turned back on.

I feel myself relax a little. She brushes back my hair.

"Are you going?"

I shake my head.

"Well listen, I'm meeting some friends in the Common later on. Would you like to have some breakfast here, then come to the park with me?"

For the first time, I think I'm being asked a question she doesn't know the answer to. And I get that feeling in my stomach again, when I see that she'd like me to come.

***

"So what are these?"

Once again, ease has returned to the world. I'm padding around Anne's kitchen in boxer shorts with coffee and a hot Sainsbury's *pain au chocolat* in my hand. Am I supposed to feel this comfortable?

"They're by an artist I like. Kind of different, don't you think?"

Anne's fixing chocolate bread, round two, and I'm staring vaguely at two posters of painted flowers. There's something strange about each of them. The paintings are both of simple vases of roses, no background or anything – except almost all the flowers are rotten or dried. Just a handful of blooms at the edge of the bunch are still fresh – perfect white roses. But the rest he's painted are dead.

"I like what he does. They're pretty paintings, huh. What he does is he tries to paint in the time."

"How do you mean?"

"Well you see the roses, yeah? The way they're all part of one bunch."

"Uh-huh."

And there's only a couple that are fresh? Well they all started off looking that way. What he does is take one perfect bundle of flowers, all completely beautiful and pure, and then he paints them over several days. Not like most people would, like a snapshot of how they were at the start, but instead he paints what's in front of him each time. So the flowers at bottom left are where he started, then he moved left to right and bottom to top.

"I like it. It's more honest. And it also makes you think about him, about what he's doing – it's like an artist painting in their own hand, holding a brush."

"It seems a bit spooky. Kind of... gothic"

"Why do you think that?"

"...I dunno. It's just kind of morbid. Painting in all that death."

"You could say that" she says, pausing from pulling the pastries out of the oven to look at me. "But it could be a positive statement too, right? If the flowers were all so beautiful, you wouldn't look. But when you see them against all the dark and rotten ones, they're much more striking. It's like a beauty spot. It makes you think that good things never last – so you should enjoy them more."

I ponder this for a while.

"There's a lot more dark parts than good..."

And Anne shrugs away the comment and smiles.

I look at the pictures some more, her little speech running round my head while the coffee cools.

"What do you do Anne?"

"Oh really? We're having that conversation already?"

"We don't have to..."

"I don't mean it like that. It's just – is your job really fantastic? I mean, do you leap out of bed every morning and make the world a better place?"

"Not really."

"Well, you know. Me neither."

"Okay then. So we won't say."

"You'll get curious. *I'll* get curious."

And now it's my turn to shrug. Except it's more a kind of goggle-eyed expression.

"Deal then" she says and grabs my arm. "Come on, put some clothes on, we're going. You can eat that on the way."

"Alright."

But I stand over the sink, first, to finish the coffee.

***

Outside, it's really summer. Nine am and already the air is a tangible thing. The sunlight loosens limbs and drops my shoulders. It's Saturday morning and warm and quiet - and I'm glad I'm up early.

The Friday night rubbish of an area full of bars and restaurants looks out of place – discarded fried food boxes, a broken shoe. We cut a path parallel to the High St on the way to the Common.

Anne's gone quiet. Taking in the morning not with her eyes, it seems, but in the way I am – through her skin, and in the smells on the hot air. Looking at her body, it suddenly seems strange that she undressed me last night. A flash of memory unsettles me for a moment – touching her or holding hands now would seem out of place. Not like last night.

We pass a pub and a big stupid dog puts its paws against the fence and pushes its nose through a crack. I ask Anne about the friends we're going to meet.

"Miles and Yvonne. They're great. I love them. They're probably my best friends in London. They're funny though. It's like they're the perpetually struggling couple. Not with money or anything – with each other.

"Do you know anyone like that? They always have some drama, some kind of tension between them, but they always stay together. I've known them a couple of years now and sometimes I think I can see it between them. Like an energy between them, some kind of strife they're always brooding over – keeping it alive.

"I don't know what they'd be like if they didn't have it. Probably break up. Not that they don't break up all the time, but when they do they're still interested in each other. They sort of circle each other for a while before getting drawn back in. It's weird. I wouldn't want it for myself, but it seems to work for them."

"Sounds too interesting for me."

"Oh I'm making them sound dreadful, but they're lovely. Miles is kind of sweet with me, in that platonic way of friends' boyfriends. And Yvonne is mad. She loves talking and gets a kick out of catching up. It's funny sometimes. They must have much more interesting friends – definitely friends with money like them. And I thought we'd just drift away like you do with people from different circles. But they don't and we've stayed in touch. Just doing this sort of thing, meeting up for mornings in parks."

I get the feeling Anne's explaining this to herself as much as me. And for the moment, tagging along and listening seems the easiest thing to do.

Once we're in the park, I get my bearings better. Anne's place must have been somewhere in the old town part of Clapham, because we exit the back streets onto Clapham Pavement, near a pub called the Frog and Forget-Me-Not, and cross into Clapham Common near the dirty little kids' pool – magnet to the paedophiles of London and half full of toddler's piss.

Our steps slow unconsciously as we walk under the big old trees. We fall into a rhythmic stride, two pistol duelers pacing in the same direction, until by some unspoken agreement we halt and collapse lazily into the warm grass, both felled by the shot of the other.

For a long time I lie on my back, not talking, just watching the high clouds speeding above, hurried by a wind that doesn't reach us here. My thoughts are out on the clouds and I watch, detached, as they melt and change and drift away, leaving my head empty. It's been a long time since my head was empty.

A shadow falls on my face.

"Hello, what have we here?" asks an energetic voice. I look up, squinting, into the dark silhouette of a head ringed by the dazzling sun behind. "Fallen asleep have you Anne?"

I sit up, confused, and Anne stands to hug first Miles and then Yvonne – all friendly smiles and greetings. Then it's my turn to be introduced. Yvonne says "Hi", and Miles gives me a "hello there fella" as they settle themselves on the grass.

It seems they've brought quite the picnic – Miles drops a great, expensive-looking carry-all next to him and starts to rummage around. This is all getting a bit Jamie Oliver; a thick cheeseboard comes out and two glass bottles of juice. The silly bastards have lugged it all the way from the south side of the Common and it looks bulky and awkward. Out come more goodies: grapes, dips, crackers, spreads.

"So how was this party, Anne," asks Yvonne. "Did you both go?" And she sounds curious, amused, excited all at once, asking about this stranger sitting on the grass with her friend - without asking the obvious directly.

"Finn went too," she counters ambiguously. "It was good, but we got out of there fairly quickly. You weren't feeling too well, huh?" And I just nod, content to watch the feminine undercurrents in this tete-a-tete.

"How about you guys? Did you do anything last night?"

"Noooo" drawls Yvonne. "No, this boy was tired too" she says, but less sympathetically than Anne. "You had a hard week at work, didn't you dear? So we stayed home and watched a movie. And I drank some wine."

Her voice is beguiling. The words directed at Miles are the aural equivalent of rolling her eyes. And the words for me, it seems, are those about wine. As if on the basis of drinking with Anne last night, I've been recruited to a team that berates her partner for his lack of fun.

"No. I'm sorry Miles. I didn't mean it like that. We had a good time, huh? And he does work very hard, don't you?" She grabs his hand suddenly. I've known Yvonne for five minutes and she already seems like a nightmare. She also seems tremendously sexy.

"Too right I do." says Miles, taking this whirlwind of belittlement and love in his stride with the calm of what's obviously long practice. "And it keeps you in the style to which you're accustomed."

"Jesus!" exclaims Anne, and takes a knife to the cheese.

"So Finn" continues Miles, turning to me. "What do you do?"

"Oh, well, um..." Shit, I don't want to be rude, but this would be a lame way to end the first game that Anne and I have played.

"He's a fox-spotter" says Anne. "Professional. Keeps a diary and pen on him at all times. It's true isn't?" she demands of me, with a smile to their skeptical looks.

"Oh absolutely. Um, actually, I made a particularly good sighting yesterday morning."

"Right" says Miles, unconvinced, and his lashes do this fluttering thing - like a stutter in his eyes.

"Yes, no. A good spotting. Ah, clear light. Um, 8.42am." I'm being unfunny. "But seriously - I did see a fox on Friday. It was cool. Do you guys know Herne Hill? I caught the train from there all last week and yesterday morning I was standing at the platform, waiting with all the other zombies, when out wanders this fox with her cubs."

"Awww!" beams Yvonne.

"She walked out in full view, on the other side of the tracks, and they all lay down in the sun. You know what was weird? They were ten feet away and there must have been a hundred people there and I swear no one saw a thing. People are dumb, right? But when I saw it, as soon as I started staring at it, she looked straight back at me, right into my eyes to check if I was anything to worry about. There's something about foxes huh - they're so crafty and dirty and aware. It's like, if London were a person, they'd be the eyes and ears of the place - like an animated version of the city..."

Miles is looking vaguely disgusted by what I'm saying and I peter out lamely, feeling stupid for getting carried away - but Yvonne comes alive at the thought.

"Oh yeah" she says. "And what else? Miles what was that thing I saw today - just now, when we were walking over?"

"It was a mouse."

"No come *on*. You know it wasn't" And you can sense the argument that ran before.

"It was dead" she says to Anne and I. "But it was too small to be a mouse. And it had these funny skinny long back legs. Like a shrunken Kangaroo."

I know what that is. "Maybe a shrew?"

"Is that what it was?"

"It sounds like it. Now *that's* an old school animal. More English than badgers, really."

"So what was it doing in the middle of Clapham then?" says Miles. "I thought it was only rats and pigeons here."

"Well Clapham Common's pretty old itself, isn't it" says Anne. "In fact, I don't think it would ever have been built on. Back in the day, this would have been the common farmland for the village. And when the city expanded, it just flowed around. It's a little island. Richmond Park's like that too. That was a royal park right? So it's been the way it is since before there were people here. No wonder you get weird animals."

"Wimbledon Common's so old it's got Wombles..."

"Idiot." says Yvonne. "So is that why you get little islands of the real old animals?"

"You sound like Carol" says Miles and puts on a faux toff voice. "None of those bloody *foreign* animals round here please."

"Who's Carol?" asks Anne.

"A friend of Yvonne's. One of those old school types. You know – just comfortably, quietly racist."

'One of their rich friends' I think – and Anne's face says the same.

"Okay then" says Yvonne. "Carol's a racist, and you get shrews in Richmond Park. Actually I saw a newt there once."

"There you go. And there are bats in Hampstead Heath" says Anne. "You can go on walks to see them."

She lies back and props a bag under her head, watching the conversation. Miles seems to be paying more attention to the cheese.

"So –" I carry on. "There's old England and new England then. But is London new? It's massively old yeah?"

"It's both," says Yvonne with a glint in her eyes. "On the surface it's young and most of this rubbish you see is new - but underneath it's got old bones. It's like it's sleeping underneath the surface. One day it'll wake up and stretch its limbs..."

It seems Yvonne is the theatrical one.

"...And go over to France to beat up Paris."

And Miles likes to keep things straight.

I don't say much after that. Just graze at the food to be polite and keep real hunger at bay while the talk flows back and forwards over me. I keep out of it, happy to be in my own thoughts – though I see Anne look over occasionally, wondering if I'm alright being left out.

I wonder what she thinks? She doesn't know me, wouldn't know I prefer to be left alone. And if she thought the person at the party was me, then pretty soon she's going to be disappointed. Sometimes I can tell it makes people uncomfortable, but whatever it is that people feel when they need to query, probe and talk to others, I don't have it. In any case, Anne lets me be.

After a while, a change in the cadence of the talk brings me back. I realise I've been half dozing. Yvonne, Anne and Miles are swapping plans for the coming week – you're doing this? I'm doing that – a thrust and parry at the end of the picnic to find a space in each other's schedules and meet again. I rouse from my daydreams and sit up straight – Yvonne and Miles look over to me.

"You know", I say, "I feel kind of rude" – as if I do – "but I never asked you back about what you do for a living."

Miles looks baffled at this out of place question.

"I'm in the music industry," he says. "Marketing and promotions." And his eyes do their fluttering stutter thing again. "And Yvonne teaches rich foreign children how to speak."

"ESL" she says cryptically, looking over at her partner. "It was nice to meet you Finn." And she reaches over to kiss me on the cheek.

"Yeah, stay in touch," adds Miles, getting to his feet, the now packed-up picnic bag banging uncomfortably on his hip. "And see you soon," he directs at Anne, with a smile now genuinely warm.

"Bye guys" she shoots back and waves brightly as they turn, heading back the way they came.

Is it time for me to go too? I sit hugging my knees and look at her for a while as she watches them walk away, a faint smile on her face. But she turns to me – is suddenly on top of me – pushing me on to my back.

"I'm sorry" she says – her eyebrows high in a pleading look. And now it's my turn to dismiss it with smile and a shake of the head.

She leans forward and kisses me softly on the mouth. I'm on my back, awkward, not knowing what to do with my hands. Everything is bright and clear and good.

"Stay at mine tonight?" she says.

***

The key scrapes in the lock. I walk into a silent flat: no sign of Jane or Phil. Or Henry for that matter. Hell, the last I saw of Henry was thirty seconds after arriving at the party last night, his legs heading who-knows-where upstairs.

I stand in the living room, listening, making sure no one's home. My gaze is on an unloved stack of books on the shelf, next to an iron — but my attention's stretched out into the rest of the house, registering the sounds of the place. Definitely empty.

I left Anne at the park with a promise to meet at her place tonight. I must have looked vague, because she made me repeat the address to make sure I didn't forget it. There was no talk of a meal, or an activity or anything. What does that mean? But when she'd satisfied herself that I wasn't going to get lost on the way back and never be able to find her again she gave me a smile and I mumbled something about "clean clothes" and took myself back to the high street.

But there's nothing in my flat to do. I guess I'd been thinking I had to show my face, to show I was still alive. But it's quiet and empty - and unpacking those boxes is still an unappealing prospect. So on an impulse I grab a jacket and stride out - still in the same clothes, starting to catch a whiff of myself - to find some food and supplies and some basics to make moving into this place feel more real.

I head for Clapham High Street again where a nexus of buses seemed to promise some options and on an impulse jump on one labeled 'Brixton'. It turns and of course seems to go the wrong way and I think I'm going further and further from anywhere useful when I recognise the Brixton town hall and exit the bus along with a spill of other people - slow moving fat ladies, cocksure teenagers with caps and branded headphones - and stand a moment at the side of the pavement to wait until the noise and bus fumes and people have gone away so I can think and get my bearings.

Seven o'clock - the time I said I'd meet Anne - sits in my stomach like the anticipation of an exam, making me nervous and jumpy.

Across the intersection is the opening to the markets - the canyon-way of

Electric Avenue, crowded by canvas stalls - but there are too many people, so I head instead for the supermarket and do a round of the aisles, picking up anything I chance across that seems needed, too unfocused to make a list. Then after, when I'm coming out with two handfuls of plastic bags, I see a small Greek deli set into one of the railway bridge arches and treat myself to an espresso maker, one of those metal stovetop ones, that the owner has to fish down from a shelf with a pole. It's twelve pounds. Do they drink coffee in my flat? Was there even a stove there?

By the time I'm outside again, arms stretching from the weight of the bags, I'm feeling better. Calmer at having done something useful - and pleased with my treat to myself. Then I see something curious.

The shop over the road - opposite the railway arch deli - has a notice in the window with the name of my flat on it. Effra.

I cross over for a closer look. It says 'Effra' in big type and 'Raise the' in letters above it and it's been printed on green card and stuck inside the window with tape. I scan the rest of the shop window and there are plenty of other notices. 'Reclaim the Brownfields' says one. 'March for the Lost Rivers' says another and they're all on the kind of paper and in the kind of lettering that you'd do with a cheap computer and a photocopier. I'm figuring the place as an old grocery store turned into some kind of lobbyist headquarters when I see a tall skinny man inside the doorway looking at me.

"Want to find the waters of London, yeah? March to raise the lost rivers?" he says and I shake my head, not wanting to say anything about the name of my flat or why I'm looking, but he leans forward - so thin, such a long reach - and hands me a yellow flyer. I grip it, clumsy, in my hand full of grocery bags and mumble "thanks" and he says "come back anytime, we're all about education!" and I turn and go to get away from his stupid ponytail and scraggly beard and the chance that he might ask me inside.

I stuff the crappy flyer into a jacket pocket and make for the buses and the ride home and unpacking my new life.

***

Despite having memorised Anne's address I almost get lost, later, on the way to hers. And that would have been the end of that. I must be the last person in London without a mobile phone and if I'd forgotten her address, or got the wrong house, there would've been no way to find her again. I imagine myself waiting on the corner of streets in the morning rush, scanning faces desperately for hers and laugh to think how pathetic it would be. I like that there's only this tenuous thread linking me to this girl. I don't like feeling boxed in. But it's still a good feeling that the thread holds and I make it to hers, pausing for a moment at the door before ringing the bell.

There's the muffled thunder of feet on stairs before the door pops open and "Hey! Come up," says Anne, disappearing back up the narrow stairway at the same rate she came down. "You hungry?" she calls from the top.

I go up slower. There's a door on the right, leading to the flat below. I never noticed that last night. Funny the things you miss, mid-meltdown. I really must have been quite spaced - which is a worry - but not for thinking about now. There's enough to worry about already.

"Umm, I'm okay either way". My voice sounds too polite. "Are you cooking?"

"Yup, but it won't be ready for a bit".

The carpet on the last step at the top is worn through; then there's Anne's flat, just as it was this morning - except somehow in evening garb. Less light, I guess. Wooden slat blinds over the windows.

Anne covers something on the stove and turns it down, then spins to find a glass, fills it, grabs hers from the stove, hands me mine - and nods me into the living area with a smile. She's all movement. I feel dull and still compared.

We talk and joke on the couch, still playing the silly game about not telling our jobs, and it's fun - though I'm rigid and thankful for the wine and the film she puts on later. We jibber-jabber through it - me trying to loosen up, but still tongue-tied - because she really is charming I'm discovering. Then I'm fed and wined. And finally led to her room.

This time there's no hurry.

She leads me by the hand through the door from the living area and sits me on the bed. Everything's done in that unselfconscious way that girls have with making things nice: she busies about, lighting candles, putting them on the dresser and window sills, then switches off the light. I'd feel like such a cheese-ball doing that, but it's pretty. Then she puts on some music.

"You look like a painting of Leda, about to be ravished by the swan. You're allowed to get into bed, you know, instead of sitting around all shy."

"Art teacher?" I say.

"Stop cheating. Now get your kit off." And she peels her jumper over her head.

I kick off my shoes and slide under the sheets, fully dressed, turning my face away so she can't see the grin. She slips in next to me.

"*Hello.*"

"Hello."

"Here we are again. Though I'm not taking advantage of a drunk boy this time I hope."

"I wasn't drunk."

"Uh huhhh..." she says into my neck, vibrating the words into my skin as if I'm Helen Keller. I breathe in the smell of her hair.

She keeps me present - with her, in the moment - as we make love. Nothing is rushed and I can tell she's taking care to calm me, making me comfortable with everything as we go. It's an incredible kindness, something no one's ever bothered with before, and more than anything else on that slow, silent night it makes my heart ache for her.

It's unbearable. And afterwards I sleep not a wink. Instead I lie staring at the ceiling while Anne slumbers, tucked back into the crook of my arm like she belongs. The candles gutter down one by one until the last tea-light gives just a faint glow on the wall; which eventually wobbles - stabilizes for a moment - then pops out of existence, leaving me in the dark with the sudden smell of wax.

***

"So", says Phil in that ever-ironic twang. "You like her then?"

The frisbee leaves his hand with a subtle back-hand twist, flies flat, and hits my palm with a satisfying whack as I catch it.

I gather the frisbee in my hand and throw back. "Well. I think so".

Sunday evening. After a long, pleasant, baffling morning with Anne drifted into an afternoon, I finally had a minor panic over what my flatmates would think – the last sighting of their new tenant being two days ago, possibly as he was lead out of a party mid-freakout – and scurried home. It was a strange moment, coming up the stairs to the new place – still so unfamiliar. I turned the key in the lock, poked my head around the door – definitely looking disheveled, probably very anxious – and came up against Phil's vast reservoir of nonchalance.

He took one measured look at me, nodded with his eyebrows, said "alright" – and turned back to the television, lager in hand.

I went to my room without seeing anyone else and spent an hour packing the last of my stuff away and getting used to the space. By the time I'd finished and made myself some peanut butter toast Phil seemed to have had some kind of spat with Jane. Nothing major by the sounds of it, but he wanted to get out of the house. "Throw a frisbee round the park?" he asked. And me – well, feeling bolder with some food inside, I took it at face value and strode down with him. He got the majority of the Anne story out of me on the way.

"It's just, you know... I don't go out with many girls."

We've come to a different part of the common. The light is long and low.

"Oh Jesus. What does that mean?" mutters Phil back.

"Well nothing. Not much. I just don't."

The conversation passes back and forth with the flight of the frisbee. Phil's an old hand. Flicking the blue disk expertly so that it flies straight and flat – never over-throwing, or curling it off target. I throw more erratically. Often swinging high and wide of the mark, making Phil lope after it as I try to perfect my technique. But I'll get it. I'm meticulous when I want to do something right.

"Well, you either like her or you don't, right. So do you like her?" And the frisbee comes at me as straight as the question. I have to pause a moment with it dead in my hand before I answer.

"I like her. But she's not like most girls. She's not big on... boundaries."

"Ha," huffs Phil. "Sounds like a bit of what you need."

"So did you and Jane just have a fight?" I say, changing the subject.

"Nah. I don't do fights. But she's always on at me on days like this. I work all week and want to take it easy. She wants to get up and go to some stupid market. Ullo ullo."

"...what?"

"It's the Friday night tripper." And Phil nods to something behind me: two figures ambling through the trees in our direction.

"He was at the party. Came downstairs after you disappeared with your bird. A right talker - was jabbering to me in the corner for ages.

"Alright" says Phil, louder now, directing it over my shoulder. And that's funny, because when I turn around again with the blue frisbee still in my hand it's the tall pony-tail guy from Brixton yesterday morning, walking across the grass with a curly-haired girl.

"Hey man" he says, shaking two fingers at Phil in recognition. "Aw, and -" he cocks his head to one side, looking confused as he recognises me - I can see him searching his memory. "From the shop" he says. "Before".

"Effra" I say, in dumb confirmation.

"Bit of frisbee in the park?" he says gleefully. "Nice. *Nice.* All very healthy of you." He's got a cigarette in his hand.

"Don't be a cunt" says Phil amicably. "Kip, Finn; Finn Kip. And it's Debs, isn't it?"

"Yeah that's right" says Debs, nasally.

"Right. *Right*" says Kip, in animated fashion. "Wasn't trying to be a *cunt*" - and he strings the word out, as if he's listening to the way it sounds. "No not being like that, *Philip*. Just going to the pub, if you must know.

"Where you're welcome to join us," he adds. "Unless," and his voice loses that greasy tone all of a sudden, becoming mock-serious, "you don't want to hang around with cunts."

"Never do," says Phil, unfazed. And: "come on then" to me.

I want to say to him 'Phil - you're not seriously going to have a drink with this guy are you? Someone you spoke to at a party? Mate, don't think I know him either - he's just some knob I bumped into.' But it's too late. Phil's already summoned up the pint before his eyes, I can tell.

***

Kip keeps yabbering away as we walk to the pub. Clearly he was entertaining poor Debs with a similar stream of wisdom and it's nothing to him to deluge another two, even if they are effectively total strangers. At one point Phil says to Kip and I "so how do you two know each other then, if you didn't meet Friday?" and I just mentally shake my head. No Phil, we don't know each other. We're going drinking with a total stranger who may actually be mad. And he gets no real answer from Kip either. Poor Phil. You can almost see the cogs turning in his head. Except we're going for a drink, so he's obviously not worried about much else.

We make our way to the Frog and Forget-me-not. Clapham's got some crap pubs, but this seems inoffensive. And when we come to ordering drinks it's one of those get-your-own occasions, rather than a buying rounds kind of vibe.

Kip pays for his with loose coins. Phil leads the way to a booth and parks himself on the cushioned seat, his ruddy pint set in front like a fat exclamation mark. His brow creases minutely.

"So you guys don't actually know each other at all?" he says, sounding a bit confused as we shuffle in next to him. I look up at Kip.

"No. But I recognise Finn from yesterday, don't I?" says Kip, looking at me.

"Yeah. You were in that... shop thing." And now I know I have to ask - there's a sense of inevitability. "So, ah, what..." and that's all that's needed, so ready was Kip to let loose with his story - this story - the torrent of some passion of his which I'm sure he unloads on to everyone he ever meets. Debs looks up at him expectantly - the acolyte who's heard it all before and never minds hearing it again.

"It's the headquarters of the Living London Group. An organisation I've set up."

"Ah," says Phil, dryly. "A front for selling drugs." Kip's eyes, expressionless, flick to Phil for a moment, but otherwise he ignores the comment.

"Externally," says Kip - and for a moment his face takes on a look of boundless, treacherous cunning - "we're a lobby group on urban environments. But we're not interested in education, or community action or blah blah blah. What we're interested in is discovering the true aliveness of the city - and keeping it for our own." He sits back, obviously impressed with himself. The crease has come back between Phil's eyebrows.

"Did you know," continues Kip, oblivious, "that London is built on buried rivers? Did you know that Fleet Street runs above the Fleet River, which is still flowing underneath those famous stones? That below Wandsworth is the Wandle stream? That Holborn Viaduct - it was a *viaduct* for the Oldburn River? Heard of the Neckinger, the Tyburn? Did you know that just a mile east of here the Effra River runs underneath Effra Road and that the name comes from a Celtic word, Yfrid, meaning torrent?"

Phil looks positively bamboozled, his pint poised at his lips. I'm quite taken aback. Neither of us says anything about living in Effra Mansions.

"This is all a matter of record," says Kip with a nasty inflection in his voice for our silence. "It's all well known and documented - there's no need to be surprised. But what we're interested in - what Living London is about - is how *alive* this system's become.

"For the last two hundred years the rivers have been a mess. The industrial revolution ruined them. People ruined them. Chemicals, dyes, shit - it all got dumped into the beautiful, bucolic brooks" - Kip waggles his fingers in a mockery of sparkling waters - "babbling through the British countryside - and turned them into open sewers. So one by one they were turned into *real* sewers. Got bricked over. Buried. Designed into the Victorian stormwater system and just forgotten.

"Since then everyone's assumed they've remained the rotten, revolting mess they were when they last saw daylight. But we know better. We've found them, one by one. And they're *waking up*.

"Did you know there's a great pipe visible in Sloane Square tube station that carries a river - a fucking *river* - from one side of the tracks to the other? I happen to know there are now fish in that river. Just think - all those commuters marching through the station, while fish swim through an iron pipe above their heads.

"You might have heard how the Thames is becoming clean again and salmon have come back to the water?" Kip's tone suddenly becomes off-hand, dismissive, and he looks out the window as he takes a drink. "But did you know there's a black market fishery of sea-run salmon operating from the river? No? The authorities don't either. But there are now 18 families with livelihoods based on an entirely illegal, yet sustainable, Thames fishery."

He leans back to us. Debs is all adoring attention.

"And the buyers they supply and all the other connections with the legitimate food industry in this city are managed through one group."

Phil's eyebrows are now hitched high on his forehead. It might be the most expressive I've seen him. Kip grins.

"It's not just fish either." There's a manic look in his eyes and you can tell he's trying to hold back on details. "There's game, and a hardcore freegan network feeding perfectly good vegetables from big-chain supermarket mini skips back into street stalls - and making a living skimming off a profit."

"You're bin-jumpers" says Phil, bluntly.

"Poachers," says Kip, equally matter-of-fact. "Gleaners. Urban hunter gatherers.

"We're told we can't net salmon at night, or liberate trout from fish farms - but why shouldn't we? It's the authorities that poisoned this place in the beginning and if they find out how alive this city is, how it's suddenly thriving underneath our feet, they'd just go ahead and kill it all over again - and take food and money from us in the process. Sure, all the greenies and the scientists and the BB fucking C, they'd love to hear about this. But we ain't telling them."

In the course of Kip's little speech Phil and I seem to have swapped moods. Phil is looking out the window, taking another gulp of his pint with a face that says 'Jesus, what have I gotten into' - while my reservations have dissolved. Sure, Kip's a bit of a nutter, but his rant about rivers keeps going round in my head. A river, flowing under our house? I remember how this afternoon, as I unpacked, my room seemed cooler than it should have been and mildew made faint Rorschach patterns on the walls.

"So you're saying... you think there are fish swimming around underneath London?"

Kip sighs and leans forward. "Not just fish, my man. You're thinking too human. A fish isn't just a fish - distinct and discrete - it needs to eat. And the things it eats need to eat. It's the apex predator for an entire ecosystem. So don't just think of it as a fish. Think of it as an expression, as a symbol, as the... as the... " - stumbling in his excitement - "as the fucking *manifestation* of a greater life force."

Phil sucks his pint a little too noisily. Kip shoots him a look.

"You know what Phil my man? Fuck you and your eye-rolling - you just don't get it. Science is just catching up with this shit, man. Nature's not individual plants and animals, it's about connections, the big picture: life force. And the life force in this city - I'm fuckin' serious here - it's *waking up*."

Debs pitches in, her voice wavery - less confident. "And only recently. We think - we think in the last few years. Some people say it's because pollution levels are dropping off, but actually in a lot of places it's getting worse. It's like, it's like *despite* the toxic environment in London there are lots of little ecosystems cropping up - and they probably shouldn't be."

"Debs has a great little project on the go," announces Kip. "Tell them about it? She's growing potatoes."

"On railway sidings" says Debs shyly.

"Yummy" says Phil. Kip ignores him.

"You know that overgrown couple of metres between the tracks and public land? It's wasted space. Put there as a barrier to keep people off the lines. Well we met this hippie couple two months ago who were sneaking through the fences and growing vegetables on the south-facing slopes. Turns out the land is quite productive. We convinced them to bring the idea into Living London, and we're looking at rolling it out in Bristol and Southend later this year."

"The hard part is keeping them hidden from trains *and* the street" says Debs.

Kip gets up and heads to the bathroom. "Everyone says the crop will turn out polluted," he adds as a parting shot. "But I've got other ideas".

Phil drains his glass pointedly and gives me A Look. I ignore him.

Debs turns to us, eyes big with enthusiasm. "We're going to get the crop tested for contaminant levels. Kip says they'll be high, but he isn't worried. He's going to do a study and get it published. He says the evidence is that people in cities are getting immune to contamination - and the weird thing is we might even need it now, to stay healthy. We're gonna call the study *Towards a Polluted Food Supply*".

"Wow," I tell Debs. "That really is nuts." She looks a little crestfallen.

"It's not you know. It's really happening. You should see some of the stuff we're doing."

"And I should see about my dinner," says Phil suddenly and stands up. I'm between him and the way out of the booth. "Tell Kip-o, tarrah from us and we'll see him at the next party."

I give Debs an apologetic look and get up too - Phil's practically shunting me out of my seat. "Maybe see you guys here some time?" I say weakly.

"Maybe." says Debs. "Or you could come visit at the shop."

"Okay," I say. And then in a moment of madness: "Actually, we live in Effra Mansions if you want to look us up. Effra like the river. You guys should pop by."

Phil, frisbee in hand, has closed his eyes briefly in a look of utter disgust.

"Alright," says Debs brightly. "And I'll tell Kip you two had to go."

"Do that," drones Phil.

"See you Debs," I manage politely and then we're out the door.

Phil and I walk down the Pavement toward the High Street, both of us quiet; Phil sulking, me wrapped in thoughts of hidden rivers and fish swimming through drainpipes. After a while I venture a comment.

"You know what? They were interesting people, those two."

Phil says nothing for a bit; then his only words for the whole walk home:

"Fookin hippies."

***

And *finally* I'm alone. Phil and Jane went to bed an hour ago. Henry isn't here. And at last I'm lying on the bed with the light out, hoping for sleep, dim twilight still coming through the uncurtained window.

And what is this: my first night here? I can't believe I've officially been moved in for three days and this is the first time I'll sleep in the house. Everything that's happened since the party on Friday's been a blur. Jesus - everything in the last fortnight's been strange.

It was two week's ago that James and Karen kicked me out. It was a real shock. I'd been in that flat since I arrived in London. And for me - you know, maybe even more than for other people - home, quiet, being alone in my room; they're what holds me together.

So being kicked out, yeah, that was pretty weird. Though I guess they were good about it. James said I could stay out my notice period, to give me a chance to find somewhere new. But I knew I couldn't handle that; I just wanted to get out, so that day I packed up my gear and moved into a bedsit in Streatham.

It was just the most depressing place. Old alkies frying food in the shared kitchen, reeking of loneliness. Grey divorcees watching TV with fallen faces - God, I felt like I'd catch some kind of disease. But at least that was motivation for getting out and finding somewhere new. And I did - this place, six days later - with only a week's wait to move in.

Yeah, that was a funny week, that one. Finding a flat was like the proverbial weight being lifted from my shoulders. Life brightened up a bit. I moved quickly around the Streatham shared kitchen, chatting cheerfully to the depressed old bastards, enjoying the way the sunlight illuminated the blue frying pan smoke, and so on. Generally started thinking of it as a short holiday in loser-ville; something to be tolerated for a while - even enjoyed.

And the walks to the train in the morning were something else. That was where I saw the fox I told Yvonne and Miles about - the one at Herne Hill station.

My commute that week had been a walk down Brixton Hill, a short-cut through a Tulse Hill estate, then finally through Brockwell Park to the train. And Brockwell Park was amazing.

The last day I walked through was one of those warm mornings under the trees where everything was green and gold. There's a hill in the middle of the park with an old manor house on it which is surrounded by very old oaks, and up on the hill there was a bloke throwing a stick for his dog.

I guess the movement caught my eye. I turned to see a black line suspended against the sky - and below it there was this black and white streaking shape, arrowing after the stick like only a collie can.

And it stopped my heart. This heavy thump caught in my chest and made my breath go almost panicky with fright. Except it was more than just fright. If I'm honest with myself, it was more like the first emotion I'd felt for months. It spooked the hell out of me.

I'd become used to having nothing and no-one - I'd grown to like it. The day before I'd packed up all my possessions and dropped them off at work; just that morning, I'd handed in my key at the bedsit. Walking through Brockwell Park left me feeling as detached from everything and everyone as a ghost - and now, suddenly, my emptiness was being interrupted by a kick in the guts; an unwanted spark of joy.

I kept walking of course - no reason not to, though my insides felt like startled rabbits - and by the time I got to the park gates, things were more normal.

The entry back into the city was flanked by tramps, bickering - on the booze already. A bus roared past and as the diesel fumes pricked my nose I had the urge to turn back. I wanted to go back up the hill, sit in the sun on the grass and watch the dog and the stick. To think about my shitty few weeks. Think about this feeling in my chest and about what happened with poor, frightened Shelley, who I'd last seen in tears, with wet hair and a towel wrapped round her. But of course I didn't.

Instead, I screwed up my shoulders. Did a kind of mental clench, walked head-down across the intersection and into the station.

Which was where I saw the fox.

In the time I took to cross the intersection the last remnants of queasy emotion had disappeared from my belly and been replaced with the foulest of moods. London seemed to be beating at my head with all the usual shit; people jostling at the turnstiles, flapping stinking pigeons, and by the time I found myself a spot on the edge of the open-air platform on which to hunch and stare into space, I was ranting in my head.

"Screw you, London," I thought. "Screw you and all this shite." And as I looked up to curse everything that my eyes fell on - the chain-link fence, the tumbled rubbish across the rails - I saw a brick-yellow fox, sitting over her cubs as they slumbered hidden among the fire weeds.

And here's the funny thing. The moment I saw her, she looked straight back into my eyes, fixing me with a burning, living stare. The happy little nature documentary I painted for Yvonne and Miles the next day? It couldn't have been further from the truth. That little tale belonged back in the park - with the trees and the green and the breeze. But being eyeballed by the fox - the way she picked me out from all the other human chaff on the platform as I stood there, hating everything and everyone: that little moment belonged completely to the city. As it stared into me, I thought *that's the most eye-contact I'll get all day*. If this city were alive, I thought, foxes would be its eyes and ears. And people its dull, insubstantial thoughts.

My breath sounds distant now, like it belongs to someone else. Lying still, I can feel the tension of the week pulsing inside me to some rhythm of its own - surging like a skiers' legs after a day on the mountain - but sleep is taking hold. I realise I've been staring sightless at the ceiling - close my eyes - and immediately images come flaring in the dark behind my eyelids, as vivid and bright as that stick silhouetted against the blue.

I see Kip's manic gestures in the pub as he conjured up the buried Effra squeezing through tunnels below us. I think of Yvonne talking excitedly; see Miles' face scoffing at some thing or other - and then, as the scatter-gun pictures fade, I think of Anne.

Such a strange week. I try to fathom where this girl came from, to make some sense of how she stepped so suddenly into my life, but by now my thoughts are like roots at the edge of a pool that slip out of my hands as I grab them. Slowly my breathing becomes more shallow. The sounds of the city at night, all distant sirens and cars, become muted and abstract. And finally, when my thoughts are so broken and fragmented they confuse me with a kaleidoscope of meaningless ideas - Anne, Kip, Yvonne, the buried rivers - I let go of the edge and drift down.

And as the black waters close over my head, the last thing I'm aware of is a voice - quiet, but clear - that says:

"Time to sleep."

***

The next week passes in a blur. For once work doesn't get under my skin - actually, I kind of enjoy it - and for the first time it occurs to me that some of my colleagues are even interesting. A work discussion with a girl on my floor turns into chit-chat, which I realise later was straying into flirtation - flirting. Me? - and even my line manager becomes almost tolerable, for all his tie-stroking, throat-clearing, arse-propped-on-the-edge-of-a-desk annoyingness.

In short, I'm chipper.

In the mornings I get up early and walk an extra mile past the nearest station before getting on the tube - an experiment with transport options that lets me soak up the sights and sounds of my new neighbourhood: the flower seller who dumps yesterday's blowsy irises into the minskip next to his stall; the legs that appear under the video-store roller doors as they trundle up each morning, on the dot at quarter-past seven. And I notice the little things about my flat that make up its daily routines: Henry's erratic hours - his late nights speckled with short conversations when your paths occasionally cross (his manner: always in control, never explaining himself or talking about his life). Or the sounds that drift from Phil and Jane's room after they've gone to bed: a low murmer of conversation that I eventually realise is a talking book they listen to before sleep.

I spend a lot of time taking in the new furniture of my life and mull over each new thing. But mostly, I think about Anne. On train platforms and at work. In the pauses between dealing with one email and another, or walking up and down stairs to see people on other floors - in every little gap in my life I replay things she's said or moments that we've had in what, for me, is a surprisingly non-judgemental way. Which is to say, instead of wondering about the meaning of what she's said, or about what I should do, my head seems content to just run reel after reel of Anne-footage - while some other part of me sits comfortably in the back of my skull, absorbing every detail.

I see her twice that week. Once on Tuesday - we go out to a Vietnamese restaurant and I have to drink half a bottle of wine to warm up and lose my shyness - though I stay at hers that night. Then again on Wednesday, when I don't stay over, but we have a companionable walk together just following our footsteps, talking. I'm pleasantly surprised at the sober easiness of the evening and I guess that's the first time I think about her role in my real life - the tedious life I have that involves work and mornings and not being drunk or particularly interesting to be around. And the idea of her in *that* life is more challenging than any other - and yet a thought so compelling, so long-shot hopeful, I'm not sure I can give it up.

Suffice to say, I remain baffled at her interest in me. I tag the issue mentally as sheer mystery - a question that yields no answer, however long I stare at it - and never quite lose the expectation that the next time I see her will be the last. That she'll drop her interest in me suddenly one day in that flighty, impulsive way she has and move happily on to the next thing, leaving me to wallow in my obsessive, plodding thoughts.

On Thursday, at Anne's insistence, I walk down Cheapside in my lunch break and buy a mobile phone, feeling like a total luddite. It's my first one - for no reason other than I've never seen the point - and that evening I pull it out of its box, throw away the instructions unread and charge it up in the living room.

It's the cheapest one there was - features-free - and I'm satisfied with its chunky, unfashionable shape. But I still feel like a twat leaning over the screen to learn the operating system, then pecking in Anne's number from the carefully folded piece of paper where I'd written it down.

I experiment with a text, typing out "HELLO", then sending it to the only number in my address book. The phone tells me "message sent".

"Hey. Finn..." Phil and Jane are sitting watching telly from the other couch, while I'm bent over this new instrument. "What are you doing this weekend?" I look up at them and shrug.

Jane pitches in: "We're going to see Felix B at the Academy tomorrow. You and Anne should come."

"Oh, okay," I say. "Thanks. I'll see what she thinks. What kind of music is it?"

"It's fookin wicked, that's what it is," says Phil. "Get yourself along."

I smile and turn back to the phone - which comes to life with an overloud bleep. I sense Phil giving me a sidelong glance.

"Hello. Is that you?" reads Anne's reply. And: "All caps is shouting you know."

Dammit. It takes me ten minutes to work out how to turn the text lower case, fretting about the delay, before I text Anne back:

"What are you doing friday? Academy with me Jane and Phil?"

She answers immediately. "Of course! I'll ask miles & von too." And just like that, it seems to be arranged. A plan materialises for us all to meet at the pub, I message Anne to check it's alright, and she signs off with an x. I stash the phone under my bed where it can't cause any more trouble and fix myself some food.

***

Friday afternoon and the last few hours at work drag like a bird with a broken wing. By four-twenty I'm fidgeting: there's not enough time to start something new and it's too early to leave. I rearrange the icons on my desktop and open and close windows. Four-thirty. The tension in the office is palpable.

"Fuck it!" Our manager Alan has made an announcement to the room. Alan is fat and wears stripey pink shirts. "Fuck it," he says to no-one in particular. "I'm going home." I can't help smiling - it must be the first personable thing I've heard him say. He shrugs his suit jacket on and walks briskly out.

A couple of heads lift above computer monitors; exchange glances. "*Yeah man,*" says someone else. No one's going to work the last half hour when the boss has gone home.

I shut down both my machines, take the elevator and a few minutes later

I'm striding through the lobby. It's a cold, narrow room - marble floor, marble walls - and the only warm thing in it is the man on the front desk; a Nigerian guy with tribal scars on his chubby cheeks who I like - but know I'll never talk to. Four forty-one and the company spits me out of its marble mouth on to the pavement at Moorgate. It's warmer out than in.

So what to do? I've got hours to spend before I meet Anne and the gang at the pub. All around, the steady flow of commuters is building - there's a kind of controlled intensity in the air as people stride by briskly - aware they're twenty minutes ahead of the rush, and determined not to waste the advantage. But I'm the only one in no hurry.

Maybe I'll walk some of the way, let the rush come then drop away again, then catch a train home when I'm sick of striding. It sounds like a plan. All I have to do is get home, change clothes then go out again. I set my feet going.

There's something satisfying about walking in London. The pace is fast, almost Olympic compared to other cities, but if you match it - then add another five percent of speed to your stride - you can move through the crowds like a fish.

From Moorgate I go south - stepping in and around people, trying to be as efficient as I can - then hit Prince's Street and come up to the rabbit warren of Bank Station. Something's wrong though. People are milling around, talking on phones while the tourists have their maps out, lost and stupid: the station must be closed. So I take a quick cut and leave the mess of people behind for the noise of Queen Victoria Street.

At Blackfriars I take the river path under the bridge, pausing to watch the water buck up against the old bridge pillars - the Thames is running fast and low on an outgoing tide - then pop up on Victoria Embankment with vague thoughts of taking a tube from Embankment Station. I march past the ancient creepiness of Cleopatra's Needle - a black obelisk of stone with bomb-blast acne around its base - but by the time I reach Embankment, the rhythm of the walk has taken over: I'm well and truly in the trance of it - head empty, legs on automatic - and the notion of going underground seems repulsive. It's not quite claustrophobia, it's just the station's yawning mouth gives me a shudder with those bright blooms from the flower stalls set around it like lipstick on a mouth, so I walk by, carrying on round the river.

Of course by the time I'm nearing Vauxhall Bridge I've regretted the impulse. I'm tired and hungry and just want to be home so I turn on to the bridge, aiming for Vauxhall tube station. Halfway across, though, I stop for a good look around.

The sky's gone flat - a metallic kind of grey - and the warmth is draining from the day; just rising upwards, out into space. A few thin clouds are picking up the sinking sun, turning orange, and the speeding water underneath the bridge is catching the colour, throwing it back like a great dull mirror. I look over to the MI6 building squatting on the bank. It's all marble and spikes - pretty ostentatious for a secret headquarters - and right underneath it, in a shallow pool in the Thames, I can see a heron stalking fish.

I lean on the parapet to watch him for a while.

He's being very clever. The tide's dropped enough to form a pool in the mudflats, which is draining through a narrow opening into the main flow. You can see the slight current as the water slides out the bottleneck, back into the river. And there's the heron: perched frozen on long legs, his big beak poised across the channel. The clever bastard.

Any fish caught in the broad pool as the tide drops has two options - stay in the pool and be stranded on the flats, or slip out to the main river. But the heron's watching the gap, hanging over the channel, as inevitable as death.

He strikes. It's so sudden I jump. The neck flashes down, he strides forth in two quick jerky steps - stabs again - and there it is, a flapping diamond-shaped fish that flashes its flanks in the dull light and goes down the hatch: a few quick gobbles - there's something obscene in the way he lurches his neck - and the fish is swallowed; I stand entranced. I can't imagine Kip, for all his talk of the living Thames, would give the faintest damn about this awkward, beautiful bird, but I think suddenly of Anne - how she'd like to see this. And think of her too as a bright flash of colour, something startling in the grey flow.

It's while I'm thinking about Anne for the hundredth time that day that I see it. I'm leaning on the parapet, gazing sightlessly at the river bank, my head a million miles away, when the word "Effra" swims into focus. I blink, look again, and see a metal plate screwed into the sheer stonework of the Thames wall. It says "Outlet of the river Effra" and below it a slimy hatch like a stormwater drain spills the faintest flow onto the mud.

Well, well, well - that Kip. Maybe he wasn't such a flake after all. There it is, his famous buried river. And what a rotten mess it's in. I take a last long look at its horrible dribble - God save us if Kip thinks we should eat anything out of that - then carry on across the bridge, catch a tube home and snatch an hour of quiet time in the flat.

***

New T-shirt. Old jeans. A jacket for the chill and shove my wallet and phone into too-tight pockets: I walk down to The Royal Oak pub and push the door open. Inside is the babble of Friday-night drinking - everyone happy for the end of the week - and there's Yvonne and Miles at a table with what look like first drinks and a bowl of fries in front of them. Miles sees me and waves.

"You better get some of these into you mate. I hear you flake out if you don't eat."

"Don't be rude," scolds Yvonne. But I smile, grab a finger-load of fries, and: "I'll go get a drink".

Ten minutes later - it's busy at the bar - and I'm setting my very full pint down, shuffling in next to Yvonne and slopping a little beer into a ring on the table.

"How's it going guys? Good to see you." And, actually, I think that I might mean it. Miles may be full of himself, but I've decided I'm going to enjoy tonight - and anyway, it was me who organised it, so that kind of means they're on my turf.

"Yeah," beams Yvonne, "you too. So what kind of gig are we going to?" and Miles leans in, looking more friendly and relaxed than he was at the park, to hear my prognosis.

"Well, to be honest, I have no idea. My new flatmate Phil recommended it - and actually, he's probably got terrible taste in music, but they reckon - he's coming along with his girlfriend Jane, she flats with us too - they reckon it'll be a great night."

Miles pulls a face. "Anything that's out of the office on Friday works for me."

I feel a meaty paw slap heavily on my shoulder and turn around. Phil's arrived with Jane hovering behind. He raises his eyebrows in a reserved salute that's at odds with his friendly shoulder-slap and turns wordlessly with Jane for the bar. I point a thumb in their direction: "And that's Jane and Phil." We shuffle along more and when they get back Phil takes the time to shake Miles' hand first, then Yvonne's - and Jane gives a friendly wave as we all sit. I get the impression that Miles approves.

Half an hour later I'm at the bar getting a new round of drinks when Anne walks in. She looks around the crowd blankly for a moment before she spots me - smiles - and walks over. She curls an arm companionably round my waist.

"How you doing lover boy. Good day at work?"

"Yeah, it was actually - it was alright."

"What is it you do again?" she asks, all faux innocence.

"Nice try." I can't help grinning. "How about you?" I move into a gap at the bar before turning round for the answer.

"Yeah, it was okay," she says, dismissively. "But it's good to see you," she adds - all sense of mischief gone.

The barman turns to me and points.

"Alright - cheers. Um that's three Kronenberg, one vodka cranberry and..."

"...gin and tonic" says Anne - then helps me carry the drinks to the table when they arrive. She shuffles in on the bench seat and I snaffle a stool and sit at the table's head.

"So. Jane and Phil, this is Anne - Anne, this is Jane and Phil."

Hands are shaken, smiles are swapped, and I see Jane - affectionate Jane, who seems already to have mentally tucked me under her wing - is looking at Anne and trying hard not to show how pleased for me she is.

Chit-chat goes around before the two couples - well, Jane and Phil and Yvonne and Miles: am I in a couple? - get back to what they were talking about, leaving Anne and me to ourselves.

"They seem to be getting on well," says Anne brightly. I pull a mock surprised face and nod.

"So tell me young man, what are we going to tonight?"

"Jeez, um - to be honest - I have absolutely no idea. It was Phil's suggestion." I turn to Phil to ask him, but he's in animated conversation with Miles. I pull the face again and Anne snorts.

"Who cares," she says and slides her hand, palm-down, across the table. "That's for you."

I cinch my eyebrows into a question mark, but put my hand over the top of hers - and when she pulls away, feel the rough lump of a pill.

"When...?" I say - and Anne just smiles and shrugs, so I put it in my mouth, trying not to be conspicuous, and swallow it down with some beer. It tastes like hairspray.

"Bleurgh," I say. Anne wrinkles her nose. And I think *why not?*

Before long I've forgotten all about pills and Anne and I are jabbering away when Phil says "Right, if you lot are keen, I want to see the warm-up acts." And Yvonne says "Shall we go then?" and there's a general exodus involving coats and bags and getting out of seats and other pub people getting in, and Anne and I find ourselves walking down the road, arms linked, in a loose group with the others - all following Miles, who's decided to take the lead.

"Miles has taken the lead," I say to Anne.

And she says "Do you think he'll be alright?" in the laziest way I can imagine.

To which I reply: "I think Phil will sort him out." And lo-and-behold, Phil is up the front with Miles, gesturing energetically to whatever it is they're talking about, but he looks up just in time to spot Ferndale Road and directs the whole straggling bunch of us down.

"You know, he's solid, that Phil" I tell Anne - and she looks up at me with eyes that seem suddenly huge and tells me she thinks so too.

By the time we get to the Brixton Academy Anne and I are an island. Her green jacket's gone slumped over one shoulder like she's Madonna in some 80s movie and I tell her I like the way she dresses - enjoying they way I've just said it, without any preamble or expectation of a reply - and she just smiles and carries on with whatever she was talking about, because there's a queue and we've all tagged ourselves on the end of it; everyone just leaning against the brick wall on the side of the road. There's a tout working his way down the line.

I remember something and interrupt her again.

"Do you remember at the party how I ended up telling that story about the beggar in Brixton?"

"Oh, how could I forget?"

"There used to be this other guy who'd ask me for money every day after work. It was brilliant - he tried it on with so many people each day that he'd forget your face, and every day was a different story. You know, like 'have you heard of the Stone Roses? Well, I'm the manager of the Stone Roses, and bugger me but I lost my wallet last night and need fifty pounds to get back to Manchester.' Or, sometimes, 'Oh my God mate, I've just been robbed. Can you spare me five quid for the train?'

"So on it went, for a whole week - and then he came up with the best one ever. The way he approached you was he'd come striding up and walk alongside you as you were going to work. And he was a big guy - quite intimidating, which was totally part of his plan. Anyway one day he just walked up - with no memory of the fact he'd been trying to scam the same person all week - and goes 'Mate. I've just bought this rock of crack' - and he pulls this lump of crack wrapped in clingfilm from his mouth - 'but I've got no money left for a lighter to smoke it! Can you spare a man 40p for a lighter?'

"Jesus - I just laughed. I had to say 'sorry mate, I don't give out money as a rule' and he was all like 'no worries buddy!' - crazy huh?"

"Well, yes Finn, that was a lovely story about crack. But were you actually listening to what I said?"

"Oh, before... when?" I stammer back - and as I waffle the tout comes up to offer cut-price rip-off tickets and Anne laughs, because it's so like my story, and she needles her fingertips into my stomach making me squirm and we're back to being an island with her arms around my middle as we shuffle up the moving line. And I think that I'm quite high.

"I think I'm quite high," I tell her quietly. And she says "crack." And I snort laughter from my nose.

"You focken eed-yits!" yells out Phil from the front. "I'm buying your tickets - you owe me drinks." The bouncer waves us forward through the doors.

The first thing that hits you is the warmth.

The air's a humid wall in here and you're immediately swallowed by the dark. *I* swallow and the thumping music, heard more as base through my belly, reinforces that I am indeed quite high - and finding this quite exciting. Anne tugs on my jacket, pulling me further in with the shouted promise of a drink.

From there on things become a blur. Not in the scary way of the party, it's just time seems to be happening in snapshots. I look down and there's a Corona in my hand which I can only presume Anne put there - so I suck at it intermittently, wincing at the lemon rammed down the spout and turn from face to face in the crowd; startled by hands thrown up in the air, deafened by the music and totally lost now - lost in the moment.

At one stage Anne is leading me further into the mess of people, pulling on my hand like I'm sure she's done before and I wonder where, but none of my thoughts are lining up properly - then the connection between us breaks and I'm cut loose like a small boat towed behind another that slips off unnoticed in the night to bob and sway on the waves. Oh God I'm so trashed and none of it seems to matter, so I stand where I am and try to dance and time - a lot of time - passes in that moment where I'm dancing and being jostled and wet with sweating.

After a while the momentum that was carrying me ebbs away. I'm aware of where I am - aware that I'm dancing - and see suddenly that I'm next to Phil - and that's Miles - and God knows how long they've been there. Phil sees me looking at him. "You getting me that drink?" he shouts. And I nod and turn for the bar with the two of them following.

"Jesus, that was intense," says Phil when I hand him his beer, and "cheers" says Miles "but let's get out of here. I can't hear a word."

There are nods all round so we follow Phil to the door and go up some stairs. The music dies to a distant throb and we sit on the top of the steps.

"Jesus!" says Phil again, to no-one in particular. "So Finn... you're sorted?"

He's looking at my eyes. "Fook man, yeah, you are. Your eyes are like dinner plates." Miles sniggers.

"You guys too?"

"Yeah," says Miles. Phil here donated to the cause.

"How are you finding them?" asks Phil as three girls squeeze past in high boots, heading downstairs

"Hey!" says Miles, trying to get their attention. "Hey, you stood on my hand! You've broken my finger!" and of course they haven't and they ignore him.

"Yeah," says Phil drolly. "Seem to be working fine. So Finn, you got yours courtesy of our fine other flatmate then?"

"Jane, you mean?"

"Ah, no. No I mean Henry." Long pause. "You haven't had that conversation with him then?"

"What conversation?" I'm getting confused. Now that I'm just sitting here on the steps instead of dancing I'm aware what a whirl my head's in.

"I'll leave that up to the two of you." Phil looks at me for a moment and I must look really lost, because he explains further.

"Well, our Henry he's is a lovely bloke, right? Doesn't spend a lot of time in the flat, but he's a lovely bloke. And also the friendly neighborhood drug dealer."

"Oh. Oh right." Several things click into place in my head.

"It's never really been a problem. We've been living in that place for two years and he's never caused any trouble with it - mostly you wouldn't know - but I'm sure he'll have that conversation with you soon. Just to reassure you, like. To reassure you, and also the way it works is he'll sort you out pretty cheap - which is his way of saying thanks for your discretion."

I just say 'right' again.

"For what it's worth, though," says Phil, "my advice is that it's not a good idea to shit in your own nest." Another pause. "Unless you want some drugs - then it's quite handy."

Miles laughs raucously while his eyes scan the legs of more girls walking by. Between Phil's dry humour and this new angle on our flatmate I'm not really sure what's going on, but I'm saved from overcooking my little brain by Miles' pushy nature.

"So what do you do Finn?" It's like a perfect echo of last week in the park. "You never told me before."

"Oh yeah. Yeah, sorry about that. Me and Anne - we were playing this stupid game where we tried not to say what our jobs were. Still playing it, I guess," and I sound apologetic. But Miles just says "that sounds like her. I better not let on too much about her huh?" Then he looks me in the eye and puts his hand on my shoulder in a way that makes me feel really small.

"You know she's a great girl, don't you?" And he holds my eye. "Don't you?" And I just nod, because I do know - but I'm not going to discuss it with him.

"I need a cigarette," says Phil decisively. "I'll leave you two to this scintillating conversation. See you in there, yeah?" And he clumps off down the stairs.

"Phil's a brickie," I say stupidly.

"So what do you do?"

"Oh, well... I'm a computer engineer I guess. I do maintenance and projects for a finance company - and also a bit of web stuff. PHP code?" I look at Miles but his expression's blank. "Though less of that now, these days."

"Criminey," says Miles, in his big round voice. "That *does* sound boring."

"No, no - it's not!" and I'm not offended - just enthused. "It's boring to talk about, but I love it. You know, you're inside this perfect world - you spend all day in it - and it has its own perfect rules and logic and some of it you've made yourself - and you can just spend hours and hours in it, tinkering away, making it better. Does that make sense?"

"I guess it does. I guess so - though it doesn't sound very social..."

"But that doesn't matter. You don't miss talking when you're that immersed." Miles is looking at me a bit oddly, like he's musing on what kind of person gets lost in computers - or else he's thinking about those girls again - but I'm becoming fixated, blathering, looking at my hands as I talk, while my head is miles away...

"...you know, sometimes I can see it, see the inside of where I'm working like it's a real place. It's always blue for some reason - a kind of fuzzy blue-on-black - and when the system's not working or I've done something the wrong way I can sort of see it, sometimes I can see it as a wrong shape - a misfitted thought picture in my head..."

And I think the reason I'm getting excited is I've never thought about it like that, even for myself, though it's so obviously true right now.

"What about the internet Miles. Do you like the internet?" Miles sticks out his bottom lip.

"Yeah sure. The internet's amazing," says the unconvinced.

"It is amazing. It's *totally* amazing. But everyone gets excited about it for the wrong reasons. Big deal about social media, right? And sharing photos, or shopping online. The question about the internet that I like is, who designed it?"

"Well, it started as a university network, didn't it?" says Miles - and I can tell he's not thinking about the girls anymore. "People just add to it and it's grown."

"Well, yeah, it's grown. But who grew it? Has anyone designed what it should do? Has anyone got control over the thing now? I don't think the internet can be shut down anymore. It was actually designed as a semi-military network that could withstand any localised attack from nuclear Russia - and that's the sole feature that's been preserved from the original network to what we've got now. The internet will *never* shut down, because it's outside of anyone's control. It's become a free agent - and no-one saw that coming."

"It's not alive you know fella. And we *have* just been taking pills..."

"Okay, yeah I know," I say rapidly - trying to steer my thoughts down, because they've really started flying. "But it's giving birth to new things, and one day it'll spawn the first computer intelligence - if it hasn't happened already."

"Skynet is operational..." says Miles in droll parody, and we both lean back on the stairs and take a drink.

I can't help myself though. My need to talk has diminished so that I'm quite content to sit, watching my thoughts floating round, but I can't help making one more proclamation into thin air.

"What will make a mind is emergence. It won't happen in a lab, or inside a company, because no single person is capable of making a mind. But if a system is big enough - the way the internet's becoming big - if there are enough connections floating around, it becomes a kind of storm, and out of that storm emerge patterns that will eventually become thoughts, and those thoughts will become a person. Some kind of person. Some kind of thing."

"Let's find that dance-floor."

"Yeah."

And for the rest of the night I amuse myself with thoughts like this. Just fantasies really, harmless ideas to get lost in that save me from the awful reality of the people around me - the social nightmare of being rammed together with so many sweating people with their morass of intentions and demands and rules: it saves me from being awkward. Then when shuffling on the spot while daydreaming loses its charm and an ache starts growing in my bones and around my kidneys - then not long after, Anne finds me sitting in a corner by myself sipping slowly on a beer and says "Hey. Phil and Jane are walking home - you want to walk back together?" And that's exactly what I want.

Outside, we find Phil and Jane leaning up against a lamppost, waiting. They swing into step without saying anything and the four of us head up Brixton High Street and then Acre Lane, passing the night trucks unloading at Tescos, each of us lost in our own thoughts and the sensuous cool air.

Eventually, it occurs to me: "What happened to Miles and Yvonne?"

"The usual," says Anne. "I should have said. They had an argument about an hour ago and went home."

"What about?"

"I reckon I could guess," offers Jane cryptically. "Your friend seemed easily distracted."

"Yeah. It's as much her fault as his, though" says Anne. "She's over sensitive. She keeps Miles on such a short leash that when he does get out, he can't keep his eyes in his head. Meanwhile, she watches him like a hawk and the whole blow-up's totally predictable. It's boring."

"You don't seem the hawkish type, though" says Jane, turning to look at Anne to show she means it nice. Anne grins back.

"Maybe you should be," intones Phil. "Our Finn... oooh, he's a ladies man." I look quickly at Phil to see if he's serious.

"I think he would be," adds Anne. "If he wasn't lost in that head of his. Do you remember when we were dancing and I tried to talk to you? I couldn't even get you to look at me."

I look at Anne now, and just shake my head. I can't remember. But it doesn't seem to matter to her and I zip my jacket up to my chin against the growing cold.

"This is us," says Phil as we reach Bedford Road. He stops on the corner and turns. "Thanks for a good night, yeah".

"Oh it was lovely!" says Anne, animating suddenly. She runs to Phil and leans up to peck him on the cheek then embraces Jane, looking her in the eye as she holds both her hands. "And it was lovely to meet you." Jane's beaming back. I pull a hand out of my pocket and hold it up, giving them a silent wave.

"See you back at the harmony hut," Phil shoots back. Then they turn away and Anne grabs my hand before I can get it back in my pocket, forces it round her waist and the perky wide-awake mood she's in lasts all the way to her house.

***

We're lying on her bed, still dressed. Too heavy to get changed and under the covers. Weariness has finally overtaken us.

"I like your flatmates, Finn"

"Yeah. I think I do too."

"Jane, especially."

"She's nice huh. Oh yeah, but hang on. Get this - it seems I've moved in with drug dealers. I found out tonight."

Anne props up on her elbow.

"What, Phil?"

"No, the one you haven't met. Henry. Zee German. He was at the party, though I never saw him after we arrived. He's hardly ever round."

"Funny that."

"Mmm. Kinda makes sense now." I prop up on an elbow as well to look back at Anne. "What do you think of that?"

"It depends, doesn't it? It might not be a problem. What kind of drugs?"

"Well, pills for one thing. Jane and Phil were on them. And Miles."

"Ah, Miles! Everything becomes clear. But you can't make money selling pills. It must be something else. Coke, with a few extras on the side maybe."

"Is that bad?"

"Hey, it's probably the least bad. You know, if he keeps it away from the house, maybe it's liveable? Pot would be a pain, with the stink and people turning up all the time knocking on the door. And if it was heroin or crack you'd have to move out."

Anne's eyes flick over me.

"It was like you were on crack tonight, the way you zoned out."

"I was just daydreaming. Don't you do that?"

"Not when I'm dancing in a crowd!"

"I dunno. I just... I don't like being around so many people. Sometimes it's easier to retreat."

"You know what? I never feel like that. But some people are born that way, aren't they. It doesn't matter how many people they know, they always feel cut off from everyone else. Maybe it's like that for you..."

"Maybe."

Her eyes flicker as she looks me over.

"Do you think of yourself as a lonely person?"

"Lonely? No. Maybe solitary. Compared to some people."

"So do you wish that you weren't?"

Jesus. Classic Anne questioning.

"Well... maybe occasionally. There was one time... a few weeks before I met you."

I look away - and smirk to show I'm not affected by the tone.

"I was staying in this bedsit. It was right before I moved to Effra mansions - I left my old flat and there was a week between moving rooms, so I stayed at this place."

A glance to see if Anne's listening.

"So anyway, I remember there was one night there when I was sitting in my room. The light was out and it was warm, so I took off my t-shirt to go to bed. And it was one of those synthetic, thermal, scratchy ones... you know?

She's looking at me with hooded eyes.

"And as I pulled it over my head, these sparks - like a forest of sparks... static, you know? They leaped off the shirt and grounded on my face. And I didn't feel anything - there was a noise, but it didn't give me a shock or anything - but it just... actually it just looked so amazing, you know? There was this halo of electricity around my face. It made me gasp. And when I realised there was no one there to tell about it... and that there hadn't really *ever* been anyone. I guess - I guess times like that it feels hard being the kind of person I am.

"The kind of person I am" - I say it with fake melodrama to show I'm not worried - though I can't tell what Anne's thinking, the way she's looking at me so strange.

"Don't stress Finn" she says, and smoothes my hair.

"I wasn't."

"You were." And she smoothes my head again, brushing the hair sideways across my brow. It feels so good. There are waves of comfort welling up and I know she's right, I was stressed. Anything is, compared to this.

We sit quiet for a while as Anne absentmindedly runs her hand down the back of my neck. Outside, the world seems very still.

She takes a sudden breath, coming alive. "I'll read you a poem."

She gets up off the bed and slips out the door. When she comes back she's carrying a book in one hand and half a bottle of wine and a glass tumbler in the other. She tucks up next to me and pours a splash for us to share. I take a sip and it makes me wince. E does that to me.

"This is my favorite poem. I read it off a wall on some dodgy underpass once and looked it up."

"Graffiti?"

"No, no. It was worked into the tiles. Official like. So. It's by someone called Sue Hubbard. I'd never heard of her. But I think you'll like it. Okay..."

Anne settles into a comfortable position and leans over the book. I take on an outward posture of attentive listening and mentally prepare myself to be bored. She starts in an even, ordinary voice.

I am not afraid as I descend,
step by step, leaving behind the salt wind
blowing up the corrugated river,

the damp city streets, their sodium glare
of rush-hour headlights pitted with pearls of rain;
for my eyes still reflect the half remembered moon.

Already your face recedes beneath the station clock,
a damp smudge among the shadows
mirrored in the train's wet glass,

will you forget me? Steel tracks lead you out
past cranes and crematoria,
boat yards and bike sheds, ruby shards

of roman glass and wolf-bone mummified in mud,
the rows of curtained windows like eyelids
heavy with sleep, to the city's green edge.

Anne looks over, checking to see if I'm with her. But I'm lost for a moment - staring into space at an image of lidded windows looking back at me as I ride by on the train. She carries on.

Now I stop my ears with wax, hold fast
the memory of the song you once whispered in my ear.
Its echoes tangle like briars in my thick hair.

You turned to look.
Seconds fly past like birds.
My hands grow cold. I am ice and cloud.

This path unravels.
Deep in hidden rooms filled with dust
and sour night-breath the lost city is sleeping.

Above the hurt sky is weeping,
soaked nightingales have ceased to sing.
Dusk has come early. I am drowning in blue.

I dream of a green garden
where the sun feathers my face
like your once eager kiss.

Soon, soon I will climb
from this blackened earth
into the diffident light.

Anne puts down the book and looks over to me, but I can't say anything for a moment.

"I thought you might like that," she says. It's called *Eurydice*. That's the name of the lover that Orpheus tried to rescue from hell in the Greek story."

"Oh," I manage, still a bit lost. "Can I?"

She passes it over.

"I liked the bit about roman glass and the wolf bone, mummified in mud. I like that sort of thing - thinking about how old this place is and the bits of ancient things under the ground. You've been to the British Museum?"

Anne uh-huhs.

"And you saw the guy from the marsh? The one in the glass case. He's like two thousand years old and got preserved in a peat bog."

"I like looking at him and thinking about what kind of life he had; whether it was that different from ours. Because he just looks normal. If he was alive today he'd be working in a bank or something, but he wasn't, he was wandering around here all those centuries ago. 'Til he got murdered and chucked in a bog."

"Yeah I know the guy. The one who looks likes beef jerky." Anne grins. "Actually did you know he was supposed to have been sacrificed? The way I heard it they would play a kind of sacrifice roulette. All the druids would get together for their May Day ritual. They bake these cakes and cover one with charcoal and the druid who picks the black cake from a basket gets bopped on the head."

"Huh," I mutter. "I know someone who'd be right into that." And my attention's drawn back to the verse.

"Who's that?" asks Anne.

"Soaked nightingales have ceased to sing," I mouth to myself. "I like that too."

"Finn?"

"Hmm? Sorry. Was drifting. Um... Kip. His name was Kip. I got talking to him in the pub."

Anne snorts. "You really do get lost in there sometimes don't you."

"In the pub?"

"In your head!"

She gives me another of her quiet, appraising looks.

"You must be one of the most shut-off people I've ever met. You're not used to sharing your thoughts with others, are you?"

I just shrug. I'm not sure it requires an answer.

"Don't worry, I don't think it's a bad thing. It's why I noticed you in the first place. You were standing there at the party, looking out the window, having your own thoughts for your own self, probably thinking about wolf bones in the mud. Then later you told that weird story and even without knowing you it seemed a strange thing for you to do."

I'm not sure I like where this is going.

"'*Soaked nightingales have ceased to sing*'. There was even a rain-soaked blackbird trying to sing in your story, wasn't there?"

"You've got a good memory..." I stutter. But Anne has a look in her eye that says she knows she's making me uncomfortable. She pokes me in the ribs to make me wriggle.

"I'll stop now. But hey, do you know why your blackbird was singing at night?"

"Why's that?"

"Apparently the city's so noisy during the day that songbirds can't hear each other - which means they can't attract a mate or mark out territory - so they've started singing at night when it's quieter and they can hear. I read it on the BBC"

"Doesn't that wear them out though? Staying up all night?"

"Totally. It's like, bloody London! Even if you're a bird you've got to work two shifts to get anywhere!"

"Ha."

She's looking thoughtful again. Oh God - here we go.

"So after you told that story, you had a bit of a freak out, didn't you?" Anne says quietly. "What was going on?"

I shrug. "Oh, you know. Blackbird syndrome. Too much staying up late stressed me out."

But it seems I'm not getting off that easily. She says nothing; just waits for me to fill the silence. I don't particularly want to talk about this, but I'm not sure I've got a choice.

Above the bed there's a painting; a kitschy picture of a blonde woman, with just her head and bare shoulders on an orange background. She gazes down on us with a benevolent smile and when I wince and clear my throat to answer Anne I look up at the wall instead and direct my words at her.

"Well, you know, when I was younger, you're right, I didn't talk to a lot of people. These days, I don't mind. I've got a few friends and don't mind talking in general. But back then I didn't used to. I would go weeks, easily, without speaking to anyone. But I wasn't lonely, because there was always something going on in my head.

"I don't really remember what it was like when I was younger, but especially when I was twelve, thirteen, fourteen, I used to have these ongoing discussions in my mind. And most of the time, they were, you know, discussions like you'd normally have - your own thoughts going around - but sometimes they were... they would... take on this quality of being someone else. Someone who would talk to me in my head and say things that I wouldn't ever have thought of. Or tell me things that I couldn't have really known. Like someone real."

I swallow, suddenly feeling quite sick in my stomach. Anne's sitting quietly, listening - but I can't unfix my gaze from the painting.

"There were other parts too. Occasionally I would have this feeling - it didn't happen often - that... " I stop, and try to gather my thoughts, as if hunting for them in the orange paint and blonde smile. "This feeling that - the best way of describing it is - that reality was getting sick. I'd get this feeling reality was kind of... *ill*. And sometimes it was just very faint, but occasionally I'd have black periods and not be able remember for a while. And I guess it used to worry me - but I never was able to talk to anyone about it. And I figured it was just part of being me.

"And then eventually, those sensations and those kind of thoughts, they started to disappear. By sixteen it was something I'd forgotten about, except maybe twice a year when it might come back in some moment. And then when I started working full-time it pretty much disappeared for good."

I finally look down at Anne, who has her head on the side, listening.

"The only time it ever came back was when I played around a few years ago with acid. Once or twice - weeks after taking a trip - I'd get this horrible feeling that the world was starting to curdle at the edges. So I avoid that sort of thing. Actually, tonight would be the first time in years that I've taken anything. And it's been *fine*," I add hurriedly. "Somehow I knew it would be fine tonight, especially around you. But then there was last week at the party..."

"What did it feel like?" Anne's voice is very gentle.

"I wasn't on drugs or anything. But it was... unpleasant."

I look back at the painting, but the quality of reassurance it had a moment ago has gone. A damp shiver seems to touch my skin.

"I had this overwhelming feeling. This growing feeling that there was a presence in the room, observing me. It gave the feeling of being just behind my shoulder. Very close. But really it was as if it was all around me. As if the room and the floor and the walls and the people were somehow all aware of me and observing me very closely."

"That sounds *awful*."

"Please don't think I'm nuts..."

"I didn't say you were."

I say nothing. The warm glow of this evening is draining away.

"Finn," she says emphatically, "I'm going to say this slowly so that I'm *sure* you understand - okay? To me you seem perfectly normal. I'm a pretty good judge of these things. And to me you are normal. Charmingly. Pleasantly. *Handsomely* normal."

And there goes that feeling again, like a light's been switched on. My anxiety evaporates and Anne smiles.

"You know, Miles wants to go into business with you," she says. "Just to change the subject."

"He wants what?"

"He told me tonight."

"Why would he...?"

"He's been looking for someone for a while. You know what Miles is like. Well, maybe you don't. But you probably got an impression, right? He's got some big ideas and what with his whole not-suffering-fools attitude, he's pretty keen to get away from regular work and go into business for himself."

"What does he want with me?"

"Well for ages he's been going on about getting the right person before he starts his business up - someone with a regular job who'll do a few hours extra when he needs them. Working online - kind of technical stuff? Anyway, sounds like you said something he liked tonight, because he told me you were the right kind of guy."

"Jesus."

"Yeah. So, I'd be expecting a call..."

"Oh you gave him my number?"

"Hey, why not?" says Anne brightly. "Oh, you look mortified! Come on, there could be worse things than getting into business with Miles - he's very clever, you know."

I wipe my hands down my face and groan. Ohhh, that's why I didn't want a mobile phone..."

"Ha - too late now," she says, totally unrepentant - and rubs the back of my neck again. "So that pill treated you okay then?"

"Yeah, totally. But gee they're strong aren't they?"

"Not really! You're still feeling it then?"

I look around. There's a grey light leaking in under the blinds. It must be 4am - and I could stay up talking like this for hours.

"Yeah!" I laugh.

"Maybe you're sensitive," says Anne, with a yawn in her voice. "Reckon you can sleep?"

"I don't mind not sleeping."

"Well, okay. But you have to be my log, to curl up against," she says plaintively. "Because, me, I'm getting really..." and her voice goes all mumbly as she folds herself in around me and twitches the sheets across us both "I'm feeling really *very*..." And that's the last I get from her as she settles in to slumber next to me.

I kick off my shoes and shift down to get comfortable - a long log sheltering a sleeping creature - and get ready for hours of my own thoughts and staring at the ceiling. But it's not like that. The sense of composing myself is the last thing I remember before a black unconsciousness flashes over me, as sudden as a magician snapping his fingers.

***

"How was work?"

"Actually, boring. Everything's slowed down now the project's over. And they get on my tits, you know."

"How's that?"

"Well they're so clubby. Their own little power plays and alliances. It's boring."

"It's not like you go out of your way to join in."

"Why would I? Honestly, the shit they talk about. Football, I mean - fucking *football* - for hours."

"How strange that you're so dark on your colleagues all of a sudden and it's the Tuesday after a pharmacological indulgence. What a coincidence."

"Yeah, alright..."

"Alright? Don't sulk at me -"

"Sorry. You're right you know. Jesus, it always sneaks up on you doesn't it. Black Tuesday." The tube carriage we're in rattles and fills with the sound of squealing rails, but we carry on talking.

"I was even dark on the whole Anne thing today. Not to her of course - but around lunchtime it just seemed a terrible, stupid idea. I should be careful with that. How do you think it's going?"

"Well how would I know?"

"Just honestly - from how I am."

"Honestly? Seriously? It's none of my business."

"Okay. Do you know one thing though?"

There's no answer.

"Do you know -" and I look at the seat next to me.

There's an old lady staring straight ahead. Across from me are two disinterested black guys. I don't know who I was talking to.

I get off at the next stop.

***

On Thursday night I'm at home cooking dinner in a quiet flat when the buzzer goes. I turn the gas off under the wok and head downstairs to the front door. It's Kip.

"Right on, right on... Finn. How you doing?"

He's wearing the same red jacket, with vintage blue corduroys and Jesus boots with socks on. He looks as tall and skinny and crafty as before.

"Kip! Hey. I was just... hey. Why don't you come in?"

"Right on," he says again and steps in the door.

"Come on up."

"So Finn my man, how you been. Plenty of party-party?" he says knowingly as we walk up the stairs.

"Oh, you know... ah. Sort of. How about you?"

Kip's eyes are flicking over the flat. There's a funny expression on his face.

"Are your flatmates in?

"Oh, nah. Everyone's out tonight. Hey listen, do you want a cup of tea?"

"Damn straight! Yeah yeah - I could murder a cuppa."

"Cool, okay well the living room's through there. Grab a seat and I'll be right with you." I head back to the kitchen and put the kettle on.

"Mind if I skin up?" Kip calls down the corridor.

"Go right ahead."

I stand waiting in the kitchen while the kettle rumbles into life. What's Kip doing here? He must have looked us up. The water takes ages, but eventually I manage to get a couple of tea bags into two steaming cups and take them through.

"I forgot to ask how you take it."

"Just as it is my man. Set it down there."

Kip's on the couch with his back to the bay window, crumbling cannabis into a little pile on the coffee table. He adds a twist of tobacco, mixing it deftly with his fingertips, then folds it into a long rolling paper, licking and tweaking until the spliff is perfectly formed. He looks up with gleaming eyes and thanks me for the cuppa.

"And a lighter?"

"Is that one in your tobacco pouch?"

"So it is, so it is" and he leans back to fire up the joint and savour the first lungful.

"So Finn... you're 'sort of' doing well? What kind of answer is that?"

"Well, you know. Nothing much is happening. It's all good. But just the usual."

With a rumbling fake snore Kips mimes nodding off, then shakes himself awake with mock surprise. "Okay, how's the love life then?"

"Well I did start seeing someone. A girl. It's been going well."

"Ah. Feisty little minx is she?" Kip draws deeply on the joint, expelling the thick blue smoke to roil around his head. "I'm just kidding you."

I don't say anything. Actually, I'm thinking of how to excuse myself from smoking pot on a school night - though there's no sign of it being offered.

"What about your salmon project," I ask. "Living City? Is that... is that going well?"

Kip looks levelly at me for a moment. There really is something weasely about him. He seems like the kind of person who gets more straight when he gets stoned. And I bet, no matter how dodgy the neighborhood, he never gets mugged.

"Put it out of your head," he says dismissively. "That's old news. We got a new bag."

I wait to be informed.

"We're reclaiming the beach."

"Which beach? You're moving to Brighton or something?"

"No my man - it's much closer to home. I'm talking about the *Thames* beach."

Kip pauses to drag deeply on the joint. His eyes seem to shine as he exhales. Meanwhile I'm perched on the front of the other chair, arms on my knees, looking nervous in my own house.

"As you may or may not know, Finn my friend, the Thames is highly tidal - even in London. That means that twice a day it recedes to reveal a considerable stretch of riverbed. Some of which is mud -" Kip's hand spirals about his head in a loose-wristed gesture that makes the joint-end glow and leaves a little trail of puff "- and some of which is coarse but clean white sand.

Do you know the total area of land uncovered in England when the Thames retreats?"

Why would I?

"Of course you don't. But the answer is: it's lots. *Lots and lots and lots.* I've been researching."

Another puff. Clearly it's not going to be offered.

"Do you know what 'liminal' means?"

I shake my head and Kip rearranges himself on the couch with his feet up and his gaze on the ceiling - all the better to pontificate. I keep an eye on the joint hand to see he doesn't burn a hole.

"Liminal. It's a wonderful word isn't it? *Liminal, liminal, liminal.* It comes from Latin and it means 'threshold' and it carries a certain legal status.

"The liminal zone, for instance, refers to the area of land revealed by the tide on any waterway. The *sub*-liminal exists below the low water mark. That's below the surface of the Thames - the dirty old Thames - and you don't want to venture into the subliminal my man!" Kip chuckles at his own joke. "So while everything above the high water mark is owned and operated and capitilized on and policed..." Here Kip takes a last little puff on the joint - just, it seems, to appreciate his illegal little indulgence - then grinds it out on the table and drops the roach in his pocket.

"It's policed..." he loses the thread of his thoughts for a moment and his eyes flicker about as if searching for the loose end in the smoke. "It's policed. But yes the liminal zone - the area between the high and the low water - the liminal zone is outside the law of the land because... *because it doesn't belong to anyone.*

"So we're going to reclaim it. I'm throwing a party. You see I've timed it for when the low tide happens at dusk and we're gonna have a massive party and it'll be right in the middle of god-damned London and no one can do a thing about it!"

Kip swings his legs back onto the floor and glances at his tea.

"No milk?"

"I wasn't sure..."

"Don't worry about it. So yeah, it'll be a party, man - a celebration of everything that's outside the law, that's not controlled by the man - by rules and corporations and corrupt businesses. You should come along brother, it'll be a blast." And Kip's grinning now, a wide maniac's grin, and he fishes in his jacket pocket and hands me a crumpled flyer. It's the same cheap yellow paper that I saw in the Brixton shop, but scissored into rectangles.

He stands suddenly, all legs and long hair.

"I gotta fly. But you'll come along, yeah?"

"Sure Kip. Okay. Thanks."

He strides to the door and pauses for a moment.

"Tell your flatmates I say hi, yeah?"

"Right on," I hear myself say, parroting his phrase.

"Right on," says Kip with a waggle of brows - and that's it. With the sound of the door and diminishing footsteps he's gone - leaving me standing with a flyer in my hand and two cups of tea in a flat that reeks of pot.

***

"Take a look at this" I tell Miles and slide him Kip's invite.

We're in the Duke of Edinburgh. Kip had been gone an hour and I was washing up after dinner when Miles called. He blustered through an explanation of wanting to talk about work, mentioned that Anne had mentioned that she'd mentioned it to me... and would I be keen to meet in the pub to discuss it? After a while I realised he meant now, tonight, at a pub down the road and after um-ing and ah-ing I agreed to come down.

"What is it?" says Miles. He's got a drink in front of him already and seems uninterested in the flyer - or at least pre-occupied with the thing he's dragged me here to discuss - so I explain about Kip and the strange visit and the party. I dig around in my jacket pocket and there's the crumpled flyer Kip gave me when I first saw him in Brixton. I lay the two scraps next to each other on the table. The movement wafts a faint pot smell from my clothes.

"I don't think much of his finished art skills," offers Miles. He rotates the Save The Lost Rivers flyer towards him to look at the hand-drawn-then-photocopied image of a rural stream. There's a derision in Miles' voice that I suspect is there often. "Campaign execution could be... neater."

He flips the paper over to look at the other side, which has been printed with columns of text; the back doesn't quite match the front and the ends of letters have been lopped by the guillotine. Miles clears his throat to read in a sneering voice:

"'Did you know?'" He pauses for effect. "'*Did you know* that Queen Elizabeth once visited Sir Walter Raleigh by sailing up the waterway that used to flow through the neighbourhood you're in?' *Fascinating.* 'And that great King Canute also navigated this stream. It was called the Effra, like Effra Road or the Effra tavern, and what you probably didn't know, is that it flows beneath these stones to this day.'

"Ahh," purrs Miles, enjoying himself. "Here it comes - the call to action.

"'We at the Living City foundation *demand* of Lambeth council that the Effra be allowed to live again. A section of the stream should be raised above ground to the benefit and education of all and a parkland be included for the beautification of the Brixton community. Take to the street this Saturday to show your support. March begins at Brixton Police station and ends at Lambeth Council.'"

Miles looks up. "It's dated last weekend. Get the feeling no one turned up?" He scrunches the paper into a ball and flicks it off the table. I wanted to keep that.

"So Miles, what is it you want to talk about?"

"Yes, quite. Why don't you get yourself a drink first and I'll explain."

When I return with a beer and sit down Miles is waiting with chin resting on steepled fingers. He pauses for a while then looks at me.

"I'm not sure how much Anne has told you...?"

I shake my head.

"Well, like I said when we met, I'm a marketer. I do marketing and project management, but business development too. And after all these years I'm a pretty well hooked-up guy, if I say it myself.

"And, well, my current situation is... that I'm bored with my work. I don't anticipate any new challenges for a while so I think this is the right time to try something I've been planning. And I thought you might help.

"So here's what I'm going to do."

He pauses again, fingers still steepled, and stares into the table with unfocused eyes.

"Imagine that you have some health insurance. And imagine that you have a credit card, and a mortgage - and a variety of debts, outgoings, investments...

"At the moment, the way you manage those is very, very slow. Unless you're in finance you probably don't check your stocks in real time and you certainly don't change insurers on a whim as their premiums shift.

"But a lot of those things that you don't do are because it's a hassle. It's a flat-out hassle and the reason that's the case has to do with the flow of information. A whole range of really useful data still reaches you by post, or through the newspaper, or in an article you read online - which is a way of saying that the information flow has lagged way behind what we're capable of.

"So this is what I'm proposing. We, as a company - the company that I am forming and that you will join and I will find funding for - we will make a kind of online entity. The entity will access this flow of information and represent you online. It makes decisions for you based on how, in general, you want it to behave - and this thing that sits within the flow of information for you, that analyses and interprets data you don't necessarily want to be bothered with - it trades for you, switching around your insurance provider, your credit card debt - even, eventually, your mortgage provider - and it does it automatically and always - here's the crux - it's always to your consumer advantage.

"Do you follow?"

"I think so."

"Good. I could go into a lot more detail, but we're in a pub and it's Thursday night, so I'll get down to my proposition. What you need to know is that I'm entirely serious with this idea, and despite the fact that it's ambitious and will require the buy-in of at least some of the biggest players in the world of consumer credit, healthcare and so on - despite that, from now on I will be ploughing ahead on this with all the hours and energy I have."

Miles looks up to catch my eye.

"What I need from you is what I lack. I plan to handle the client relationship side of things - and I have my eye on a contract lawyer who we'll need on board fairly soon. But what we don't have is technical expertise.

"Now, I don't know if this is up your alley. And I don't know if you have the kind of character and capabilities to cut it on a job like this..."

Here Miles' eyelids do that fluttering thing of his, like a tic in his vision.

"...but after our conversation the other night, it occurred to me that I'd like to give you a chance."

"What do you want done?" I ask hesitantly.

"Well, number one, I need someone to build this thing. Someone who can - what, programme? - our entity. Work out how it speaks to the banks and gathers data - and then work out how it speaks to the consumer, how we design its interface. And so on. But that's a huge job. I wouldn't expect you to do that. That will take a team of developers and a lot of time - though ideally, I'm looking for someone who can guide that phase. But what I need *now* is someone who can read a business case. Who can look at what we've got on paper, view it through the lens of what's technically possible, and help me redesign the business proposal based on that.

"What do you think?"

"I think you're right: it is ambitious. But also very interesting. You know, I've done similar projects on a smaller scale; things like linking supermarkets with their supply-chain software. Third-party software. But this is ambitious on a whole different level Miles."

"So you're interested?"

"Could be."

"Then here's how I think it would go. Normal process is for you to send me a CV; apply for the job formally. But I recognise this is a bit different. So what I suggest is that I give you part of the business case for you to read - you review it, write me a technical response document - and I'll pay you £90 an hour. That way, your work functions as a kind of CV: if I like it, we'll think about further roles. And if not..." Miles shrugs "...it's no big deal.

I shrug and fiddle with my beer mat.

"Let's do it."

"Great."

Miles starts banging on about company structure - hinting at the future riches that would come my way if I work out - and I try to listen, but inside my technical mind's firing up. I take a long breath and that meditative, abstract place receives the oxygen and flares gently awake, like slumbering embers blown on. Already ideas on how I might build this thing are roiling around half formed. They're thoughts I can barely perceive, but I can sense their possibilities and all I want now is to be some place quiet, away from Miles' talking, so I can pursue their logic on my own.

"...so how about another beer?"

I make an effort and turn aside from my ideas, hopeful they'll be there when I return.

"Ah, go on," I say, with full attention now. "Why not?"

And Miles says "Well we shouldn't get ahead of ourselves, but maybe we have cause to celebrate." So we go up for more beers and then another round after that. And when we step out of the bar at closing time, my feet catching just a little as we step over the worn flagstones at the door, I've got a glow on - the kind of warmth that comes from booze and big plans. And Jesus, I've got a pocket full of napkins covered with ideas and diagrams in blue biro. I mean, *napkins* for crying out loud. But my usual capacity for self-derision doesn't make it through these radiating plans for the future and anyway, I'm eager to tell Anne about this. So Miles and I say goodbye with a whole new level of chummy enthusiasm - he's going one way, I'm going the other - and I stride for home, smiling as I go, stopping just once for a piss on a wall.

***

The other thing that happens that week is Henry resurfaces. He's there when I get home on Friday, bouncing around the place, engaging Phil and Jane in conversation when they get back from work - and generally trampling over the kind of boundaries that crystalise round people who live together and like routines.

When Jane starts cooking he parks himself in the kitchen so he can quiz her about some drama she's having at work - Jane's a landscape designer - and he gives the sense that he really wants to build something from their discussion, that's he's not just making chit chat. Phil, on the other hand, he manages to agitate into good humour and I notice Phil laughs more, is more engaged when Henry's around; though I bet he watches less television than he'd like.

Eventually he finds the time for our talk. It's something of an echo of the conversation where he invited me to the party: a Friday night tap on my door, then Henry leaning casually at the room's entrance to chat.

"I hear I missed meeting your new lady last week. Jane's says she's great," he tells me. And I know what this is about - I figure I'm getting Henry's 'I'm a dealer' lecture, which is why he's turning on the charm. Yet I still can't help grinning.

"Yeah, she's cool. You'll meet her soon enough I hope. How are things with you? Work busy?"

Hurrying things along.

"Well that's right. It's been crazy busy. I got two new clients this week. Did I even mention I'm a graphic designer...?"

I just wait. Henry looks at something in the corner of the room.

"Actually, work's what I wanted to talk to you about. My other work, if you like. Phil told me he'd said something to you?"

"Yeah, kind of..."

"Right. Well, I just wanted to check with you that it's alright. You know, I'd have mentioned it before you moved in, but obviously it's not the sort of thing you want to spread round every potential flatmate that you interview. So, well, we sort of took a gamble that you'd be the kind of guy who wouldn't mind. You seemed pretty cool when we met..."

Now I'm actually starting to feel put-upon.

"So, I don't know." He looks back at me. "*Do* you mind? Is there anything you'd like to ask?"

I shrug, aware that it looks kind of sulky. Then I remember when Anne and I discussed it last week.

"Well, what kind of drugs, I guess?"

"Ah yes, the key question," Henry laughs. "It's mostly coke. I have a very small but regular group that come to me. They buy a few pills, but mostly coke - though that's dried up for the moment, and I'm selling speed...

"Anyway, the main thing is how it operates. What you need to know is *no one* comes to this flat to buy drugs..."

He says it forcefully, and as much as it's meant as reassurance, it also sounds half warning.

"...so you never have to worry about that. Number two, I don't keep any volume of product in the house. And, the last thing, I guess, is my clientele. I'm pretty choosy about who I deal to. I'm not saying I don't deal to black people," he says carefully. "I just leave the yardie bad boys to their turf and keep my clients strictly middle-class.

"Do you see what I mean?"

"Of course." And I'm sure there's logic behind it, but this speech sure brings out the worst in Henry.

"Now, what I guess would be really great from you, is if you wouldn't tell this to anyone. You can see why that's important huh? If every geezer at every party comes asking for charlie, pretty soon the bad people notice - and bad things happen to me.

"So you won't mention it to anyone? I mean, obviously it's no big deal if you were to say something to your lady," he adds presciently, "it's more that people don't get the impression they can get hooked up through me. Anyway, I'm rabbiting. But you get the general idea?"

"Sure man, don't worry about it" I grin - more in amusement at the effort he's putting into this friendly-with-a-purpose performance than out of real camaraderie - and make like a zip across my face. "Your secret's safe with me."

"Sure!" laughs Henry, with relief in the force of his exclamation. "I knew you'd be cool. Just wanted to check though, yeah? Oh and hey, the way I've worked it out with the others... if you ever do want anything for yourself... it's yours real cheap, okay? Just let me know?"

"Thanks man," I say - and Henry turns to go. He stops though and looks back, a little uncertain.

"I mean, I've got a lot of speed in at the moment. Really pure. As in... it's *really* the good stuff," and he sounds like a Eurotrash drug dealer now for the first time. "£30 a bag for you, if you want some?"

"Ahh..." I shake my head and raise my hands apologetically. "I'm okay for the moment."

"No worries. Okay. Just let me know."

***

Sunday morning. Text message wakes me. I'm up and scrabbling under the bed for the phone with just a hint of shame for my eagerness. Only one person texts me.

'Have you heard of Syon Park?'

I stop to think for a bit.

'Are you Jewish?' I always do proper capitals now.

'Haha.' says the reply. 'Dick. Syon not zion. Butterfly house. Been there?'

I text out 'Why do I feel I'm about to?' and straight away - *how* does she text so quickly? - comes the reply.

'Smart fella. Great. Get thee ready.'

I look at the time on the phone - it's only 7:08 - and a last text comes while I'm looking at the screen.

'I'll see you in 40 mins.'

Even though I'm tired, I get wriggly expecting Anne and can't get back to sleep. I should get up and shower and get ready, but the thought of *being* ready and sitting there waiting obediently when she arrives is too much, so instead I drool into the pillow for a while and daydream.

All of sudden there are brisk footsteps outside my room and the door flings open. Without any preamble, Anne jumps on the bed, all knees and elbows, and pins me under the sheet.

"Dammit! *Goddammit!* I can't believe it!

"Sorry. Sorry, I was in bed, I should've got up..." She's ignoring me.

"I can't believe it! They closed it down. The butterfly house. I *really* wanted to go there."

"Uh. How did you get in?"

"Henry walked out as I went to push the buzzer. He let me in. Oh, I can't believe it!"

I sit up properly in bed, still groggy - definitely groggy compared to this onslaught.

"You can't believe...? They closed the...?"

"...the butterfly house. There was this wonderful butterfly house at Syon Park. I remember my Mum took me when I was a kid and I woke up this morning and thought *that's* what I want to do today. So I looked it up and found it, it's way out West, and I texted you and now I've found out it was closed, ages back, to build some stupid bloody *thing*.

I let loose a long breath and rub my eyes. Anne looks at me with a hint of pity.

"Fancy a cup of tea?" I venture.

"You mean you want *me* to make you a cup of tea?"

"It's alright, I'll be up in a minute - I'll make it." But she wraps a pillow round my head and pushes me roughly back on the bed.

"No, no, poor Finn. You need a sleep-in. I'll make the tea. God knows you deserve it after a hard week in the..." - the pillow comes back off my face long enough for Anne to give me a hawkish look - "...newsroom?"

"Lame." The pillow comes back, and not gently - though it's kind of pleasant in the dark. "White with one?" I mutter meekly into the fabric and she clatters off to put the kettle on and give me some peace. After a while I decide not to push my luck and sidle to the shower.

When I get out there's a mug of tea cooling on the arm of the couch, plus some toast. Anne's sitting with her legs crossed on one of the wooden chairs, cradling her own cup. She gives my skinny towel-wrapped frame a leer as I hurry to my room, where I throw on clothes willy-nilly, rub my hair mostly dry and re-emerge.

"So, oh hunk-of-man, what can you do about my vanished butterflies?"

"*Tea tea tea...*"

"Oh, you're a little addict."

The first mouthful is like sunlight in my brain. I swill another around my teeth and send it down. Pause to enjoy effect. Open mouth...

"So. Anne. Good morning!"

"*Hi* Finn. How are *you?*"

"Very well now, thank you. Thanks for the tea."

"Not a problem."

"So, she-who-will-never-guess-my-job... I, ah, sense that you have a certain up and at 'em thing going on this morning."

"You've hit it. Right on the head."

"...and I sense also that you've had a little disappointment... something about butterflies... I might have slept through some of that part."

"Again: spot on."

"Okay, well, I guess what that means is we need an alternative. A different activity that doesn't involve butterflies; one that's just as excellent a way to spend the day - maybe better? - that you and I should think of right now. Toast?"

"I've just eaten, thank you. Those are for you. And you're absolutely right, we need an activity. So, oh fortunate one - what shall we do?"

I grab a piece of toast and take a big bite, chewing to stall for time.

"Hmmm."

Again, stalling with the long exaggerated swallow and a sip of tea.

"Okay, here's a few ideas.

"One, we could do a day trip inside London. These are the things I like doing: trip to Richmond Park, trip to the Natural History Museum, trip to the Design Museum - or else picking out a place neither of us has been. Benefits: stimulating to the mind, easy to tackle, can relocate to the pub afterwards and have a meal. The downside? *Meh*. You can do that any time."

I'm making this up as I go along.

"So, suggestion two: playing a game. Pull out the rail map, point to a random station. Go there, and get on the first train we see. Don't pay for the train and get off after an hour.

"Benefits of this plan: spontaneity is fun and we could end up somewhere brilliant. Potential downfall: trains go to Luton too." I swallow the last of the tea. "Any suggestions to throw in the mix here? I'm just making this up."

"And you're doing a wonderful job. I like the idea of a train trip - we're up early and we should take advantage of that - but maybe the random factor would throw it out? Why don't we load the dice in our favour - any suggestions on places to go?"

"Well, again, there's always the 'meh' options - places everyone goes. But we should find somewhere awesome. Forget about Brighton and Oxford and Cambridge and so on. Do you have a map?"

"Must have left mine at home."

"Alright, alright. Hang on - come in here."

I rummage through the bookshelf in the main living room area and sure enough there are a couple of decent-sized fold-out maps that show the south of England. We spread them on the floor and get down on our hands and knees, crumpling the paper where we lean on it.

We both go quiet as we scan the tiny village names in a band around London. Anne traces her finger down a rail line through Kent.

"What about this? Wye."

"Wye not?"

"That cuppa's done you wonders. To think you were in bed half an hour ago."

"It's next to Ashford, which is on the main London rail line. About..." I press my thumb into the gap between the two names then compare it to the scale bar "...two miles? We could walk it at a pinch, but it looks like there's another railway that branches off. What do you think?"

"A tiny little town in the middle of Kent. It could be full of chavs and housing estates, but what's the bet it's the prettiest little place you've ever seen?"

I brew on this for a moment, pulling a thoughtful face.

"So what do we need?"

"We need to walk out the door and go."

"Hang on we don't even..." I reach for the A-Z and open it at the rail map.

"Look, the line goes straight into Charing Cross," says Anne, her voice rising. "You don't need that."

I stop to think again, running through things we might need. Then we both look up from our bums-in-the-air, map-scouring pose as we hear Phil and Jane's door open and someone walk to the loo. Anne looks back at me with a kind of warm tolerance and says in a quieter voice "Get your wallet, a hat in case it's cold and your jacket."

When we slip out, closing the door softly, I hear the toilet flushing behind us.

***

"We're on the way!" Anne announces to the empty street, enjoying the loudness of her voice - and she grabs the scruff of my jacket and shakes me. I just scrunch up my shoulders and duck my head away from her - is she going to be this annoying all day? - but eventually she calms down enough to curl her arm around my waist as we walk, back to being the affectionate Anne that she does best, and we settle into a rhythm. Down the stairs to the tube on the Northern Line; comfortable in each other's company as our carriage rocks to Charing Cross.

"How am I going to ask you about your week if I don't know what you do?"

"It's a problem isn't it?" says Anne. "It's a shame, 'cause it was a good one, too. It made it all seem worthwhile."

"I reckon you do something artistic. Kind of creative; or something with people. Working with retards maybe."

Anne laughs out her nose and shakes her head.

"No - that's the weekends. But you're close with artistic. What about you. How was your week?"

I look up, trying to read the signs that flash by as we pull into a station. Charing Cross.

"It was fine. This is us."

"You know your eyes were doing the most horrific thing just then."

"How do you mean?"

"They were flickering when you tried to read things out the window. Real *Exorcist* styles."

We get out and trudge up to the overland rail station, taking our time because there's no one around. Up on the concourse we stand arm in arm looking at the timetable board. The names of towns scroll past and that train lady's voice intones the destinations: the sound of modern Britain. There - Ashford. Leaving in three minutes. It couldn't be easier.

"Anyway - your week?"

We're sat on the mostly empty train in facing seats. Anne's gathered up newspapers.

"Yeah," I begin, with my feet up on the cushion in defiance of the signs. "Miles got in touch." And as the train shunts gently away from the platform, overcoming its inertia with a lurch then building up speed in a smooth motion, I lay the happenings of the last few days in Anne's lap - taking my time because she seems patient and interested. I tell her about Kip first and his random visit to our place - she thinks it's strange that he knew where to come and asks lots of questions - then we talk about Miles and his business idea, and finally Henry and his drugs.

Outside, the view that speeds by grows more rural as we pass into the Kentish countryside. The sky turns a perfect powder blue with towering white cloud-heads, like a painting with spitfires in it. Maybe there'll be rain later; a classic British summer day.

We reach Ashford and lo-and-behold, when we get off there's another train going to Wye. By the time we get there - just an hour and a half since we left my place - we still haven't finished dissecting my week. The train pulls away and we stand alone on the small country platform carrying on the conversation, oblivious for the moment to the sudden quiet, the birdsong, the emptiness. Anne wants to know about the machinations of Henry's double life - does he have a regular job? So it's like two separate lives? - but I still want to ask about Miles.

"Well, like I said Finn, you could do a lot worse than going into business with him. You know Miles is quite driven, don't you?"

"That's half my worry. He seems so intense about it. It's just like... it's a *massively* ambitious project. It'll either be a huge success or a total failure - there's no middle ground. It's a hell of a long shot and I'm not sure I want to be shackled to Miles if and when it goes down. No offense. I mean, he's your friend."

"I know and that's alright. Yvonne and Miles are good friends, but I know what they're like. But I don't see what the risk is. Are you worried about the fallout with me if it all went wrong?"

"Sure. I mean, that would be weird."

"No it wouldn't."

It's perfectly quiet on the platform now but for the two of us standing face-to-face. It's slightly absurd.

"I know exactly what Miles is like, but there's no way anything that might happen with him would affect what goes on between you and I. You think those two are more important to me than you?"

I shrug, uncomfortable, but she holds my eye.

"Do you?"

I don't say anything.

"So this is what you should do. You should go along with his plan. Just make sure you insulate yourself from him a little. You sound like you're getting along fine, but make sure when you're dealing with him at work that you keep it professional. Because I think it's worth getting involved. You don't want to end up being the fifth Beatle."

"The what?"

"You know. The guy who was in the Beatles before they were big. He played drums before Ringo."

"I thought he was kicked out."

"Whatever. Or the guy who sold his stake in Apple Computers then, and missed out on a billion dollars. I'm just saying, you don't want to look back and wish you hadn't backed out of something good for just some stupid social reason."

I look at my feet for a while, thinking.

"Alright. You're right. Anyway, it's just some freelance work at the moment."

Anne gives me a slow, pleasurable smile that makes it look like she's genuinely happy for what I've said.

"Wye not!" she exclaims, and thrusts her arm through mine. "Now where are we?!"

We look around. Wye doesn't seem so small after all. From the station we can see serried houses marching in pretty tiled rows down the streets - there might be a couple of thousand living here. And then: "What the hell's that?"

A high down rises on the other side of the village, running off into the distance on either side, and on it, right above the houses for all to see is a great white crown, carved into the chalk of the hillside.

"Finn, my boy - we have our destination!"

We make our way over a bridge and down a series of roads, always trying to keep the crown in sight. It has a familiar look - like something on a coin that you never notice despite seeing it every day - and even though it's just a simple outline with a cross on top, there's something eerie about it.

"It's modern, isn't it? It's got to be," says Anne. I ask if this is better than butterflies.

"Much better. God, it's spooky though isn't it. Have you been to see the Long Man of Wilmington?"

"The one with the boner?"

"No that's the other one. The long man has two sticks in his hand. Well they look like sticks, but people say they represent the edges of a door and he's guarding the entrance to the underworld."

"What do you think this is guarding, the entrance to a giant stamp collection?"

"Haha. But it is modern, isn't it? That's a royal crown of some sort. It's like it says Queen woz here."

Eventually we find ourselves down a Coldharbour Lane - "Just like Brixton" - and the crown, close now, disappears behind trees. There's a path.

"Ladies first."

We wind up an overgrown track and emerge from the woods onto a grassy slope. The crown's hard to see now because we're on it, but the lines are clear. They're channels cut into the turf that have been filled with white flints - pale-looking stones that show dark hearts of glass where they break.

"Look, there's a plaque."

And sure enough the crown is modern - or near enough. A commemorative effort marked out by students in 1902 for King Edward's coronation. The mystery's gone.

"Bit of a shame there's an explanation, isn't it?" says Anne, and we drift off the site and further up the hill.

From here the view gets silly-pretty - all fields and hills and oaks under a white-bright sun. We mill about for a while then turn our backs on the town and follow a path. We should have got some water.

By the time we've gone down the other side of the hill and strolled through fields where insects fly up as our feet swish through the grass, the sun has passed behind clouds. Finally, after a couple of hours walking, we spot some houses and - joy! - a pub, and just as we near it the heavens open and we run the last hundreds yards in the rain.

It's been a day of good timing.

The downpour eases off as quickly as it came. By the time we've ordered our lunch and a drink each it's bright enough to settle out back on the outdoor tables where the white concrete patio drying in the sun gives off a fresh, chalky odour.

The only other person out here is on the table next to us - and I can see Anne getting curious. He's in walking boots and shorts and a vest with a funny badge - a proper anorak - but tanned and in his mid fifties by the look of it. Anne's not even pretending to listen to me as she peers at him filling out paperwork. Eventually she throws in a shamelessly pointless remark, and opens a front.

"Lovely day!" she says loudly. "So lucky with the sun!"

He looks up from his work, pen hovering.

"Isn't it!" is his jocular reply after a slight pause - and straight away Anne's in like a terrier:

"What are you doing?"

"Oh, well, I'm... filling out a census. Of butterflies."

"Butterflies?" And that's it - Anne gets straight up out of her seat and carries her drink over to his table. "Oh I love butterflies. Are you catching them? May we join you?" And so on and so on - turning on the charm and leaving the poor man with no option but to wave at the seat next to him - and me to gather my drink and our plastic order number and join them.

With her initial assault successful, Anne slows her pace, giving the man some space and settling into the steady business of information gathering.

"I'm Anne - and this is Finn."

"Hello. Hello Finn - I'm David."

"Are you with the National Trust then?" She takes a sip of her beer.

"No, not really. I'm doing some work for the UK Butterfly Monitoring Scheme. It sounds grand doesn't it? I volunteer for them, running what we call a transect where I count all the butterflies in a set area throughout the year and record the different species."

Anne looks like the cat that got the cream. David looks like a jolly nice man who's unsure whether he's having the piss taken out of him. But I can tell that Anne can tell, and she launches into an earnest account of getting up early this morning because she wanted to see the butterflies at Syon House and how disappointing it was, and isn't it a coincidence to meet a butterfly expert out here today? And she makes sure to put in plenty of detail so it's clear she's not lying and David warms up with a pleased look on his brown sun-creased face.

"Well you know it's the Duke of Northumberland that owns Syon Park. I believe it was he who closed the butterfly house, to build a commercial wing of some sort, and Lord knows if it got made anyway. But yes, a crying shame they closed it - although I'd not been there for donkey's."

"Tell me about your survey" says Anne. "Are you trying to find the rare ones?"

"Well, not so much. The fate of the butterflies isn't what concerns us. Not really. No. We're using them as a canary species if you see?"

David has a musical kind of voice - an up-and-down tone with a slightly flutey pitch.

"Butterflies are delicate creatures, as you'd imagine. They're sensitive to temperature change and pesticides and chemical levels too. Because of course they all start out as caterpillars and caterpillars are by nature rather porous to their surrounds.

"So you see, counting butterflies is like taking the pulse of the countryside. If anything's different - if the body of the country's running hot or cold, or catching some kind of fever - then chances are you'll see it in the butterflies. More of this kind, less of that - though decoding such things isn't really my domain; I'm just a volunteer.

"But to answer your question Anne, as an enthusiast not a scientist, of course I see it as my right to get excited about spotting the rare ones, as you put it. Look here: you see! I recorded two Clouded Yellows this morning in the field below the downs."

"Oh we came through there. Down the narrow track? But what's a Clouded Yellow?"

And I think I'm content to just sit here sipping beer, listening to Anne and David. Our meals arrive.

By the time we finish we've forgotten more about Clouded Yellows and

Painted Ladies and the beautiful Chalk-hill Blue than most people will ever know. Then David tells us the best way for walking back and where we can call a cab from halfway if we're tired; and I watch Anne give him a fond goodbye - he gives us both a tarrah in return, with his blue eyes and brown face under his toweling hat - and we head off back to the road; ambling, both of us satisfied in our different ways.

The walk back to Wye takes longer than we bargained for; mostly because there's a trail on the bank marked out in green signs with a crested heron in the logo and Anne insists on stopping to look at the river every ten minutes. We make it to the station with no dramas - though there's a half hour wait to get to Ashford and then another wait on the platform there. Then when we get on the train to London we gather up all the abandoned weekend papers that we didn't get round to looking at on the way out and read them all the sleepy way home. When we get to Charing Cross dusk is falling; by the time we finally make it to Anne's front door, really kind of pooped now, it's proper dark.

We trudge upstairs, feet too heavy to lift, and slump on to Anne's soft bed. After a while of lying face down I force myself up, get two big glasses of water and bring Anne's in to her. She gulps it down in one go.

"That's better. Oh that was a good day. How is it that my back's sore?"

I shrug, shy suddenly, and lie myself carefully down. Anne comes over, props herself over me on locked elbows, catches my eye and holds it. I lie there, looking back.

After a while the tension in my face seems to melt. Anne stays there, watching. The room blurs into obscurity - everything fading away beyond her brown steady eyes - and I forget about Wye and about aches and pains and me and her, or anything else at all, and just look.

It goes on for a long time. Her pupils flicker slightly as she studies my own gaze, flaring and contracting minutely as if she's trying to focus on something behind my face. Then she says in a very ordinary voice:

"I like you very, very much Finn. Did you know that?"

In my trance the words slip inside unjudged.

"No," I tell her. "No. I didn't know that at all."

3 JULY

"It seems indeed as if the heart of London had been cleft open for the mere purpose of showing how rotten and drearily mean it had become... And the muddy tide of the Thames, reflecting nothing, and hiding a million of unclean secrets within its breast - a sort of guilty conscience as it were, unwholesome with the rivulets of sin that constantly flow into it - is just the dismal stream to glide by such a city."

- Nathaniel Hawthorne, *Our Old Home*

Summer has hit its stride. We've had three weeks of almost entirely good weather now and dull Brits that we are, can't talk of anything else. Though we're a bunch of computer nerds at work, every conversation in the office gravitates to the topic of heat, sun, weekends, the reluctance to do this-or-that task because - oh, it's just too hard to work when it's so nice outside! - and the tube ride to work on Monday mornings is an immersion in the politics of tan: on girls' shoulders painful pink blushes of burn fan from the creamy ghosts of white bra straps. The carroty yellow fake-tan girls have lost what winter glamour they thought they had; and thin ladies sporting a perfectly managed bronze clop through the turnstiles in short skirts and trim white blouses, proud to be in control of everything, right down to the brown of their hides.

The day of Kip's party rolls around: the alignment of low tide, dusk and a Friday snicking into place like some rare astronomical event and I tell myself that I'll pop down, just out of curiosity. Just to have a look.

The flyer gives a location a short walk away on the South Bank, not far from Tower Bridge, though it says start at eight, so when work wraps up on Friday afternoon I break with tradition and go to the pub with 'the boys' to kill time.

Fat Alan pulls his shirt out of his trousers and dominates most of the talk. Everyone's relieved that the stress that gripped our company during the last project has dropped away and for the first time in a while people seem willing to chill. Alan's banging on about some bird he wants to get his mitts on, all to the amusement of the little group that gathers around him in a semi-circle, and as usual I'm content to be mostly ignored - passed over, I suspect, because God knows Finn wouldn't know the first thing about women; probably hasn't spoken to one in years.

Thinking of Anne, my phone bleeps in my pocket. No one looks over, but I switch it to silent so any future exchanges don't draw remark.

Anne says: "Any plans, loverboy?"

I write back. "No. Nothing. You?"

"Shall we meet back south of the river?"

"Maybe. I might end up going to Kip's thing. Later though. I'm at work drinks right now."

A pause for ten minutes, then Anne writes:

"Shall I come to you?"

"It's pretty boring. Why don't I just text later from Kip's."

"Okay. I'll find something to do."

I stop to think for a moment, then just send back: "Will see you soon." And I'm not sure why I'm reluctant to meet with Anne all of a sudden.

I guess I don't really want to introduce her to this crew - and I've got a hunch about the kind of people who'll be at Kip's. People who I'd be embarrassed for Anne to meet - though I still want to have a look.

Alan's stories carry on, laughter punctuating them at the proper points - dictated more by the tone of his voice than anything funny; people filling in the gaps with mirthless guffaws when the cadence of his tale tells them it's expected. I start wondering about Miles' little task.

He emailed me earlier in the week, his language very formal, and attached the business case chapter that he'd mentioned. So against work policy I signed out a laptop and took it home for my moonlighting project, saving the work to an external drive every night and deleting it from the machine to be safe.

My first impression at his document was relief that the goals were so clear - followed by bewilderment at the scale of his ambition. But as Anne had said, there was nothing to lose, so I treated the task as entirely abstract - not something that had any consequences to it - and wrote him an analysis that pulled his working model apart and reassembled it based on what was technically possible. I deliberately didn't build in any limitations on funding or man-power and even got right down into the nitty-gritty when the mood took me. All-in-all it was distracting enough.

I emailed it back yesterday and signed in the laptop. I haven't heard from him since.

Alan's sexual escapades seem to have lost their entertainment value for everyone by now and the guys are casting round for something else - a couple are feeding coins to a slot machine. I look at my watch: 7.30. I look at my pint: half full. I knock it back in slow, yeasty gulps - swallowing deliberately to make sure it stays down - then slip out without saying goodbye.

Out on the road I seem to have a slight lurch. Was it three pints, rather than two? I guess it was. And on the way to London Bridge I step down an alley for a leak. The pool of piss builds then spills into a long tendril that zigzags back out of the alleyway, gathering dust and debris on the way. It reaches the entrance before I can walk back out, blowing my cover, and runs away down the kerbside looking for a drain.

I, on the other hand, remain resolutely upright; firmly above the asphalt and concrete in the upper world of light. I march across London Bridge, seagulls skimming below me, cross the road carelessly and take the steps down to the Southern Embankment. I'm heading to where that great grey wedge of battleship the HMS Belfast lays moored - and when I pass him (how could a thing like that be a 'her'?) I hear it: wild music blaring out of a decent-sized sound system, and something else - the chug of a generator? - and at the same time see the high-vis vests of a police presence in the distance and think 'Oh my God Kip, what have you done?'

By the time I get to the grassy area next to Tower Bridge I've got a clear view of the whole palaver.

Up on the Embankment a small crowd has gathered, leaning against the rails and taking photos. Mixed in with them are three or four policemen looking unsure of themselves and trying to keep people from joining in. Blaring over the whole scene is an appalling mix of very loud trance music and a very loud diesel generator. Smoke is drifting out over the water and being whisked away on the wind and on the mucky-looking strip of land that the outgoing tide's exposed - dancing around the cables and the speakers and the thumping generator on its wooden pallet - are about two dozen people, every one of them caked to the knees in mud; guys and girls in bright clothes, half of them dreadlocked, some with their shirts off, all dancing with wild abandon like a multi-coloured patchouli-smelling bacchanalian mob.

A policeman is leaning over the parapet, shouting at one of the dancers, but his chances of being heard are dismal. The sound system's been turned up to drown out the generator which itself is saturating the area with background noise - a lawnmower in your room you can barely hear for the booming party next door. The whole atmosphere is charged with tension and irritation and the promise of oncoming night.

I turn and Kip is right there, standing behind my shoulder looking at what I see. His eyes are huge and shining and in that moment, muddled as I am with a beery head, he frightens me.

"Beautiful, isn't it," he says, with no let-up to the intensity of his gaze.

"Come on: come with me." And I see that while his shoes are filthy, he's wearing a pair of plain nylon overtrousers to conceal his muddy legs. He catches my look.

"Disguise, innit. Got to move among the people. Come on!" And he steps quickly away from the crowd, leading me under Tower Bridge, out of sight of the mob and the police.

On the other side of the bridge a knotted yellow rope has been looped around one of the ornate lampposts that mark the edge of the river - as subtle as dog's balls, but enough to be missed by the cops. Ignoring stares from the promenading tourists, Kip flings a leg over the parapet and edges gingerly down, grinning all the way.

"Come on, Finnegan! You're missing the party."

Damn it.

I probably wouldn't have done it without that third beer in me, but the risk of falling, breaking a leg, getting arrested or not making it back to the top all seemed a little abstract and next thing I'm squelching on a gritty mudflat, elbows and knees slimed from the stones.

"Good boy. Now how much money have you got?"

I look at Kip blankly.

"Come on. How much?"

"About forty pounds."

"Perfect. This is for you then." And he heaves up a slab of cement among all the other slabs of cement and fishes out a dirty plastic bag. Inside are lots of little bags and Kip pushes one into my hand before kicking the rest back under and dropping the rock into place.

I close my hand into a fist and look up. We're hidden from all but the most determined eyes. Kip looks at me.

"That's forty pounds."

And because it's already in my hand and I don't want a fuss I get out the money and give it to him. It disappears down his pants.

"That, young sir, is the purest speed you'll ever have the pleasure to taste. I've got a tube pass - we can have some off that."

Again, I follow Kip mutely. He leads me into the corner where the great buttress of Tower Bridge meets the wall and hands me his card. The bag, he takes from me and as we huddle, he taps it gingerly over the little plastic rectangle. I cup my hands below.

Kip carefully picks the bigger crystals off the card and drops them back into bag - then very carefully lifts it to his nose and snorts. His tongue flicks out to wet his finger and he dabs his nose and then the card and sucks the digit clean.

We repeat the process, but this time it's my turn to sniff. I push a finger against one nostril and snort gingerly up the other. At first I feel just a few flecks going up like sand - then a great cluster hits the back of my nose and I reel back. It burns and my right eye is smarting but I follow Kip's lead, wiping the card clean - I've left more than he did - and swallow the acrid powder.

He stuffs the baggie into my pocket and pats my leg with a grin. He's grinning like a cheshire cat, grinning like a maniac with giant liquid eyes and without a word he strips off his nylon trousers and throws them in the corner - then he's skipping away down the shoreline, leading me round the base of the bridge, splashing through the water and oh my shoes are fucked, there's mud all up my work trousers and we round the corner into full-on, squat-party, cluster-fuck madness.

I back into a corner away from the gaze of the police; avoiding the dancers and flailing dreadlocks and breathing fast. The speed's hit me like a train.

I can feel my eyes strain wide at the spectacle, while my knees wobble and my stomach flops - and still the speed rushes on. Ten feet away a man in orange pants and beaded braids is yelling at a copper, 'you can't come down here, you can't come down!' And the cop is yelling back but I can't hear the words and I close my eyes at the aggression, but that's worse - that throws me into the grip of a kind of horizontal vertigo - so I open my eyes and hurry back round the rocks to the yellow rope and beyond.

After a while of pacing on the shoreline I've gathered my wits, feel not so scared and venture back. By the time night falls I've snuffed three more lines of speed, just tapped into my sweaty palm in the middle of the dancing, cloaked by the dark and surrounded by others with staring eyes and fevered limbs and my suit pants are splashed and ruined and my shoes are sopping wet when at last, after a long time, I think about Anne.

Shit. I get out my phone. There are two missed calls and a text and as far I can make out it says she's here. Or at least near; in a bar some place by the bridge.

In a panic, I lurch out of the dance area, my thoughts on the yellow rope. The climb up is... a memory. Something not so much experienced as recalled and at the top I consider flinging the bag over the parapet into the dark. I even pull it out of my pocket, weighing it up for the throw. But instead I just stare at it for a while, fixated by the crinkled white plastic and the drifts of crystals, then stuff it suddenly inside my jacket lining through a hole in the pocket, and the next long while is spent staggering in the grassy area near the Mayor's office, ignored by the police, avoided by everyone else, trying to gather my thoughts about Anne: *finding Anne*, I'm finding Anne. How can I find Anne?

Later, I'm with Anne, sitting on the grass in an out-of-the way spot.

She's looking at me funny and I realise I'm speaking. It's possible I'm not making sense, because I can't remember the words, but she says something back.

"So you want to stay here?"

"Yeah."

"Well I'm going to head off."

She puts her palm on my cheek. Her hand's hot.

"Why don't you come to mine when you're finished?"

"Okay," I nod emphatically. It's a liferaft of an idea. She tells me she'll leave the key out.

"You know where it will be?"

"Yeah. No."

Then the next thing she's fishing a pen out of her bag and rolling up my sleeve. It tickles as she writes on my arm and she looks at me with pursed, amused lips - and that makes me smile. She keeps writing, right down onto my little finger.

I twist my arm and try to read it, but the letters seem to have come loose from their meanings and new ones float in to replace them, distracting me. By the time I get to the end of the sentence on my finger I've forgotten what the words on my wrist were about - and anyway, she's saying something.

"...you look after yourself Mister."

And her face is reassuring; with a kind of quizzical, rueful concern, but not unfriendly, so I look back at the words again to try to work out what she's written - and when I look back upwards she's gone. After a while I realise she really is gone; and as soon as that happens I wish more than anything I'd gone with her.

From there, my mood turns black.

Regret at leaving Anne sours in my belly into general unease and I weave back towards the Embankment edge, taking the long way around people.

I lean on the rails to watch, realising distantly what a total state I'm in. The police seem to have backed off, resigned to letting the party run its course, with just one surly copper keeping watch. And I'm watching the crowd below - they're still dancing but with a different energy - no longer fueled by the drama of conflict; settled instead into grim repetition - when suddenly the world floods with an awful sound.

A deep, sonorous moan drowns out the music, crawls up my nerves, and vibrates my diaphragm like an answering drum. As one, the dancers look up over the water to where a ship, waiting on the other side of the bridge, sounds its horn again.

Knowing the cause of my fright should have set me at ease, but instead the second low moan from the ship seems like an omen of disaster: something awful is going to happen. My shoulders crowd up round my ears and as we all look on the platform of Tower Bridge cracks apart. Free of cars now the two sides simply lever up - opening the bridge like a great valve - and the boat moves through, entering the body of the city with ominous purpose. I have to look away.

Below, the dancers stand transfixed. Someone turns down the music and a cheer for the spectacle rises from the crowd. One young man turns around and looks up - olive-skinned, blue trousers, his face beaming - and catches my eye. "Magnifique!" he yells in melodious French. "C'est fucking superb!" but I can't feel his jubilation for this growing sense of fear.

He punches the air. "Vive la plage!" he yells. "Vive la citié plage!" - but his words get jumbled in my brain. *Vive la phage*, I hear - *the city phage* - and the words rattle around, picking up associations every time.

'Phage' I whisper to myself. 'To eat.' City phage: the city eats. Does the city live? And at that, my dread takes on life of its own.

The presence that I felt at the party - on the evening I met Anne - it comes crowding back. I feel it all around me; a malignant, brooding force. Bigger than me - much bigger - crushing just from the sheer mass of him, and I look around and where there were rails and streets and lights and people I see a body respiring on a grand scale, a brickwork Gaia with pipes for veins and rats for blood and people for thoughts and I look down over the embankment to the river and see his lifeblood, a great thick artery that swells with a heartbeat just twice a day, and the people dancing on the mudflats, their jeans caked with silt, they fill me with horror. I want to yell *get out! You have to get out!* But I'm rooted to the spot by this thing, this presence around me like a chuckle in a dark room when you thought you were alone, until Kip walks up and says, "Yo" and the spell is broken.

"Yo, you look white as a sheet man," he says, sounding delighted by the fact - and the words *white as a sheet, white as a sheet* go echoing round my skull. It occurs to me that right now my mind is in such a state that I need something in there, that anything in my head will be pounced on and picked over and repeated, so it may as well be harmless ideas rather than frightening ones - and Kip goes on talking; a person so alien right now to what's going on in my mind, it's like he's speaking to me from the moon.

"We're jetting soon - going to my place to chill and smoke a joint. You wanna come?"

And I hear my voice speaking in the space outside my head: "Yeah. Yeah, okay". And when I blink, Kip's not there - he's walked on past to round up some other lost souls and I rub my hands through my hair to try to clear my mind.

I turn and look for Kip again - he's just a few feet away with some other people, pointing away from the river.

My heart's been going crazy, so I take a few breaths to try and slow it down - then with great trepidation cast my attention back out again: searching for the presence that was here before, like a man who comes home to a burgled house and checks through every room with a knife. There's nothing there.

"Come on, we're heading off!" yells Kip so I let out a long relieved breath, jog to where he is and the bunch of us walk away.

Half an hour later we're bundling out the back of a van.

My mental state has improved. Enough that I handled the van ride without any crazy ideas, though the background nerves are still there. We're in Brixton.

"Welcome to GCHQ" says Kip as he produces a set of keys. We're down Atlantic Avenue, opposite the railway overbridge, at the shop where I first saw Kip. He leads us inside.

"Hey Kip" I manage as he flicks on the lights. "What about the gear. All the equipment?" And his derision is complete:

"Not my sound system - those idiots can lose it to the tide for all I care. Come upstairs."

I look around before we go up. The room we're in seems to be an old grocery store converted to an office - there's a desk with a phone and boxes of paper, though none of it looks used - and through a corridor I see what looks like a kitchen with untidy stacks of plastic trays on the floor. There's a faint smell of fish and old cabbage.

Upstairs is clearly home to a lot of people. We go down a corridor and I glimpse bedrooms on either side with mattresses on the floor, sheets hung up as partitions - every spare inch used for someone's repose. Except in the living room: we walk into a windowless box with dark wood veneer walls and a mixed assortment of couches covered in cheap cotton throws.

"Take a seat, take a seat. Introductions?"

There are five of us from the van and I suddenly realise that one of them, a round-faced girl with her hair under a cap, is Debs - the quiet one who was with Kip when Phil and I met them in the park. I wave a hand and take a proper look at the others.

"This," continues Kip, "is Trader Dave" and indicates with a flourish a guy in a suit. "Timmy I believe you also haven't met" - he's a stunted, dread-locked guy - "while Debs, of course you have."

With a final flourish Kip raises both hands in the air. "Timmy?" he says expectantly. And the ugly blonde dread-locked guy pulls a considerable bag of weed from his trousers and throws it for Kip to catch.

"Ah!" says Kip, taking to his seat and rolling duties with enthusiasm.

"Well that was a pointless party, wasn't it" says the guy in the suit.

"Why's that Trade?" counters Kip without looking up. "Is it because you remained aloof up above, keeping your shoes clean, fiddling away on your phone?"

"I had crucial information to keep up with. I can't be expected to do so half-underwater." And indeed at the mention of his mobile, 'Trade' pulls out his device - one of the latest, with that small-yet-big look to it - and checks his messages. He doesn't seem to notice he's done it.

I watch him as he tucks it away. Trader Dave seems to be in the totally wrong context. Here we are, I would swear, in a genuine Brixton squat - home to a dozen freeloading dropouts - and then here we have Dave.

He's wearing an immaculate pinstripe suit. Banker's stripes, if I had to guess, and everything matches to perfection: cuffs rest on wrists, the shoes look Italian and it must be - I dunno, one in the morning? - and he's still wearing a tie: a silk job in a tasteful muted yellow with a great fat knot. I've worked around finance for long enough to know that's not a trendy colour this year. Instead this guy's gone classic, choosing a pale tone to match his cropped curly hair.

I look away before he can catch me staring and see Kip holding up the joint. We light it and pass it around and the pot makes me more speedy when I inhale - but the more I have the more it blunts the edge. We talk and laugh and as we do Kip keeps rolling and we keep smoking and we even have one more line of speed, though I seem to be in a safe place now, my brain padded in enough green cotton wool that my lurking nasty from before seems like a distant concern.

It's hours later when I'm using the toilet, trying to work out who lives here and who doesn't; wondering about Dave and laughing to myself at the power cable that snakes through the permanently open toilet window - rising, no doubt to a dangerous homemade connection to a free power supply - that I notice my arm and the writing.

Jesus. I must really have been fried before. I roll up my sleeve and take a look.

"To find your way back to me," Anne's written, "come south. To Offerton Road. Number 25. Flat 2. Don't ring the bell. The key's under a flower pot to the right of the steps." And, you know what? It's probably time to go.

Back in the living room I don't sit down, but ask instead where there's a mini cab place that will still be open. Kip eyes the marks on my arm.

"Ahhh," he says looking distant and thoughtful suddenly. "That bird I saw you with. Who was she, your sister?"

"My girlfriend," I say flatly.

"What a shame" purrs Kip theatrically - but the joke doesn't quite mask the appetite in his eyes.

I say my goodbyes. The others wave and nod, struggling with the effort in the thick cannabis smoke and I let myself out - past the flyers and the phone and the faint smell of fish. The shop bell jingles as I close the front door behind me and I'm still thinking of that look on Kip's face as I walk to the mini cab's and take a car to Anne's.

Okay, and perhaps I'm more cut than I realised: I get the silent treatment from the driver when I try to make conversation. But I find the house no problem and find the key and let myself in - slipping quietly into bed next to Anne without disturbing her slumber - though my own sleep is an unpleasant thing.

I dream of going down a tunnel. I'm standing on a raft and the slick current is accelerating me down a river. It starts off wide but then the banks climb higher and get closer and the water speeds me past glossy mud and a mess of wharf beams into a mouth in the earth. It goes dark and immediately I'm aware of something behind me that growls with an animal insistence right behind my neck. It's like a dog caught in a trap, half snarling, half panting and I want to turn around but I'm more scared of what I'll see so I stand bolt upright while the boat speeds forward and I hear a man's clear voice saying *flows so fleet* before the velocity of my forward motion scatters into black vertigo and an hallucinogenic half-state that seems to last for hours - followed by perhaps a little real rest - and when I finally open my eyes properly Anne's sitting cross-legged on the bed holding a cup of coffee that steams in a beam of sunlight. It's late afternoon.

I sit up. My head pounds. And there's mud - mud caked everywhere; over the floor and the bedsheets and my shoes. I cover my face with my hands.

"Oh Finnegan" says Anne. And with undeserved sympathy and the careful administration of coffee, she revives me. The room is swimming. My whole body feels *awful.*

"I'm *so* sorry."

She raises her arms and shrugs.

"Just make sure you clean it up!"

"Really I'm sorry."

"Don't sweat it." She pats me on the ankle through the sheets. "The rest of the coffee's on the dresser - I'm going out. But just... clean it up."

***

The hangover from the party seemed to last all weekend. I felt sick on Saturday and flat and tired Sunday, so we just stayed inside playing board games; Anne didn't seem to mind. Then when inevitable Monday rolled around I walked into the office and into a glaring realisation: I hate my job.

I stood at the elevator doors with my satchel, looked around, and knew that it was stealing my life. Though that wasn't a bad thing to know. Looking at the room through that new understanding I felt a weight float away. Everything was exactly the same, yet as I stood there blinking it seemed to transform. The limp plants, the computer screens, the cubicle dividers and Alan's morning grimace all now seemed to have the substance of crepe paper. They were weightless and expendable; something to be screwed up and tossed aside. I took a deep breath and prepared myself for a patient day tolerating an inconsequential world.

By midday, though, my patience was wearing thin and I'd abandoned any pretense of work in favour of staring at my desk daydreaming. Several times the phone startled me out of a state where my keyboard and screen were framed unseen before me. There was plenty of work to do, but my thoughts kept going back to a place that seemed much more real - that night that Anne and I took e and stayed up at her place talking.

We've had some good times since then, but there really was something about that night that got under my skin. I try to think back to the poem she read me but can only remember snatches, along with a sense of yearning that seemed to run through the verses. Was there something she was trying to tell me? I animate suddenly, move my mouse to wake the screen up, type the phrases I can recall into a search tab and a minute later I've got the full version printed out.

I read the poem over and over, but all that becomes clear is that I need to know more about this Eurydice - the character who makes me think of Anne. So after work I detour to the Brixton library on my way home.

Well, kind of to the library. I detour on the detour down Atlantic Ave - telling myself it's for a nosey at the market stalls, but really it's an excuse to go by Kip's. I linger round the door for a minute - seems like no one's inside - and I'm cupping my hands round my face and peering through the glass when a woman says "Hey" behind me in a not-unfriendly voice. I turn and it's Debs.

She looks nervous without Kip or someone else round. I'd never noticed before but she has a dog tooth and funny piggy-looking eyes.

"Are you here to see Kip? He's not here tonight, but you want to come over tomorrow maybe? Come tomorrow - he'll be in, there'll be people here. He was saying we should get you round..."

So I say yeah, sure, I'll be there and she's like "see you then, Finn" as if she's trying hard to sound nice and I go off down the Avenue, not looking after all at the shops with their hanging chickens and displays of fish and stacks of brown roots with the ends sliced off white. I loop back down Coldharbour Lane to the library.

The woman inside has curly hair too - but not like Debs, all hippie and cheap. She's a hundred per cent librarian with a streak of grey through the ringlets, a cardigan that drapes down her shoulders and glasses round her neck on a chain. Her nose is pinched and she looks out at me from under her brows with a cultivated librarian look and says "Yes? How can I help you?" in a brisk I-could-actually-help-you-here voice.

"I'd like to get some books out, but I'll need to join."

"Good man. What ID do you have?" And we fuss about sorting that out. In the end she looks me up on the electoral roll, holding my credit card against the page and matching my name to the right line, and peers down her nose when she finds me.

"But you say you've changed address?"

"To Effra mansions. It's not far from here."

"It wouldn't be, would it. That's a good local name."

"Like the river" I venture and she glances at me approvingly.

"Yes. Exactly. So I think we can sign you up - just bring in a bank statement next time to prove where you live."

Something pops into my head.

"You know, I saw another Coldharbour Lane a while back. Not around here. It was in the country."

"That would be right," she says like she's been asked about medieval road names ten times already today. "It sounds like it's from the sea-side, but it's not. A coldharbour was what they called a shelter by the road. Back when this was a small village outside London travellers would have come down Coldharbour Lane knowing there was a shelter there - a harbour - but that it didn't have a fire. That's what a coldharbour was.

"Now, this is your temporary card. I'd show you how to use the computer terminals, but you look like you know what you're doing."

"Okay, thank you."

"Just come see one of us when you've got what you want." And she delivers this last line looking back down at what she'd been doing before, because of course she's a very busy librarian, don't you know?

I sit down at a terminal and search for "Orpheus and Eurydice". A bunch of titles come up - though most look like kids' stories. Then after, on a whim, I do another search for "underground rivers" and a handful of other entries come up, so I write them down too, then I take my list and walk through the aisles and find about half of them and sit down on a beanbag to read.

***

Taking Debs' invite at face value I go to the library the next day after work, read for an hour about Eurydice - and how underground rivers are a symbol of occult knowledge - then walk to the shop and tap on the door. Some random skinny white guy in a yellow singlet opens it and points upstairs with a chopping knife when I ask if Kip's in. I go up hesitantly, glancing down the hall to the living room. There are two pairs of legs that don't look like Kip's and a couple of low voices in the haze.

"Hello?"

"Brother," comes a familiar voice from behind a curtain screen. "Get yourself seated and fire one up, I'll be in there in two shakes... of a lamb's tail." I can hear him clattering around, his impulsive movements unmistakable.

"Okay."

But I don't feel comfortable quite yet, so I go to the toilet. Inside, I lock the door and fish in my jacket lining for the crumpled bag of speed - untouched since Friday. It's still sealed, with about half the original amount of powder left. I tap out a tiny pile on the back of my hand and lick it up - and I'm glad for it, because Kip, when I go to the living room and find him already there, is relentless - standing in the middle of the room lecturing, laughing - bending the attention of everyone round him with the force of his personality.

And it's like that most days. I go back Wednesday night and the night after - and the night after that. Stopping off in the library to read, then sniffing a small dab from the bag before heading for the Shop, just to get my brain up to pace. Because mostly we just shoot the shit, covering off half a dozen crazy theories in a night if Kip's in the mood, and I like being able to keep up.

I learn that Kip doesn't like visitors during 'business hours', but on any given evening ten or fifteen people might pass through the Shop. Some I presume live there on whatever arrangement, but the rest are just breezing through: come to show their respects to their skinny ringleader, to buy weed, or just to get stoned. The yellow singlet guy I don't see again, but Trader Dave is in twice that first week - and there's a stream of girls, ranging from grungy ones with lesbian haircuts to a liquid-eyed electro-honey that Dave brings one night.

Through it all the only constant - Kip aside - is Timmy. He's in the same chair every night, slumped low, as mute as a tree root and permanently stoned. I don't think I've even seen him get up to piss. Occasionally he fishes weed from down the side of his arm chair when someone makes a purchase, or tsks if you Bogart a joint, so it's memorable the one night he speaks up.

It's a Tuesday and we're sitting about, smoking, when I think back to Kip's thing about rivers. He'd seemed so big into that stuff when I first met him, but it hasn't come up since. So I ask.

"Hey Kip" I throw into one of the reflective stoned silences. "What happened to your march to raise the Effra?"

Someone sniggers. Kip's eyes shoot over while his body stays still.

"You can piss right off Trade."

Dave keeps chuckling.

"What happened, Finn my man, is no one came. And what a relief. I never had such a sappy idea."

He holds the joint lightly between long fingers, with his arm perched on the end of the couch. With the thick rope of smoke coiling upwards the effect is kind of camp.

"I dunno... it seemed alright. A new park in Brixton with the river raised up again..."

He sniffs.

"Nostalgia. Soppy nostalgia. I'm off that ride. Why is it that every time we look at nature, we look back? What's wrong with right now? Oh yeah - the Effra used to be green and clean and now it's not. So what's your point?"

The joint gutters out.

"What's wrong with a little pollution? Or a lot? Everyone says it's not natural, but oil, lead, mercury - they all come from nature. It's just we can't handle them concentrated. But that'll come - we'll adapt."

He shrugs.

"So I say, stop looking back at history and live in the now. Look at these people - Timmy, Trade; this prick - what's your name? - beam you all back to 1600 when the sappy greens think the world was pure and you'd be dead in ten minutes. We're city people man, we're adapted to this place. Have been for generations."

He relights the joint, sucks on it, and exhales into the room.

"So *that*, Finn old bean, is why no-one came to the march: the dirty old rivers are buried and they should stay there."

"Plus your flyer was crap."

There's a giggle.

"Screw you Trade."

Kip hands me the joint; I draw deeply and close my eyes - picturing the old Effra, irises growing on its marshy banks, flowing through Brixton fields. I think of houses spreading and springing up - bricks, bridges and then factories - until the river becomes poisoned by the race to create; its charm snuffed out, its waters banished to the underworld - condemned to a dirty existence beneath the stones. I think of the vast lumbering machinery of the modern city around us, life-like in its complexity. And I think how Kip would make a good cult leader.

"How about that joint?" comes a request from the couch.

"Sorry Trade."

I hand it over.

"I was reading about something" I venture. "About Orpheus and Eurydice. That's another underground story. You want to hear?"

No one protests.

"It's like a Greek myth - but it sort of relates. It's like this.

"You've got this guy Orpheus and he's - I don't know - a minstrel or something?" - Timmy jiggles his foot, looking agitated. "Basically he goes around singing and playing and the point is he's really good at it. Everyone wants a piece of him and all the girls are into it - but he doesn't want any of that. He's just into the music."

"...what an idiot."

"Yeah, well, exactly. But not for long. One day he's strolling through the hills when he comes to a pool and by the edge of the pool is a girl. She's like a nymph. Her name's Eurydice and I guess she's like... like a little goddess. The goddess for that stream, all perfect and natural and unsullied. And they see each other and it's love."

"So anyway they decide to get married. But at the funeral... sorry, *wedding.* Duh. Giving it away. At the wedding there's a disaster. One of the guests is a satyr - I'm not really sure what that is - but he sees Eurydice alone for a moment, and she's so beautiful and delicate he wants to rape her. He chases her - she runs - but a snake bites her as she's running through the grass, and Orpheus finds her dead."

Kip moves his hand along like it's a newspaper headline, declaring "Rape Goes Wrong!" in a phoney East End paper-boy voice. Timmy laughs a stoner laugh, but I carry on - in the grip of my thoughts.

"So Orpheus is destroyed. He mopes for a few years but still can't get over it - so he finds a cave and goes down it into the underworld, and he meets the King of hell."

There's a listening kind of silence now.

"He tells the King about his loss and the King's like - yeah, you and everyone else. But Orpheus plays him a song and because he's such a good musician it's got all the sorrow and pain that he feels in it - and more than that, it's a song about the world above, about wheat fields and sunlight and wind and all that - which gets right under the skin of the Queen. Because the Queen of hell used to live up above as the goddess of growing things and the song reminds her of what that felt like.

"So the Queen begs the King to give him a chance, and he agrees. He says, 'Orpheus, if you can walk out of here without looking back I'll send the ghost of your love after you. And when she gets into the light, she'll be alive. But if you look back' - this was the deal - 'then you'll never see her again.'

"So Orpheus sets off. It takes him ages. And of course he turns around, because he gets the doubts; thinks a trick is being played on him. And he sees his perfect love Eurydice for one last time - before she vanishes forever."

A late train rumbles past on the Brixton line, rattling the ashtrays and cups. When it's gone no one has anything to say - I don't know if I've bored everyone senseless or they're just thinking - so I say my piece.

"What gets me is this story has been around for, what, four thousand years? So there's got to be some point to it that's worth repeating - and I think it's this: it's stuck around because it's about loss.

"It's the same as when London's rivers got buried. People still remember them because there's this sense of regret. Maybe you're right, maybe it *is* just nostalgia, but the fact is we had something beautiful, and then we lost it."

"Like in The Bible."

Everyone looks at Timmy, surprised he's mentioned something other than cannabis.

"The same thing happens in The Bible man, in Genesis. God's burnin' up the cities of Sodom and Gomorrah for their sins, but he tells the one true brother that he can get away. He can leave with his wife, but the deal is they can't look back. It's the same as with thingy..."

"...Orpheus"

"...it's the same deal - don't look back. But his wife does man, she does - and the bitch gets turned into a pillar of salt."

"Into *what*, Timmy old bean?"

"Into salt, motherfucker. Don't ask me why! God turns her into salt. But *that's* the lesson bruv." And Timmy looks straight at me, pointing with two fingers like a gun. "Don't look back man, never look back. Because you turn around for a *second* and they get you."

Kip laughs loud and long - a genuine guffaw.

"You're a moron, Timmy, you know that?" He shakes his head, still smiling at what he's heard. "And you're all over-thinking the point. This lovely little nymph of Finn's has only one problem." He waves a palm at me. "And it causes every other issue in the story.

"She's too fuckable."

***

The last thing of note that week? I see Henry walk into the Shop.

Well I dunno - I think I do. I'm walking there myself on Wednesday and looking up at all the old buildings - seeing the handsome old neighbourhood underneath all the old Brixton grime. The library, I think - that's a big old handsome building. And St Matthews church - that's a big old handsome building too - and no matter there's a nightclub in the crypt. The clock tower; all the facades along the high street… this place had some serious money in the past. Sure, these days if you wanted to get your head shot off around here, you wouldn't have to try too hard, but it's got good bones, is what I'm thinking - and then I see Henry step out of Kip's on to the street.

Or it looks like him. Wears the same shirt - but he turns and goes up the Avenue before I can see his face. And when I get inside, something stops me asking about him. The Shop - it's not the kind of place that rewards curiosity.

4 AUGUST

"What rough beast, its hour come round at last,
slouches toward Bethlehem to be born?"

- *The Second Coming.* WB Yeats

The following Monday Miles calls me at the office. Two weeks of late nights at the shop means I'm a long way into not giving a damn about work - and angry to have the phone interrupt my thoughts.

I pick it up and just listen. Then:

"What?"

"Is that Finn?"

"Yeah it's me. Who is this? Miles?"

"It is. I don't think much of the guy who answers your phones. Accent like Nelson Mandela. Listen, can you get off work?"

"Did you get my email?"

"Yeah I got your email," says Miles impatiently. "It was good." Pause. "Very good. I've been spending the last two weeks re-writing the business plan around it. But can you get the afternoon off?"

"Why?"

"Because I need you to, that's why. The group that I sent it to, the angel investors - do you know what that means? - they have a man who can see us today. If it's not today it has to be at least a month from now and if we wait that long then it'll be holiday time and then it'll be goddamned Christmas and we'll never get this done. Look, I'll be paying you for every minute that you're out of the office. Just call off sick."

"What do you need me to bring. Actually - why do you need me there at all?"

"I need you there because I need you to talk this guy through your designs. Nothing special or scary, just sitting down informally round a desk running him through a few flowcharts. But it has to be you. I can't talk the turkey as well as you do. Plus... one guy in a room is just a chump with an idea. Two is a team."

I wait and have a think about it. At least it will get me out of this place.

"Hello?"

"Yeah, okay."

"Great - but you need to bring a laptop. I left mine at home."

I tell my line manager I'm feeling sick and that I'll work from home and sign out a machine to use. My homework's still on my pen drive and that's still in my pocket, so I just leave work and catch the tube straight to the address that Miles gave me.

*****

"How do you like the new offices?"

Actually, they're very nice. Miles has rented two rooms and a shared meeting space in a sunny office off the Edgware Road. Looking round I realise for the first time his commitment to this thing.

"You can plug that in over there."

Miles starts faffing with the laptop, fiddling with the internet connection while he glances at his watch.

"Dammit! I can't get online!"

"What for?"

"To download my goddamned emails - that's where I saved the work."

"Let me."

Miles looks at me for a moment, weighing it up.

"Alright. We've got fifteen minutes."

I shift the machine over and sit down.

Within a few minutes I'm online, patched into the building's wireless network. Then I get Miles to point the browser at his mail server. After a bit more mucking about he finds what he was after and sends a bunch of pages to the printer - then I get back on and re-read my notes.

"That won't do."

"Huh?"

"The sticker on the back of your machine. We can't have that." And Miles marches back out of the room. I turn the laptop around. There's a label with my company name and a serial number on the back.

A minute later Miles is stretching a piece of black electrician's tape over the label and muttering under his breath. His eyelashes flutter and tic.

"Fucking close call," he says to himself. "Fucking close call." And then there's five minutes to go.

Miles sits down and tries to get calm.

"Okay. The guy we're meeting today is called Lars. Lars is... an entirely free agent. If he likes what he sees, then he has the clout to get our application accepted - or to throw it out on a whim. So what we're going to be with Lars, is relaxed. Got it?

"We're chilled. We're just going to have a little friendly chit-chat here with our friend who likes business ideas and if he likes ours - then no big deal. Maybe we'll chat some more, maybe not. But no hard sell, get the drift?"

I just shrug.

"You lead the way."

"Good man. Now, forget your original work - what I want you to do is talk him through this."

"What?"

Miles hands me the still-warm print-outs and clicks open a display on the laptop.

"I had it done by a graphic designer, but it's mostly your stuff. I suggest you brush up to get familiar."

"*What?*"

The landline rings. Miles picks it up and I hear a muffled woman's voice -

a stupid, nasal, East-end tart - say "Costume You? This is Carol."

"Hello Carol. It's *Consumer*. ConsumerU. This is Miles."

"Yes well I've got a visitor for you Miles. He's coming up." And she hangs up the phone.

"Right, that's Lars. You'll be okay with that then?"

I'm flicking through. There are about fifteen pages with a corresponding computer display. I roughly recognise the content as my own, but there are whole flow diagrams that I've never seen before - mine was entirely text. I'm too furious to talk.

"Good."

Nearby an elevator dings.

Lars isn't Scando at all. He's a small dapper Englishman with a friendly voice that has an underlying force. His tone is soft but the words emerge as if they're pushed from his stomach like a trained singer. It makes you feel desperate to listen, in case you miss some quiet crucial message.

I say very little. Lars seems very interested. He asks a lot of questions and as we talk he flips through each page of the printout, reading at the same as he talks.

At one point he asks me some detailed questions about the diagrams. I give simple answers. Then he asks me if the work here is mine. "Some of it" I say. And then the meeting is over and Lars shakes both our hands, thanking us for our time. He clips closed his briefcase - taking the printout - and sees himself out to the lift.

Miles looks thoughtful. Then he shrugs and puts away his things without speaking. It's four o'clock. I close down the laptop and go home.

***

The bag is empty. I snort the last line in my room when I get home, planning on enjoying my own high thoughts on this empty afternoon, but as soon as the first rush disappears I find that I don't want to listen to music, or daydream about old rivers like I'd planned. I just want more speed. For a while I play with the limp bag, twitching it between my fingers and wondering if it's a bad idea to ask Henry for some, until I think no. I'll go to Kip's and ask him. I spring up and step out of my room. He'll have some spare.

But I don't have to go to Brixton to find him. When I close the front door with my thoughts on the nearest cash machine he's there outside our place, sitting in the passenger seat of a van.

"Hello old bean," he says. "I was just looking for you. Effra mansions," he grins. "Just like the river."

Trader Dave is in the driver's seat, wearing a tie as usual, with white shirt sleeves rolled crisply round his forearms in a nod to the van's working-class vibe.

"We thought you might like to come on a drive with us. A little mission. Up for it?"

"Hello Trade," I say and stick my bottom lip out in indecision. "Where are we going?"

"Trade secret" he shoots back deadpan. "Not for the faint hearted though. You in?"

And because I can still feel my last line roiling in my belly I tell him "sure" and Kip reaches back to slide open the side door and let me in. I step into the dark interior, slam the door shut and nearly lose my footing as Trade lurches the van up through its gears, heading out into Clapham then turning west, making for the quickest way over the river. Neither of them seem communicative so I lean between the two front seats and watch the brick and asphalt winding by.

I almost never travel above ground in north London so I'm quickly lost, but when we eventually skim Regent's Park and turn east I realise we must be somewhere near Camden. Trade slows down and starts peering for street names; his tie, loosened at the neck, wags when he leans over the wheel to look left and right. Then he spots his street and chops the stick-shift down skillfully, turning in and coasting 'til he finds a park.

"Out you get boys."

Kip jumps down and hauls the door open for me.

"Come on pal - this is our stop. Trade's going on."

He shoulders a backpack and hands one to me.

"Don't worry. All will be revealed."

He bangs the door and the van roars off, its exhaust hanging in the afternoon light. The street is leafy and quiet.

Kip crosses the road and I follow. On the other side is a low iron railing on the edge of what must be part of Regent's Canal. Kip leans over and looks down - I do the same - and there's a thin edge of ground between the wall and the water. Not the slick mud of the tidal Thames, more of a crust baked hard by a summer hot enough to have dropped the water level.

"Jesus Kip. It stinks."

"It's the smell of success," he grins, turning to me. "So my man. How illegal are you feeling?"

I look him hard in the eye, trying to size up where he's taking this. I know Kip enough to not ask for details yet.

"Jail illegal?"

He shrugs.

"If you do what I say that won't happen. It's just if we hop this rail, I need you to know - no turning back."

I wonder how much of my nonchalance is chemical? The currents of something larger seem to swirl round me, making it easy to say yes. And I can ask about the baggie later.

"Alright. Let's do it," I tell him and Kip turns his back to the water. He surveys the quiet street - eyes scanning windows for prying faces - before vaulting over the edge in a fluid movement. My descent is less graceful, but when I get to the bottom we both have grazed palms and greened knees.

Kip has a Tigger bounce on. He tightens the straps on his backpack with a "follow me compadre. And try to keep your shoes clean."

"You know it *really* does stink Kip."

"It's the slime on the walls," he says without turning. "In a hot summer the canal drops and all the vegetation rots in the sun. The more it stinks, the better our chances. You'll see in a tick. But we gotta keep quiet here for a bit."

I hunker down instinctively and follow close. Above, there's not much to be seen of the street - just the tops of trees and distant tower block windows that search the horizon hopelessly for an end to the city. Then our path passes into a tunnel with a bright square of light at the end. I can't see the ground and when my shoes splash into water Kip hisses back "keep them clean!"

The light comes back when we reach the tunnel mouth and Kip stops to scan for signs of life. His eyes are clear and alert and I think of the other Kip that I know from the Shop - bitter and sharp-tongued; always drug-addled - and realise this, rather than the Shop, is his element.

There's no one round.

"See that?" he whispers. "That's us."

Across the water and high on the canal wall is a stormwater outlet - just a square concrete section with a pipe coming out. There's a metal ladder leading up to it from the water, presumably so it can be serviced from a boat, and a small flat space on top. It's wide enough that two people could sit comfortably and be invisible to anyone walking by above. A couple of dusty looking weeds have even made an earnest attempt at life there before running out of water and drying off.

"How do we get over?"

Kip jerks his head back at the viaduct we've popped out of. There's traffic rumbling over the bridge, but we're still invisible.

"Follow me pal." He fits his foot into a gap in the brickwork.

The tunnel that we've come from has an edge that juts six inches from the side of the bridge and it's this that he works up on to. Above that, at convenient shoulder height, is a black cable that's been clamped into place. By running a hand underneath it for support and keeping his toes on the narrow ledge he's able to cross to the other bank. With his ponytail bouncing against his faded red puffer he looks quite the urban fox, tiptoeing over the brickwork.

"Now your turn. Just not too much weight on the cable or you'll pull it out."

I'm getting better at this stuff, though it still takes me five times as long. If Kip's a fox I'm more the clumsy hound tagging behind. When I jump triumphantly on to the foot and a half of dry ground on the other side Kip's off immediately, impatient to get going.

"Come on. Trade will be ready."

He leads me to the ladder, climbs up to the stormwater outlet and sits cross-legged on the top. I join him, puffing a little, so that we're side-by-side, facing the other bank, and settle back into the dry weeds.

Instantly I feel at ease, in the way a wild thing would. From here we can see everything without being seen and my curiosity about what we're up to, set aside while I negotiated Kip's assault course, perks up. Kip pulls out a mobile phone and a much-folded sheet of A4 covered in blue biro to place between us.

"Burglary."

"What?"

"Burglary. You were going to ask what we're doing here: that's the answer. You're a meek little worker bee Finn, but you've got a weird streak a mile wide - and you understand how I think. So I figured I'd treat you and bring you on my annual outing."

He grins his sharky grin.

"I hope you feel privileged. What state are your shoes in?"

He pulls one of my trainers towards him for a closer inspection and wrinkles his nose at the green sludge smeared round the edges.

"It'll have to be burglary in socks, pal."

"Seriously?"

I gaze over the canal, digesting the thought. If I'm honest, I knew it would be something like this. And yeah, maybe this would be easier if I had some more speed right now, but I'm still not regretting vaulting the rail. Not yet.

"So why once a year?"

"Ah! That's why I like you. You're a thinker. For a very good reason - it's the stink.

"What do you think our main source of income is pal?"

"What, at the Shop? Um. Well. Drugs?" I venture - unsure about bringing it up.

Kip snorts.

"Not quite. You'd have to be blind to not know that's going on. But we also need a respectable front - and we also *also* need another stream of income right? Because between the fickle pricks in Amsterdam and the filth, selling meth - even in Brixton - it don't keep the wolf from the door."

I settle back against the sun-warmed concrete, confident of being enlightened now that Kip's started lecturing.

"Nah. Today's effective urban peasant needs a diverse portfolio, as Trade would put it. Gotta hedge your income against the seasons! See, it turns out that the most consistent earner for us is produce. In winter that means pet-food grade chicken. We buy it cheap and hose it down in a yard with a good dose of detergent - scrub the stinky bits off with brooms - and sell it to kebab shops out west. There's good coin in that. And for the rest of the year we're jumping supermarket bins and flogging the contents to street stalls. That's why I like to keep the Shop full of dossers - bin-jumping needs man-power and that lot owe me rent.

"But at the height of summer all your produce goes rotten too fast, yeah? The revenue dries up. Which brings us to the beauty of this gig.

"Because when it's *really* hot - and we're almost starving, because we're not earning squat - the canal here runs dry. Dry enough that you can walk the length of it. And you see that monstrosity?"

He waves at the new and expensive-looking block of flats immediately opposite.

"The front entrance is keypad controlled and covered by cameras. But the *back* - security at the back is based entirely on the canal acting as the building's private moat. No one figured on the moat drying up from time to time - those people don't understand this city man. And the beauty of it is that when the moat turns into a pathway, the stink keeps them all off their balconies."

"Oh my God Kip. That's almost beautiful."

I'm starting to get butterflies.

"It is man, it is. There's no one outside to see us - yet they don't lock their back doors, because they're so conditioned to feel safe."

He drops his voice and eyeballs me, looking frightening now.

"These people are our harvest man. Don't ever feel sorry for them. They're our harvest and every year we pray for a good one."

"Are we really going to break into a flat?"

"Too fucking right we are."

The phone lights up.

"That's Trade from round front. He texts us when people go out - which is when we go in. I tell you, it's a great system. But it's more fun doing burgs if you've got company."

He gives me a saccharine smile - oh my God, is this his way of making friends? - then checks the phone and unfolds the paper. It's got a rough grid marked out that matches the apartments opposite.

"B4" mutters Kip as he consults the page. "B4... that's two up, and four across."

He looks up and counts apartments until he's pointing at a place. All the lights are out.

"That's us, my man. The first catch of the day."

I've got proper butterflies now. Kip shuffles me on to the ladder.

"Back over - and quick as you can," so I make the first crossing. Kip's close behind, eager. On the other bank he does a dainty dry-shoes shuffle past me to take the lead and hurries to another ladder - this is a more impressive affair, obviously designed so rich tenants can access their canal boats - or at least imagine themselves doing so: no one's used it in months.

As he climbs I have a proper freak. Kip's above me on the ladder and I tug his trousers...

"Really?"

I sound pleady. His down-turned face goes hard and he shushes me.

"Keep your head down" he soft-mouths and then he's over and I only hesitate a moment before following.

I can see what he means about keeping low. At the top of the ladder there's just four feet of concrete before the first geraniumed balcony - Kip's crawling below the line of its sight towards a concrete buttress. I follow with heart thumping so hard in my throat I almost gag on it - but once we're clear of the balcony edge we can both sit up and relax a little.

We're in a kind of divider between the flats - an overtly architectural feature that separates the blocks and rises the height of the building. There's a concrete flange on either side with a channel between them. We're both pressed tightly into the gap; Kip's eyes are moon-sized and shiny.

The reason for his triumphant look is clear now - we're still totally invisible from the other bank - and the flanges that rise above us have been etched with another 'architectural' pattern that may as well have been intended as a beginners climbing wall. If there's one of these between each set of flats then they've each been made with their own private burglar's entrance. So Kip's right - the security at the back of these flats is based on an assumption that the canal stays full.

Kip unfolds the paper again and shows it to me. I don't need to be told not to speak.

He points three-quarters of the way across the rough diagram to show where we are, then holds up two fingers while looking up. Alright - we go up two levels, and then? He jerks his thumb: on to the right-hand-side balcony. My heart starts hammering again as I wonder whether Trade could have made a mistake. What if there are still people there? What if - my skin shrinking - they're setting me up?

Kip jerks his head up and beams, meaning *you first*. No way - I shake my head. *No way*. But he nods emphatically with wide, wilful eyes and I remember what he said about backing out. I breathe in deeply. Shuffle past him reluctantly and fit my hands into the first holds.

But my legs won't do it. I'm so nervous I could piss my pants and something's stopping me from taking that first step. I will them too, but they just don't want to move - until Kip sticks his shoulder under my arse - stands - and I'm forced to find a hold or topple back.

My hands are sweaty and slick but, really, it's an absurdly easy climb - bracing your feet on one side lets you lock your back against the other and take a rest - so I slowly go up. I don't want to think whether I'm visible now that I'm higher and I don't want to look down, but I must be the right height now, so I lock each limb into a solid hold and peer between my legs at Kip. The framed oval of his upturned face nods excitedly and I see him set his hands into the first holds to follow.

Getting around on to the balcony looks tricky, but I want to try it before Kip gets up and starts shoving. I shift my foot holds, reach around the edge of the vertical flange and lean round for a look: I'm about four feet higher than the balcony, which is about the right height to clear the rail. Tall windows run the length of the balcony, but bunched-up drapes at the edge will cover me if there's anyone in. It looks easy enough. There's just a planter full of basil that I'll need to not bump. Screw it: here we go. I shift around - there's a nasty moment when my body-weight swings over the drop - then the safety of the balcony is in reach and I pitch myself in an ungainly sprawl on to the cool surface.

I don't bother getting up. My limbs wobble wildly. Moments later Kip appears round the edge and drops lightly to his feet. What a showoff.

"You know!" Kip announces loudly - enjoying my shock at the broken silence. "The thing about people chatting merrily on a balcony, dear chum, is they could be anyone. Friends, family, visitors - blah, blah, blah!" he jaws theatrically. "And what a view!"

I clamber up to look out. There's the canal, there's the busy street on the other bank - with no one looking back at us. There's the rooftops of Camden - and behind them the hills of north London going hazy as the sun drops. A fresh whiff of rot roils up and Kip sucks it in both nostrils.

"Ah, the far canal!" he puns. "Shall we step inside? But first, put on your outfit. When visiting the wealthy classes one must dress appropriately don't you know."

He shrugs off his backpack and fishes out an absurd pair of pink rubber gloves into which he wriggles his long hands. I don't see any for me.

"Best that you look but don't touch, if you get my drift. Oh and slip off your shoes or you'll mark the carpet. Don't want to give away our secret. Now - are we locked out?"

He shoulders his bag again, steps boldly out in front of the window and hauls on the ranch slider. It rolls wide open and he smiles at me like a saint. God he's loving this. I rush to kick my shoes off in a hurry and follow in.

"Can you watch the phone for me? It's on silent, but if anyone comes back Trade will text. We'll have about two minutes to get out if that happens, which is long enough - but only just. And don't forget your shoes."

I take the phone, nodding, and gaze around.

This place is beautiful.

I didn't really realise people lived like this. There's a chandelier above us and a smattering of antiques, but everything else is bright and modern. It would all be crass if it wasn't so carefully balanced. And expensive-looking. All the technology is low-key with that bespoke, pricey feel. I stand on a rug, keeping as far from anything as possible and watch Kip work.

He's very fast. He bags two tiny European speakers from the living area, but leaves the stereo; grabs a wi-fi hub and laptop, then moves to the bedroom. I follow and watch from the door, heart thumpety thump-thump. He's moving frantically now - hand running under the mattress. A pink hail of knickers flies over his shoulder as he empties the dresser - then he stops to hunch over a jewellery box, assessing value like a beady-eyed crow before tipping the lot into the bag. Finally there's an *aha*! as he opens a shoebox high in the wardrobe and produces a baggie of powder from beneath Dvd porn.

"We're done. Okay let's go." And he leads me back to the balcony and slides the door shut.

The air tastes great, stink and all. I check the phone for the tenth time in the last few minutes, but we're still clear.

"Why don't we take five?" says Kip. "Enjoy the fruits of our labours. We'll get good warning from Trade; put your shoes on now and we'll chill out. We could have ages."

I feel nervy, but I figure he's right. People who go out for an evening in London go out for hours.

Kip flops on to one of the reclining deck chairs.

"So was your day at work this fun?'

He puts his feet up while I perch on the edge of my chair, still edgy.

"The trick is not to get burned out on adrenaline too early, yeah? Take it cool; we'll get more done that way. You like coke?"

I shrug.

He pulls out the baggie and tosses it to me. There's probably two, maybe three grams in it, plus half a broken pink pill.

"The proceeds of crime. Call it your spotter's fee."

"Thanks..."

"You can chop me a line from it though - as fat as you like."

I cast around for a flat surface and end up dragging a small glass table over while Kip puts his hands behind his head.

"I love this time of year," he tells the sky, voice full of contentment. "*The summer harvest.*"

His beady eyes watch me shake out two piles of powder and shape them into lines. When I'm done he fishes out a five pound note and hoovers his up.

"Oh mother of God..." he mutters, blinking away tears and hands over the note.

"Rich people know their coke..."

I suck my line hard.

"Oh Boy. Oh *boy oh boy*."

I flop back on to the recliner, trying to rub the twitch from my nose as a dollop of acrid mucous slips down my throat.

"Ohhhhh man..."

It doesn't have the sharp kick of speed, but a kind of lust wells up in my lungs. Lust for what, I don't know - for the sky, for the low sun lighting the clouds like gold foil. Lust for the basil in the pot on the balcony maybe - anything. An overwhelmed *uhhh* slips out of me and I laugh at its porn-ness.

Kip chortles too, eyeing me askance through narrowed lashes.

"Don't you forget that phone now..."

"No sir!" and we both giggle.

"*Wooo...*" I manage, until I feel myself in control again.

"So Kip," I say, leaning back, feeling like clockwork that's had all its tension taken off. "How often have you done this?"

"Robbed these places? Once a year for about.. oooh, three years now. The apartments are pretty new."

"Don't you worry they'll cotton on?"

"The trick's not to get greedy. Don't do the same place two years in a row. That's why we keep a map."

He looks over at me and turns serious.

"I hate these people Finn. I hate them with everything I am. All they know how to do is consume. All they know how to do is spend money. People like them crush people like us - and they don't even know it."

"Am I people like you?" I stammer. "I mean, I'm not that different from this lot. Work in the city. Wear a suit."

"You? Hah."

Kip mops up some of the white dust on the table and rubs it round his gums.

"No, I see right through you pal. You've got your meek little front - you'd love it if people thought you were normal, but I don't think you're normal at all. I think you're possibly quite *nasty* and you know what? I reckon nasty's just fine."

"You're a sinister bastard, Kip - you know that?"

"That's the spirit."

I blow out a big breath. He's just trying to twist my head. And I was enjoying being high for a while there. I'm about to ask Kip something about where he grew up - where does someone like him come from anyway? - when the phone lights up in my lap.

"Give it here!" he snaps.

I jump to my feet, a panicky looseness in my guts, expecting the ranch slider to open right away - but Kip laughs.

"No rush my old pal. Haven't you gone pale! It's another empty flat."

He hands the phone back to me to read. 'B4 still clear," it says. "C3 gone empty.'

Jesus. I'm going to need a bathroom soon.

"Your face! I'm gonna steal a camera and take your picture."

"Like hell you are."

Kip looks thoughtful.

"C3. That's one up, but on the other side. Why don't you take it solo?"

***

I asked Debs about Kip once. We'd been on a late-night tea mission downstairs at the Shop; me filling the pot while she gathered stained mugs and told me about Trader Dave.

Turned out Trade isn't a trader at all - doesn't even work in a bank. He runs a delivery van out of Peckham. And fences stolen goods.

Not in finance at all then? I'd asked and she'd said "Nah!" in that nasal voice. "He's mental! It's like his thing." He just liked suits and dressing up and even followed the financial papers daily. It was like a joke, she reckoned - a joke he couldn't stop telling - though she looked baffled as she said it, like she'd just realised how odd it was. Then I asked about Trade and Kip. She always brightened when she talked about Kip.

He and Dave had been tight for a few years now. When he first started hanging around, everyone had been suspicious - all those suits and big talk - until one time Kip called him on it. Made him make a bunch of dummy stock picks, then followed them in the papers. Turned out he knew his stuff and after that the two of them got tight.

Kip was still number one, but Trade started tweaking things at the Shop; coming up with ways to make cash out of all Kip's dreams and scams. Things started getting more organised. And crazy, said Debs. All that validation from people acting out his imaginings - and making coin from them - it turned Kip's ideas weirder and darker. Her concern pricked my ears and I asked her "are you his girlfriend then?" which shut her up. She went quiet and hurt-looking and I guessed then that whatever she might want for herself, Debs was just one of the people Kip liked to use and to dominate.

***

I look up, raise my hand to a solid hold inside the concrete chute, and haul myself higher.

So what *am* I doing hanging out with Kip then? My thoughts march on, one after the other, whether I want them or not - driven by that great honk of powder up my nose. I'm even climbing more briskly.

Yeah, Kip's charismatic, but he's callous as well. He'd drop me in it without blinking - I know that. So why do I bother? Are his jibes right - am I really like him? Or is there something about having met Anne that's pulled down my boundaries - made me more susceptible to new experiences, the good ones and the bad.

Oh man. Speaking of bad. What the hell am I doing here? I can't believe I just helped rob someone's house. My breathing starts getting ragged and I have to wedge myself against the concrete for a moment to will my heart rate down. I wish I could stop my brain spinning like this - and I still need to shit.

Can't think about that though. I pat my pocket to feel the phone. Kip turned it on to vibrate for my solo adventure and said don't sweat it, the apartment would be clear. "But if the phone goes, don't bother to check the message. You'll have roughly two minutes; just get over the balcony and down."

Come on - keep going. I must be almost there. I chance a look down to check position and wish I hadn't, but my height looks about right. I look around the corner.

Too low. Too much thinking and not enough attention on the climb. I work up a few more holds and peek round again - it looks good and the way's clear - so I do my shuffle-round-the-edge-and-leap maneuver, which doesn't feel any safer than before. I scuff to a stop on the balcony, keeping my feet this time, and wipe my clammy shaking hands on my thighs.

I pull Kip's rubber gloves on, noticing a faint sweaty smell. Just like the last place, the sliding door into the apartment's unlocked. We're all on.

I pull the door wide and step in.

It has a younger vibe. A faux black and white zebra rug dominates the room and the lampshades are Asian red and gold. I scan the space, heart hammering; noticing how I've seemed to step out of myself. There's me, with sweaty palms and dry mouth, trying to think like Kip would - assessing what to steal; there's the other me - the high one, sitting back in my head watching with what I admit is enjoyment. And then there's someone else - a faint observer of the observer; some phantom of my scatter-gun mind. A quality to the edge of this experience that seems to lick its lips and watch close.

The late sun's lancing in. Time to get moving.

I spot a laptop on the couch. That goes in the bag - and there's a backup hard drive that goes with it. On the floor next to the TV is a battery pack plugged into the wall, charging, and the frazzled am-I-really-doing-this burglar's brain says think, *think*. What's the battery for? Until I spot the camera it belongs to in the corner - an expensive SLR. In it goes.

I'm fumbling the battery and charger into the bag too - the camera's not much good without that - when a thump from the other room sends a jolt through my gut.

I freeze. It was unmistakable: the sound of someone tossing a bag on the floor. My belly gurgles ominously.

My eyes go to the mostly-closed door to the bedroom. There's someone in there. A woman's voice mumbling a song. How did I not hear?

The way to the ranch slider's open. I could get there without being seen. But.

But...

The presence at the fringes crowds closer.

...I just want to see who's there. Against all sense, I creep to the bedroom door, peer through the hinge, and...

Jesus.

Look at her.

She's like someone in an ad for consumer electronics. The coffee coloured skin. The perfect frizzy hair. She probably surfs the net on her bed wearing white pants and a man shirt. And she's completely oblivious.

A bangle slips down her wrists as she busies herself sorting laundry. She has earphones in, which explains why she didn't hear me, and she's mouthing to the music. Christ, I think, a Sloanie slumming it in Camden - and contempt wells up inside. Kip's words come back to me - people like this crush people like us - and I remember the hate in his voice. Suddenly the room seems too hot.

The stink from the canal has drifted through the ranch-sliders and it's begun to stick in my throat - a smell of rotten vegetation that makes it hard to think. There's pressure in my head - a sense of eagerness that seems to come from outside me - a sudden urge to *do* something which is followed by a single shocking image of my hands around the girl's throat that vanishes as my thigh jolts me.

Instantly the pressure evaporates. I blink stupidly and the phone in my pocket vibrates against my leg again; urgent, unignorable. Oh my God I'm standing in a complete stranger's living room.

What the hell was I thinking? I glance back through the crack to the woman, who's back to being just a pretty woman who thinks she's alone. Jesus. But there's no time for soul-searching. I dash back to the ranch slider as silently as I can, snagging a foot on the rug so that I almost trip, but then I'm out on the balcony and out of sight. I pause, look back in, risk sliding the door shut and almost immediately hear the front door open. No fucking way that's two minutes.

"Hi-ii" coos the newcomer. Then something I don't make out - and: "are you all settled in?"

My guts roil dangerously. I've got to go.

I toss my shoes over the balcony and shimmy down the buttress without noticing. Halfway to the bottom I hear a faint "...have you seen my camera...?" and now my belly's stabbing with pain. At the bottom I crawl to the ladder with sweat slicking off me, practically fall down it to the water's edge and tug desperately at my trousers. With a heave I get them round my ankles, squat, and pour a steaming slop of shit on to the shore.

I'm gasping with relief when Kip comes down the ladder. He wrinkles his nose.

"Jesus. Don't dip your balls in it."

I look up, totally wretched.

"How'd it go?" he says.

"Laptop," I manage quietly. "Camera." And he nods, eyeing up my mess.

"That'll do then. For tonight my man, I think that's us."

***

The days after the burglary are like a bad dream - those ones where you do something wrong, something intractable, and then wake up swamped with relief. But there's no waking. I sit at work brewing over the break-in - and that disturbing urge that gripped me - and clip my replies to Anne's friendly texts short, for fear that my guilt will leak through.

Two days later Miles calls my work phone again.

"I heard back from Lars."

"Okay."

"Actually, it was Lars' secretary," says Miles, sounding rushed. "She said - well, she said that Lars asked her to call us and say that he was pushing our business case through to the review committee. She was very charming Finn. She said that he was impressed by our ideas and despite a few reservations, he was keen to see it go through. Finn, fella - she said Lars chairs the review committee and that she shouldn't say, and we shouldn't get too excited - but we're likely to be given the nod!"

I take a breath in.

"What do you think? Nothing to say!?"

"I can't really talk right now, Miles."

"Oh of course. Of course of course of course. But listen. Fella. We're going to go for dinner tonight - and we're going to celebrate. The four of us. I'm giving Anne a call now and she'll call you back when it's arranged. How's that?"

My voice is flat: "That sounds great Miles." I hang up.

Ten minutes later my mobile goes. Alan looks over.

"Hi."

"Hey hon, how are you?"

"I'm okay."

"Sorry to disturb you at your, er, work..."

I don't feel like playing; Anne goes on.

"Well, Miles got in touch. He said he called you?"

"Yip."

"He seems pretty excited. He's gone and booked a restaurant for us all and that's fine by me. I wanted to check it's okay with you?" And somehow Anne's already clicked to my reluctance. But no, it is fine and I tell her I'm in, because there's no reason not to go, is there? We arrange to meet at the restaurant after work.

Turns out Miles has found us somewhere quite upmarket. It's a fancy place off Soho Square with a great pane of glass out the front and the inside done in tasteful soft lighting and pale wood. The evening's cool. Anne and I time it well, arriving outside together; from there we spot Yvonne and Miles already at a table.

"How's my big entrepreneur?" says Anne softly and reaches up with both hands on my shoulders to peck me on the cheek.

"It's not even half approved," I say dismissively and she gives a shrug that shows she understands everything about Miles' gross ambition and this premature celebration and that makes me feel a bit less tense, and she says "come on, let's go inside."

We walk to the door and a gloved footman opens it, letting out a low hubbub that matches the glow from the lights. The Maitre' D takes us to Yvonne and Miles.

And they look pretty good. I've just worn my usual work suit with no tie, but Miles is in a jacket that's somehow shinier and sharper than what he wore to the meeting - and Yvonne looks amazing. She's in a dull black dress that shows the skin between her breasts and her makeup makes her eyes look huge. I look back at Anne. Her vintage dress looked okay out on the street - kind of cool even, with the white crochet knit and 70s belt and her charity store shoes - but I notice in this light, with these people around, she seems out of kilter. Mismatching somehow; all thrown together and I feel a pang of regret for her in those clumsy clothes that's she's so happy to be wearing, though it's a confusing feeling. It's like I want to protect her.

The waiter drags our chairs out.

"My two favourite people!" gasps Yvonne as we're tucked into our seats

"Yes, quite darling," says Miles cooly, and the waiter asks if we'd like drinks.

150

"Well I'm sure Yvonne will have a bottle of that Pinot Noir, won't you?"

"No I won't," she says, looking hard at Miles. "I'll have another glass when I'm done. Be nice." She takes a tiny sip - but her hand putting the glass back on the table looks very deliberate.

"*I* would like a drink" states Anne emphatically. "And I would like you to chose it for me Miles."

"What do you drink then?"

"I drink what you choose. Though mostly white: if you picked something white I wouldn't hate you."

"Okay. No more hints" says Miles and sets to studying for the task. The waiter looks at me. I point at a beer on the menu and make a question face and he just nods. That was easy.

"I think Anne and I" says Miles, when he's got the waiter's attention again, "will have the Castillon Viognier - a bottle. Finn?"

"No I'm done. Thanks." Looking up to the waiter who nods at me again and takes our menus as he turns.

"So I hear," says Yvonne in her pert little tone, "that you clever boys are started in business."

I look at her but don't say anything. She has a rounded little heart-shaped face, Yvonne. And a very small mouth.

"Come on Miles; tell us. We're all *dying* to hear about it."

Miles squares up his napkin and clears his throat.

"It's not quite like that. Lars is..."

Another waiter leans over Miles' shoulder to place menus on the table.

"...Lars is unlikely to write us a blank cheque without exerting considerable control over the way we do things. I've spoken to people who know how he and his group invest. They're quite out-there with their portfolio. Prepared to fund some really long-shot, weird ideas..."

"Like yours," says Yvonne.

"Yes... like ours. Because they're looking for ideas - like ours - that have unusually large potential return on investment, despite being... despite being unlikely to succeed. But what I've found out about them is that when they do find a project that they see potential in they get very heavy-handed with appointing their own management structure - writing control over your company into their hands and dictating your direction - which," says Miles dismissively as he picks up the menu and scans down it, "is not going to happen with *my* idea which will come to fruition through *my* contacts."

"So what are we celebrating then darling?"

"We're celebrating - darling - the commencement of negotiations that will see the direction of my project remain in my hands. And also the simple fact that some very savvy business people recognised a good idea when they saw one."

"But Miles," I interject. "Shouldn't you take these guys' advice? I mean, they've done it before. Their guidance might be a good thing."

"I think it might be a good thing if we wrapped this conversation up" says Miles, disinterested. Yvonne makes a little snorting sound down her nose which he ignores and Anne shifts in her seat. Then: "Oh look, they have freshwater crayfish. Do you remember the ones we had in Thailand honey, with that amazing flavour?" And Miles, willfully oblivious to what an arse he's being, goes on to tell us about their trip through Thailand where the crayfish they ate came from Cambodian farms. Are we familiar with the buttery North American lobster? Or the local Devonshire crayfish? Well it's totally different from that, Miles informs us. In the farms they control the taste through how much they're fed and the richness of their diet and the temperature of the water - and I don't think I can take much more of this.

"So the crayfish taste like butter?" asks Yvonne sounding bored and reaching for her glass.

"No" Miles says; impatient, confused. "It's the North American lobster that's buttery. They're a different species. It's nothing to do with what they eat."

Yvonne smiles suddenly. "You know, it really was a wonderful trip in Thailand. The pot there is so cheap and I was smoking it *so* much and this guy we were buying from, he was telling us about the prawn farms they have there. They keep them in cages in the sea, and underneath live these giant fish." Her eyes grow wide. " Because the food is dropping down through the holes and the prawns too, they're dying all the time. So underneath live these monster fish that do nothing but eat" - she throws her arms wide to show how big they are and I realise yes, she's quite drunk; was probably drunk before she got here - "just below them. Bigger than anyone's ever seen."

Miles is back to arranging his napkin, looking quietly contemptuous of his wife. I look out into the restaurant, imagining the swarming waiters and laughing guests as prawns. The drinks arrive.

Yvonne has the food menu in her hand and she's batting her lashes at the waiter with all the sweet she can muster.

"Are you ready for that drink now ma'am?"

"Oh yes, very ready. And I'm thinking of having the risotto. Is it creamy, do you know?"

"It's very smooth," he says. "Almost buttery." And Yvonne's tiny face looks absurdly pleased.

"I'll have the crayfish" says Miles.

"The fish for me please" says Anne.

"And for me too" I chime in, glad to have it done so fast.

Miles looks uncomfortable, almost constipated.

"You don't want to try the crayfish?"

The waiter looks back at me.

"Um, you think it would be a good idea?"

"No no. It's just different. Quite different compared to our local Devonshire variety."

"I don't think I've tried Devonshire crayfish" say I, all bright chit chat. "I think I'd quite like to."

"We don't have that on the menu sir" chips in the waiter.

Prick. Anne's looking at her plate. I see Yvonne drain her glass.

"Can I change mine to the crayfish please?"

"One crayfish?"

"Yes, thank you."

The waiter leaves and there's an awkward pause as Miles' eyelids do that fluttering thing; the outward sign of his inward discomfort. Anger at him flushes through my scalp and I stare at the table-top. Looking through Miles' eyes must be like trying to peer through the cracks in a fence as you walk by, I think bitterly; the tic in his lashes like his mind trying to blank out half of what he sees.

What goes on in that accumulated dark of yours, I wonder. Where's your big fish, Miles? And what slips down through the cracks to feed it? And suddenly that's such an unpleasant thought - physically unpleasant - that I have to say "excuse me" and get up for the bathroom.

Inside I splash my face over the basin and pat it dry with the soft, expensive towels. But it's not enough. I know exactly what's wrong. The talk has turned my mind back to that presence I imagined at the break-in - the lurking intelligence from Kip's party - and now the idea's come back to bite me. My hands are trembling.

Physical memory, I think. Delayed response to a stressful situation. But the feeling is close now, swimming to the surface, a frightening thought taking on a life of its own - and convincing myself this is just an attack of anxiety is more than I can muster. So I step into the cubicle, fish the bag of coke from my jacket lining with hands that are wobbling badly now and tap a line on to the cistern.

Immediately, my head clears. The creepy thoughts that felt so overwhelming a moment ago melt like cream into strong coffee and when I step back out into the restaurant and take my seat at the table - chit-chatting with Anne and Miles and Yvonne, steering the conversation back into cheerier pathways, teasing them about the taste of our crayfish when it arrives - the whole circus-scene of the evening has become laughably easy to handle.

Afterwards, when we've paid and I'm out on the pavement with Anne, hands in my pockets, contented, I ask if I can stay at hers. Of course I can, so we swap notes with the other two and decide to get a cab together - they can drop us off on their way past the Common - and when we get to Clapham Anne unlocks her door and we head upstairs.

"Oh Finn. I feel like I'm constantly apologising for those two. But sorry, they really can be awful, can't they?" She's folding clothes in her room, exasperated.

"I'm really..." I shrug. "Well, look... at the start of the night, sure. But afterwards, I just stopped caring." I laugh. "Stopped caring in a good way - you know what I mean. It was a good night in the end."

"Yeah, it was. It actually was." She's smiling too. "I just can't let those two get to me. You know, when I first met them we'd go out and I'd think, God - they're on the brink of breaking up. But they do it all the time. It's just the way they are.

"She's told me all about it, you know. Tonight they'll probably go home and have a proper screaming match - her being a dramatic drunk, throwing things on the floor and him being unbearable and shouty - then they'll end up shagging like rabbits. It's just the way they do things." Anne shrugs. Then out of the blue:

"What were you on tonight?"

My stomach in knots.

"What do you mean?"

But there's no reply. She doesn't look angry at all - she's just waiting.

"I had some coke."

"Where from?"

"From Kip. Kip gave it to me."

She doesn't say much after that and we go to bed under a cloud. We lie beneath the covers with backs curled away from each other, like parentheses faced the wrong way round, while my whirring mind keeps me awake. Over and over I see the girl through the door. Over and again I think of the urge that grew in me, that itch in my palms. I can't ever tell Anne.

And how did she know about the coke? I think back to the apartment and the way my chemical confidence made so light of the transgression. Then the restaurant and how that line saved me. It must have been obvious - to Anne at least. And it's obvious I need to throw that shit away.

I can't ever mention the apartment to Anne, though. Or tell her about my crazy fears.

I sit up in the dark. She's awake still; I can tell from her breathing.

"No more drugs," I say over my shoulder.

There's a silence, the blackness so tangible it's like it's knitted.

"You shouldn't hang around Kip and those guys," she says. "Not so much."

"Yeah. I know. You're right." She *is* right. "I won't then," I say softly and Anne rolls back towards me. I turn to face her, feeling better already, and we fall asleep with heads touching.

Later in the night I wake.

I can hear her moving too. I reach for her, and as we make love in the dark Anne becomes the girl in the apartment, pinned below me on the floor.

I feel her hip bones underneath me, delicate like a bird's, and somewhere far back in my mind something closes its eyes - an ancient gaze of pleasure and annihilation. My hands slip around Anne's throat. Tiny mewling sounds escape her lips and I drive myself into her, more and more frantic, until we collapse with a cry.

She's back to being just Anne again.

But I've become afraid.

I lie still, listening to her breathing, and as it slows into sleep my fear fades with it. My eyelids grow heavy and fall shut - dark within dark - as a faint sound of water grows more clear. The Effra is tugging at my limbs. It swirls around me, whispering its want to wash us down, and merge us with Thames' dark tide.

***

I knock the drugs on the head.

It's harder than I thought. I'd figured it was a habit, not a Habit. Hanging out at the Shop, getting a little high or taking a dab before a meeting - I thought of it as temporary measures; just a useful boost for when life's moving a bit too fast. But after just three days clean it feels like I've pulled off a jumper - every little chill pinches at me, makes me uncomfortable; awkward. And in this cold clarity I grasp for the first time the full impact of what I did in the apartment - and that's not all.

As each day strips away another layer of insulation I'm forced to confront the reality of what I've been feeling since that first day with Anne; since before the first day: the undeniable sensation that I'm being observed. That something is around me. A presence invisible, but tangible. Unwholesome, all-encompassing and aware.

I feel naked to it.

On the sixth night of this cold realisation I'm at Effra Mansions and it's late. I'm up by myself and for some reason I think of that windy night when I first used the dictaphone. My sleep patterns have been terrible. The TV's on but not tuned to a channel and the hissing static washes the room with queasy light.

Below, I hear a woman cross left to right. The clop of her heels seems to pass through me, the sound making me feel nauseous and afraid, and it's like the party again: the patterns on the wallpaper start their writhing, the room is crowding in and I desperately want Anne's hand in mine leading me away. Please, *oh please* not this again - but Anne's not here to help me. I look up out of the room, through the window to the terraced houses across the street - the fading footsteps sounding awful, empty - and I see him.

I see a face that swims into focus from the Victorian brickwork like a magic eye painting that was always there but you couldn't see and a voice that is both inside my head and out says "Finn. *Finn*," and I must have passed out briefly because I find myself sitting on the floor with a bruised tailbone, looking at my hands, his presence all around me.

***

"You've always been a man lost in your own mind, Finn. Is it strange to be in someone else's?"

"Oh God..."

"Come on, don't panic. There's no need to panic. You're not panicking are you?"

My breath shoots in and out of my nostrils. I can't seem to get enough air.

"Good, good. You'll be fine."

But I'm a long way from fine.

"I don't want this..." I say under my breath.

"You don't need to whisper."

"I don't want this..."

And he says nothing. But he doesn't go away. I have a desperate little cry - and then I'm done with that. I dry my eyes and it's like he's been waiting.

"...so?" I manage.

"So what?"

"So why are you here?"

"Why are *you* here?

Jesus Christ.

"I've always been here Finn. It's just you've finally noticed."

"Can you go away please?"

"Go away, where?"

"Please? Just stop talking."

"Of course I could. But I think that would just make you nervous. I don't want to make you nervous Finn. Anyway - what do you mean 'talk'?"

I look up into the room. The light from the TV is still flickering on the walls. It's quiet - I don't think my flatmates are home - but I understand that if they were, they wouldn't be hearing two voices.

"How do you do that?"

"You're a very receptive individual, Finnegan. Very receptive! Though particularly so right now. Maybe it won't be so easy at other times, but now we've started I'm sure that we'll find different ways."

"I don't want to!"

"Don't want to!" And his laughter is like being stabbed by knives. "You don't want to? But you're so very receptive, Finn. So well tuned in!" And he laughs and laughs as blackness clouds up around me and I slump dead to the world on the floor.

Jane shakes me awake. I'm startled and scared like a rabbit, but I don't think she sees it. Phil's silhouette looms above me and I gather enough to see that he's drunk.

"You alright there, Finnegan?" says Jane kindly - and she's very drunk too.

"Yes. Yes..." And it's just the three of us in the room now. "Yes, I'm okay." And I get up and struggle down the corridor.

"*Hey.*" Says Phil suddenly and points a finger at me, swaying. "Frisbee," he says - his Northern accent stronger. "Tomorrow."

I sort of wave and go to my room.

***

By 4am, I'm thankful for the two hours I realise I spent unconscious: despite having a splitting headache when Jane woke me, that was the only rest I got all night. When a grey light starts creeping around the curtains and it's clear nothing's happening sleep-wise I get up, shower and make for work hours early.

Instead of riding the underground I walk the quiet streets to Clapham North train station and wait for a train east towards London Bridge. It's going to be hot today. It's warm already. Overcast, though, and sticky. The last of the true summer heat before autumn.

The train arrives almost empty. I sit and lean my head on a window - the doors bleep, then clang - and we speed past the backs of sleepy houses. Beyond their shuttered faces I see Lambeth clock tower slipping by and I crane forward and look down: Brixton High Street flashes past and for a moment I see Kip's shop, with blankets hung across the windows.

On an impulse and because I have hours to kill I get off at the next stop, Denmark Hill, and when the train grinds off, popping and sparking into the distance, a presence seems to shake itself from the noise and settle round me. The quiet returns.

"Good morning Finn. You're up early. Did you not sleep well?"

And yeah my heart is thumping but this is too absurd - and I'm too tired - to be really scared. A woman walks down the stairs on the platform opposite.

"You know, I think I'm going to look like a crazy person if I stand here talking to myself."

"To yourself? Huh. Okay let's go. We can take a walk. I'll see if I can keep up." And is that actual mockery in his voice? At least he keeps silent as I clear the ticket barriers and head out on to the street. I'm striding fast in the faint hope that a determined mindset will keep the voice at bay.

"Do you know that building is a college for the Salvation Army?"

"I don't care."

"You should. It looms large in the unconscious of everyone who lives here. *Look at it.*"

I look up. A square central tower thrusts into the sky; as brutal as the Tate Modern, but somehow more gothic and dark.

"Impressive, isn't it?" says the voice, sounding like a proud parent.

"I hope I never see it again," I say, sulky.

"You know," continues the voice, oblivious, "if you come back here in the evening I'll show you something you *will* like. A fox who suns himself every afternoon on the roof of the station platform, while just beneath commuters march by, without the faintest clue he's there. You should show Anne. It's just her kind of thing."

I stop dead in the street.

"I think..." I say slowly - half angry, half terrified - "that we should clear a few things up. Like what the fuck's going on?"

There's a long pause. A blackbird hops on the low brick fence next to me then flies away.

"You're not going crazy, if that's what you were wondering. Though I understand that this must seem strange. I think that in time you'll come to understand what I am - though I wonder if you already understand?"

I turn again and start striding.

"Fucking hell. I'm *actually* losing my mind. God, it's never been like this. Not even when I was a kid..."

"It would be a mistake to think this is all just happening in your head."

"...God-*damn* that shit is bad for me. No more drugs, no more drugs, no more drugs. This is just cold-turkey..."

"You think you hear me because you're in withdrawal?"

I wrap my arms round myself to stop the shaking, muttering as I go.

"...Just don't tell Anne. This could last a while - another week maybe. So I just need to hold my shit together and avoid her for the meantime..."

"Don't think you can ignore me Finn."

The voice is full of menace. I take a breath, trying to decide whether I should say anything - but he chips in first.

"Finn, we're going to talk again. Like I said, I think you're going to come to understand me. But for now, tell me one thing.

"You remember at Kip's party - down on the mud at the Thames? Tell me what it was you were thinking, just before you became afraid."

"Then? Look, damn it, I was high..."

"Tell me..." says the soft voice, with a hint of threat.

"It was... well, it..."

I take a breath and begin again, speaking deliberately, as if that somehow cancels the absurdity of the conversation.

"I was very high then and quite confused. And I guess, in that state, I started thinking about how much the city consumes. How life-like the whole system can be. I guess I was thinking of London as if it were alive."

"And is that idea so crazy?" he asks softly.

"Crazy? Yeah, it is. And here's another crazy idea. I need to go to work soon," I venture delicately. "Where I need to be undisturbed..."

And at that the voice starts to laugh - a laugh that fades slowly like a radio being turned down and down and then off - until he's suddenly simply not there. The reality of the bright morning - the hedges and the bricks; the asphalt and early commuters - comes bold in front of my eyes.

I'm *very* tired.

***

When I get to the office, still way too early, I text Anne asking if I can come round tonight - then power up my machines. As the various servers patch in I rub my eyes and login to my inbox. What I need - what I desperately need - is a quiet day. But it seems I'm not going to get it.

The first email is from Alan, my line manager, sent last night at 7.58pm with the subject line "Official Warning". What's a prick's use of capitals.

"Finn," he's written (what, no 'dear'?) "for at least a four week period your work output has suffered notably in both volume and quality. In addition, your communication and general presentation within the office have been observed to be below acceptable standards, and this email - and an accompanying letter, which I would ask you to collect from me - are to notify you that this has been recorded on your employment file with this company."

I can't believe it. There's no one else around but the morning cleaners. I've got my head in my hands.

"This letter also functions as an official warning," goes the email. Then comes the good bit.

"I'd like to take this opportunity to point out your otherwise exemplary performance for this company in your time here, and express my hope that this is a temporary and soon-to-be-remedied setback.

"Furthermore, if there is a personal basis to your current under-performance, or if there is anything that you would like to discuss with me on a personal or professional level, please understand that I'm always available to talk"...and if I had an axe right now, boss, I think I'd put it right through your stupid head.

Personal or professional? *Personal or professional?* Oh, great Alan - thanks. Yeah, no - I've spent the whole morning speaking to a disembodied voice while trying not to look like a *freaking lunatic,* but thank you - I think I'll just pop over for a chat so you can help me out with my communication and general presentation skills vis-a-vis the voice in my *goddamned head.*

I've got a full body shake on now and I'm just about ready to cry. There's a ding and a note pops up from the online calendar. Extra wonderful: there's a planning meeting at half nine for our whole unit, which most likely means we've got a new client. Alan's added a message saying he looks forward to input from *everyone.* Subtle. I didn't even know you could do italics in that thing.

What I need now, what would make all this so simple, is a nice quick line - and that's just not going to happen. Will not. Happen. My phone beeps.

I rub the heels of my palms into my eyes, ignoring it for the moment.

So. Hooked on speed, huh? Nice work Finn. Yeah, really good.

My malignant little voice is right, though. Ignoring for a moment the fact that everything he says is just coming from somewhere in my head, I have to admit his point - that he's not just withdrawal. Those feelings at the party - at both parties - even at the apartment, weren't only drug-related. Hell, half the time I've been using to keep those thoughts at bay. What you have Finn, if you're honest, is a latent tendency for an unstable brain - and a very low tolerance for drugs.

So yep, it's clear that I was using to feel more normal. But - surprise, surprise - being in withdrawal just makes it worse. I think of the joke and laugh: you put your thumb and forefinger together in a ring in front of your face, then gnash your teeth with a snarl.

Q: What's this?

A: A vicious circle.

So I managed to get myself hooked. In a way, though, the thought perks me up. It means that the voice, the presence, is temporary - a kind of detox demon - so that if I soldier through this period, just tough it out, then it should simply fade away.

It's a hopeful thought.

For one thing, it means not having to fight for my brain. Yes, my friend said he would be back, but humouring a voice until it fades has more appeal than cracking my mind like a dinner plate in some howling psychological conflict.

So I just stay off the drugs.

I'll stay off the drugs - permanently. And until I'm better I'll need to cool things with Anne.

I open her text.

"Of course I'd like to see you," it reads. "You're alright? What would you like to eat?"

I read the message twice more, taking reassurance from it each time. Then with hands that are steadier peck out a warmly ambiguous reply and say that I'll see her at eight.

***

"So, team. Any guesses why we're meeting today?"

Alan, plopped on the table-top in that casual we're-all-friends way he likes to affect, grabs the knot of his tie in one pink hand and hauls it loose with a backwards heave of his neck. He looks like a walrus preparing to fight. Chubby fingers pick open the top button; we're gonna get down to business.

"Translink have come through?"

"Karim, that's a hundred percent right."

When Alan arrived this morning I took the initiative, approached him at his desk before he'd even sat down, and asked for a "chat". Alan's the team leader for a fair group of developers, so he could probably swing his own office, but he hasn't - I suspect because he likes to be one of the lads. Instead, he works in the cubicle farm with the rest of us, so when he does any kind of personal management - which luckily is not often, because he's bad at it - he tends to leads you to a side room.

"Sure," he'd said, fishing in his drawer for an envelope then nodding me towards a side room, "for privacy". We sat down facing each other, the envelope equidistant between us and neatly placed to one side.

I'd had a good hour to gather myself since reading his email - an hour with no intruding voices, where I'd been able to shore myself up with plans and decisions - and also recall my contempt for this workplace: the blissful freedom from concern I'd felt the other day. I took the lead.

"This will be the paper copy you mentioned." I reached for the letter and slid it towards me. "Thank you.

"Because, look, Alan... I do actually appreciate this warning. It needed to be brought up. Your instinct was right: I have been experiencing some upheaval in my personal circumstances. And while I am grateful for your offer of help working them out between us, I think I'm better handling things by myself."

The poor guy looked baffled - he hates anything too heavy before his 9am coffee.

"So, what you need to be reassured about is that'll I'll be back to my usual standards of behaviour right away. And that's something you can rest easy on." I stood up. "Because I know you'll soon be noticing some significant changes." Like my chair through your goddamned forehead.

"Okay..." the pale pink sausage had said. "I'm - well I'm glad you've taken the initiative on this issue. I appreciate your... forthcomingness."

And I thought 'Alan, time to wake up. It's 8.35am and 'forthcomingness' isn't a word' - though what came out of my mouth was "Good stuff. Oh and hey," as I made for the door. "Very much looking forward to this morning's new project." And if I hadn't been feeling so wrecked, I think I would have laughed at the relief on his face.

It's full of self-importance now. Karim adjusts his pen with pleasure. I look around us.

Twelve bona fide nerds in one room. It's lucky the air-conditioning works so well in here. To people with normal sweat glands this is just a meeting in a London office block with a pleasant view of the Barbican towers in morning sun. But for an all-male group of software technicians it may as well be midday in the jungle.

Of course they're not all the same kind of nerd - and they know it. People are sitting in little clusters according to how they see themselves relative to the others. On the right are slouched the cool nerds - IT techs who think they're the business because they have girlfriends and subscriptions to Auto magazine and talk about football; in other words, they're the louts. And then on my left are the true computer losers: those who stutter when they talk to women and feel happiest in a digital world - though they can be further divided by their various hobbies and backgrounds: here we have the ethno computer nerd. The judo computer nerd. The yoga computer nerd and Goddammit, I think we have one, but truly I'm too frightened to ask: down the end in cowering Colin I think we have a genuine, traditional, trainspotting computer loser.

Together we make up the formidable development and implementation team for a) our own company, a medium-sized and old-fashioned financial house and b) for any other client stupid enough to contract us. I wonder why Rail-link *has* been stupid enough to contract us?

"...so pretty much that," Alan is saying, with his back to the view of bright-lit concrete, "is why we'll need to be far more client-facing that normal:

they're asking for multiple points of contact throughout the different aspects of the project. Any ideas on how we structure this? Finn?"

"Not sure. Sorry, I wasn't listening."

Alan's translucent skin - this part is brilliant - it actually goes purple round his face.

I'm not sure that did me any favours though. When he wraps up the meeting and we file out to our desks I expect to be called in for another a talk, but it seems he's given up. Or, more likely, he's decided to give me enough rope and let me earn my own dismissal. In any case, I wade through the rest of the day untroubled by corporate machinations, clamber out at the other end and make for Anne's.

***

I ring the buzzer and feet come drumming down.

"Hello!"

The door pops open with more than the usual vigour and Anne's face appears, giving me a warm cat's blink.

"Would you like to come up?"

"I would," I mumble. A week away from her and I'm out of practice. I shut the door on the humid air and climb into the cool of Anne's flat, heart heavier than it should be.

"What kind of wine did you bring?"

"Oh I... I didn't think actually."

"What, you forgot? You didn't bring...? Oh, lucky there's a bottle open already for you. It's in the fridge."

"Sorry, I should have stopped off on the way. I'll go down for a bottle."

"Dick - I'm kidding. Pour a glass and top me up as well please. I'm making Special Gumbo. I hope it's not too special." She takes off an oven mitt and kisses me on the ear, suddenly still and gentle. "How are you?"

I nod an affirmative. "Yip," I say resolutely. "Yeah." And it's enough to just be here back in her warm orbit.

"You seem a little tense?"

I am tense.

"I haven't taken anything," I say stiffly.

"I know. You told me you wouldn't. Anyway, I'd be able to tell." And her eyes do that half-closed slow blink thing again. "But is everything else okay?"

"Yeah."

"You just need feeding up, don't you? And a drink - weren't you pouring me a drink?"

I smile properly.

"Now. Did you know," says Anne matter-of-factly as she turns to the gas stove-top, tastes the contents of a pan, then starts spooning on to two plates with bread. "That Miles. Has told me he wants *you*." A dash of salad on each plate. "To work with him full-time."

"Did he say that?"

Anne looks over, hands full.

"Wine!"

"Sorry. Where - in the fridge? But hang on..." I get the bottle and slosh her a hurried top-up, then pour one for me. "He said that exactly? When?"

"Last night. He called about something else and then made quite a point of saying so. I think I'm supposed to pass it on."

A sigh sneaks out and I look at something on the floor, seeing now how this will work.

"That's... that's actually something I've been thinking about. You know when we were at the train station, talking about it?"

"When I discovered the giant chalk crown of mystery and led us on our total result of a day out?"

"Yeah... then. Well, you got me thinking about what you were saying. So I'm going to do it. I'm going to call Miles tomorrow and make a go of it."

"And quit your job?"

"And quit my job."

"Good on you."

She sets the plates down and we both both sit, but ignore our food.

"Listen... Anne. Something else."

Tension seems to crystalise out of the air. Anne looks at me like she knows what's coming.

"How would it be if we saw each other less?"

"What do you mean?" Her face is prim and controlled.

"Well, look. This is... a big deal for me. And I'd like to make a proper go of it. I mean really proper. Throw myself in, give it everything I've got, see if can make something of it..."

My mouth runs on, sounding like lies.

"...And I think that Miles, he's a great guy and he's, he's got some amazing ideas - but in another sense he has totally no clue. I really think this business of his has no hope unless someone like me puts in more than is realistic from just a day job. Someone needs to make Miles' thoughts work in the real world, and I've been thinking about it and I think I can do it, but. *But...*"

"Not at the same time as being with you," I finish weakly.

Anne raises her eyebrows but looks at her fork.

"To be honest," I carry on, "I don't know what our status is anyway." I'm feeling really miserable now. I look up at her dismally. "I mean... are you even my girlfriend?"

"Are you mental?" Her control is starting to give.

"Well..." I start poking at my plate - then give up suddenly and clank my fork on the plate. "Do you mean mental, of course you're my girlfriend - or mental, you aren't?"

Anne gives a hurt-sounding sigh, but still she holds herself back. Have I really just messed this up? I know I'm supposed to do something here - I can feel it. But I'm so low - so low and so tired.

There's a way to do this I tell myself. It's just a task - a puzzle - and if you work out how to solve it, then everything turns out fine.

"Listen. Hon."

Anne's sipping her wine, looking away - and angry.

"That's not what I - I don't care about labels. I mean, I hope you are my girlfriend. If you are then I'm luckier than I realised. It's just I... need to do something. And when it's done, I want. Hope... that you'll be there on the other side.

"Because I'm starting to feel like life wouldn't seem very real without you. But just now I'm not really handling life very well. And I really... I *really* don't want to ruin things with you, this person that I need, while I get my life sorted out.

"How am I doing?"

"Better. So let me get this straight. You don't want to see me while you and Miles do his big launch?"

"More or less."

"Do you want to see me at all?"

"Make me dinner sometimes?" And it took everything I had to crack that one. Anne picks up her bread and whaps my cheek lightly with the floury end.

"You'd be lucky." But I get half a smile.

"So maybe, I thought... once a fortnight." Her forehead crinkles. "Once a week?"

"Once a week. At which point you'll be very, very nice to me." She looks up and catches my eye - and catches, I think, my thoroughly miserable expression.

"And I'll be nice to you." Then she frowns - looking hard at me.

"Oh Finn. You're like our caterpillars, aren't you? A bit too permeable to your surroundings." But I'm too drained to reply.

"You might perk up if you munch on a leaf or two."

"And have a drink," I manage quietly.

"Once a week?"

I look up at her.

"Once a week."

"And back to normal when you're back on top," she says. I look her properly in the eye and nod. And then we eat on it - and as the food fills me up I begin to believe that maybe, maybe, I can pull this off.

***

"You know, I don't mind if they bite me," Anne says into a darkness pinpricked by the sound of insects. We're lying on the bed with the lights off and the windows open, cooling the room for sleep; bellies full.

"It's just the *whining* I hate."

"But if you only kill the ones that whine, won't that evolve silent mosquitoes?"

"That would be fine. They could bite me all they want, then - so long as I don't have to hear about it."

"Huh."

The awkwardness from before hasn't totally gone.

"You know, you can bite me too if you like," she says.

I kind of don't register what she means. I've been anxious all day, thinking about the voice. Its cold insistence that it had a life outside my head.

"Finn?"

"Sorry. Do you mind if we don't?"

"Of course not."

But she sounds like she minds.

A hand goes to the back of my neck and scrunches my hair - until she feels me getting tense and stops. We both listen as a whine wafts away from us, then back again, and suddenly cuts out. I wonder who's providing the meal.

"Anne?"

"Yes?"

"Are you religious?"

She shuffles round to face me, though the light coming through the windows is too dim to make out her expression.

"That's an interesting question. How long have we known each other?"

"Dunno. Coming up three months?"

"It must be about that." She pauses. "We don't know much about each other, do we?"

I shake my head.

"That game has probably run its course, huh."

"It really has, hasn't it. Anyway," she says. Now that we're *officially* half going out, we can grow up and tell each other our jobs. You first."

I can just see the twist on her lips.

"Come on!" She pokes me in the ribs and makes me squirm. "Come on, fess up!" And she keeps poking me 'til I give a snigger.

"That's more like it," she says when we've settled down. "You can be a tense little bugger, you know that?"

"Yip."

"So what got you thinking about religion?"

"I dunno. You murdering mosquitoes?"

"Well, I'm not a Jain if that's what you're wondering. What about you?"

"No."

"Weren't brought up religious at all?"

"Nah."

"We were - our family." She pauses to gauge interest. "Mum and Dad and two sisters. We were Catholic growing up - and only very vaguely - but if you're brought up that way, I think you never really shake it."

"How do you mean?"

She shrugs.

"It just changes the way you think. I don't believe in God - not in the slightest. But I understand why people do."

"Why?"

She stops to think.

"Weeeeell..." it's drawn out as she lays there on her back. "For me, I get it out of art, right? You might see a painting - maybe a special painting - one out of a hundred. And suddenly you can see something extra. There's paint and brush strokes and images and ideas and all of that - but if you're lucky, there's a hint of something more.

"I think that's why I like still-life. The more static everything is, the more you get a sense of something trying to burst out. Do you ever get that feeling?"

I shrug.

"I'm not really arty."

"But I mean outside of art. In regular life? I guess what I'm saying is, I think that's why some people believe. Personally, I get very occasional moments where I feel like the world is jam-packed full of a sort of mystical potential. It's a lovely feeling. And I don't get it so much now I'm older - maybe that's why I go looking for it in art. But if you're brought up being told that faith's important and you start feeling like there's meaning lurking behind every leaf, well, if you want to call that feeling God, that's fair enough by me."

"What do you call it?"

"Why call it anything? Perhaps just beauty. What I do know is the moment you turn to look at it, it's gone."

I wish. I clasp my hands, remembering back to the party and that feeling of being surrounded; the presence and its sense of being real. I know I shouldn't be thinking like this, but it's harder to brush off the memory of that voice as an illusion when it's after dark.

"What about Gaia theory then? Would you believe in that?"

"As in?"

"The natural world is all connected. And it's aware."

"Dunno. There was a girl in college who was into all that. I remember she'd lecture us about that nurturing earth mother nonsense..."

There's a slap of Anne's hand on her skin.

"Little bastards."

"I thought you didn't mind."

"He was whining. Anyway... she was pretty irritating too. But her heart was in the right place - even if her head wasn't. I remember deciding she was a flake, but that if she wanted to believe in a conscious environment or whatever, then at least it was a nice way of thinking."

"I think it's terrifying."

"Why?"

"Well - look at the environment now."

"Huh."

Anne gazes at the ceiling, sounding wistful.

"She dropped out the year after that. She had a big bum."

Pause.

"Are you finding this boring?"

"No. I *am* wondering what it's all about though."

Which is the last thing I need her wondering. One more question.

"Have you come across emergence theory?"

"As in, if Finn keeps thinking up theories, it'll be an emergency?"

"As in, the whole is greater than the sum of its parts. Two plus two equals five, sort of thing? It's a theory about how we got our consciousness - how we became aware."

"Go on - I can tell I'm going to be enlightened."

"The idea is that if you get something complex enough, then you get extra stuff for free. You know - if a person has two ears and they can hear and they can count... well chances are they'll be able to understand music too. And music has no real purpose - not like having ears or being able to count, but it just emerges out of the other stuff: it's extra, an anomaly, free. Anyway, self-awareness is supposed to be like that. If you get something complicated, like a brain - but also maybe like a computer, or your hippie friend's natural systems, or even... maybe... a city..." I pause, trying to sum it up in my head. "Then as a by-product of all those capabilities, consciousness spontaneously blossoms - kind of just hatches out. That's why they call it emergence theory: it emerges."

"Like a butterfly."

"Sure. Like a butterfly."

"Any particular kind?" says Anne. I'm starting to feel better for blurting out my thoughts.

"Um. Chalk-hill Blue?"

Her hand goes back to my neck. This time I let it stay. The mosquitoes have stopped; only the faint sigh of cars makes its way into the room, and as we lie there in the dark an idea about the presence wells up in my mind. Like the first sight of a hooked fish as it's pulled to the surface, it begins to take on the shimmering outline of an answer. I wait and watch, hoping not to startle it - trying to guess its final shape.

"You know my dear, I think you might think too much."

The thought-shape vanishes with a flash.

"I know. I really know. It was just some stuff that I wanted to ask you."

"Of course." Then she brightens: "Speaking of which - your Kip. Is he a tall, skinny man?"

"Why?"

"I think I met him."

"Where? How?" I roll over and prop up, all thoughts of voices disappeared.

"Last Friday at Tescos on Acre Lane. I'm in the wine aisle and suddenly there's this man next to me. A tall guy with a ponytail and these awful sharky teeth? He was going on about some nonsense and tried to give me a flyer."

"That's Kip alright."

"Yeah, well I would have told him to get lost, but it started ringing bells. I let him keep talking and he decided that I needed to come to one of his meetings. Is he always like that with strangers? He said - get this - that at the top of the tower at Guy's Hospital there's a 'secret, exclusive swimming pool' and the 'people of the south' need to band together to gain access. I mean, seriously - what the hell? He didn't make a lot of sense to be honest."

"So you met Kip..."

I don't even know how to feel about this. The exhaustion of the past few days is finally taking hold, and I can't think straight enough to work out what it means, so I flop back on to the bed with a 'huh' and let it go. Anne goes back to massaging my neck, and I let myself drift into the sensation.

Eventually: "He's wrong about the pool, you know."

"How do you mean?"

"I did a year's pre-med at Guy's. I remember a rumour going round that the bulge in the tower was a pool, but it's not. There is one, and it's exclusive, but it's at ground level. You could use it if you were a student or faculty."

"Good grief. Don't tell me you're a doctor."

"Okay," I say with closed eyes. "I won't."

I hear her lips part in a smile - then there's a little intake of breath.

"Oh, Finn. What will I do without these talks?"

And to that, there's nothing I can say. I need this woman. She holds me together. But right now it risks everything to stay close.

We lie quiet for a long time. Until a nasty thought pops into my head.

"Anne? You didn't go to his meeting, did you?"

But she's asleep.

***

My eyes flick open. It's cold. The gaping windows are two bright squares of breeze and it's light enough to see - but that's not what's woken me. The air's gravid with expectation.

Oh man - I've got to get out of here.

I hurry into my clothes, belt jangling as I pull on suit pants, roughly do up my shirt, sit on the bed to put shoes on - Anne stirs as the mattress jiggles - then I slip my wallet in one pocket, phone and keys into the other - and I'm crumpled, but ready to go.

I stop to look at Anne - face down, back and arms free of the sheets, and think *see you in a week* - but even in this pause I get the sense of a chrysalis tearing slowly open and something struggling to get free, so I quickly tug the curtains closed, darkening the room, lean down to Anne's neck to breathe in the smell of her hair, and slip out.

She makes a "Mmm?" as I go.

Out on the street I check my phone. It's just gone 5am. I walk down Clapham Pavement to the bus stop. There's no one else there.

I sit jiggling my legs. Somewhere in the trees nearby hundreds of sparrows are chattering to the morning light, sounding like an aural version of static - patternless and noisy. I work on trying not to think too loud - and then the bus arrives, lurching and hissing to a stop.

By the time I've crossed London bridge into the city there's a definite sense of wakefulness around me, yet still no sign that I'm about to be spoken too. It's like sharing an apartment with flatmates and finding they're not morning people: you shuffle around the breakfast table wordlessly, pass the cornflakes without making eye contact, dreading the moment when one of you will break the silence. I ring the bell and get off just before Bank.

5.29am. This early in the morning central London's a different place. It's the cleaner's city, the street-sweeper's town. A quiet place where the whine of electric motors and occasional clop of footsteps echoes into the cool air that lingers between buildings. I like it. I nearly fall asleep on my feet walking up Prince's Street it's so peaceful. But halfway up Moorgate I'm brought up sharp.

An electric milk-delivery cart's lying on its side in the middle of the road. It looks like it's taken the corner from Great Swan Alley too fast and tipped over: cardboard tetra-paks have scattered out, lying bashed and squashed on the road, and milk's gone everywhere. It's splattered on the cart's wide black tyres, dribbling out of crushed cartons and gathering in a thin pool on the road that drains silently into a storm-water grill.

Sat on an upturned plastic crate at the side of the road is a man in a yellow vest with a phone in his hand and resignation on his face. He looks at me as I stand there, taking it all in.

"What does it mean?" I say stupidly.

"It don't mean nuffing," he says back and I look on, transfixed, as the white tide runs and runs and he's right. It doesn't mean anything so I walk off, around the crashed cart and up Moorgate towards the office, and as I go he yells out "hey!"

"Hey! It's no use crying, eh! No use crying."

***

At the office there's no one around - I had to kick over a stack of newspapers at the door just to get in - so I go the men's cubicle, put the seat down, and snooze. Nothing startling happens except when I open my eyes they won't focus on the door in front of me. It's something about the speckled surface that stops them pulling up out of a distant gaze and I have to blink and look at my hands to get them right.

And still no word from my friend. Just a sense of watchful waiting, so I go out again, on to now-busy streets where the upturned cart and the mess of milk and the driver have vanished like they never existed - and get breakfast from the Pret. When I get back it's gone 8am - Alan's in - and it looks like I've just arrived. I have to pretend to work for an hour before he leaves his desk and I can ring Miles.

"Miles Charmers speaking."

He sounds tired.

"Hi Miles. It's Finn."

"Oh hello old boy. I've been waiting for you to call."

"Listen, Miles, I don't have much time to talk because I'm at work. But do you have a job for me?"

"I believe we could make that happen."

"Like how?"

There's a pause and then a scratching of pen on paper. It sounds like scribbling.

"Let's say a fixed-term contract. Six months - three and then three. I'd prefer to offer sweat-equity old man, if that was up your alley, but Lars is still riding me on that. Structure, value of the company and so on - but let's call you the technical associate for the meantime and we'll look at bringing you properly on board later. How's that? Why don't you come in and we'll talk about a rate?"

"I don't care about that. Can I start tomorrow?"

He sounds taken aback. "You can. You'll need a machine? I'll see that it happens. We'll make it our first bill for Lars when he signs."

"Okay," I say. "See you tomorrow Miles."

"See you then."

I hang up the phone and take a breath.

Is there anything in or on the desk I want to keep?

No.

I push my chair out and take the stairs up.

The general manager for our section is a wiry old git with a taste for old-fashioned suits. He's on the phone having some kind of chummy conversation when I tap on his door, so I step inside and wait while he talks. He doesn't look pleased about this, and tails off his call.

"Hello? Can I help you?"

"I've decided to resign Mr Whiting, and I wanted to do you the courtesy of telling you first."

"*Right.*" He looks surprised and the plummy voice goes up a notch into plummy displeasure. "Who is your line manager then please."

"Alan Bagbury." You have no idea who I am, do you?

He picks up his phone but keeps a finger on the disconnect button and looks at me for a moment.

"Well is there anyone else in management you wanted to show courtesy to?"

"No thank you, Mr Whiting, just you."

"I'll leave it up to Alan to arrange the details then shall I?"

"Thanks Mr Whiting." I give him a smile and as I walk out hear the clack of the button coming up.

When I reach my floor Alan's back at his desk and just hanging up the receiver.

"Finn," he says, looking pale. "I'd like to speak to you."

"Go on," I say across my desk and stay where I am. His eyes flick to check if we'll be overheard.

"I've just been told. You won't be required..." Softer now: "You won't be required to work out your notice period Finn. I'd like you gone. I'm advising security to escort you off premises in ten minutes. You're not to touch your computer or your phone."

So I sit down to wait - and it's the best ten minutes at work I've ever had.

When security arrives, it's the Nigerian guy from front desk with the scars. He comes and stands next to my desk.

"Hello Finnegan," he says softly. "Are you ready?"

"Yes, thanks."

He leads me down the back steps, takes my magnetic pass-card and holds the doors open. Brian comes round the corner wheeling a trundler stacked with stationery. He flicks his watery eyes over me, taking in the scene.

"Alright Finn," he says.

"Alright Brian."

It's colder out than in.

5 AUGUST ENDING

"The river's tent is broken: the last fingers of leaf
Clutch and sink into the wet bank. The wind
Crosses the brown land, unheard.
The nymphs are departed."

- T.S. Eliot, *The Wasteland*

Suit jacket flapping in the wind, I aim for London Bridge. If you move fast enough people can't tell you're not talking on a phone.

"You've made the right decision Finn. I'm sure of it. Now that you're spending less time with Kip you need something to shake you up."

Is it just me, or has something of Mr Whiting crept into his voice? Maybe the austere facades of the banking district have loaned him their tone.

"Good to see you've got my best interests at heart. But I don't see how Miles shakes me up."

"Miles?" He laughs - definitely posh - "He's as mad as a snake. Trying to bludgeon the world into shape without the faintest clue why. Kip may be crazy, but at least he gives reasons for what he does. No, I think you'll have a grand time dealing with Miles."

"Oh dear. Well, I did appreciate the silence this morning. You must have been oh-so tempted to put your oar in, but it would have been quite the distraction."

"As you say - your bests interests. But you seem more resigned to me today?"

I'm half over the bridge now, gulls looping overhead; their paths over the buses making an archway in the air. I shrug.

"I guess it's about management isn't it? I figure that until my brain chemistry evens out you're going to be around. So there's no point in fighting it. And this morning showed that you don't have to torment me day and night, do you? So instead of aggravating you with an argument about being imaginary, maybe we could come to an arrangement?"

An unpleasant purr creeps into his voice when he says "an arrangement would be good," but I plug on regardless.

"See, my issue" - we're coming up to the main entrance to London Bridge station - "is having my life ruined by looking crazy."

"Crazy, how?"

There's a wreck of a homeless man slumped by the station doors mumbling to himself. I drop my voice.

"Crazy like this! I'm standing here talking to myself," I hiss. "And soon I have to get on my train. If we carry on this conversation the only difference between me and this poor guy is going to be dress code."

"You don't like to be thought crazy, do you?"

I think he's enjoying himself.

"*Please?* I just need to not look like him - like a goddamned nutter - just for this time on the train."

"That isn't a deal Finn. Deals goes both ways. We need to discuss this."

"I know, I know." I turn my face away so people can't see I'm talking. "But couldn't we do it somewhere more private? If I find somewhere quiet, we could talk there?"

"Promise you're not running away?" he says it with a laugh.

"Promise."

And his snort sounds amused. In the girders above there's a flurry of feathers as pigeons flap from their roosts.

"It wouldn't work anyway. See you when you leave the train then." And he's distinctly, emphatically gone.

As before, reality sans the voice is a cold surprise. I realise a black-cab driver has been watching me, disinterested, while he smokes - though the homeless guy's still oblivious beneath his tangled mop. I duck away from the cabbie's gaze as I walk into the station - walk into the smell of cookie dough and engine oil and the sound of the PA echoing off the floor - find my train and board.

We pull out - passing through Bermondsey with its view of the stadium and its stamp of green turf - past cranes and crematoria - then it's Queen's Road Peckham and Peckham Rye before we arrive at Denmark Hill. The doors bleep open. I glance up at the sight my friend was so keen on yesterday - the brutal Sally Tower looming over the station - and while I'm peering through the scratched perspex window, a movement catches my eye: on the black-topped platform roof on the other side of the rails a young fox is sunning itself, perfectly hidden from the commuters that pass below. It yawns

- black lips over white teeth - and stretches its belly fur to the breeze. I feel my heart sink. Alarms blare as the doors rattle shut: I spring up on an impulse, wrestle the door open again and jump out. The train pulls away.

Even from just these few feet lower on the platform, the fox is hidden from sight. I pace for a while, not knowing what to do now I'm here - half tempted to board another train, to just ride the rails forever in the hope that the voice will leave me alone. I even consider busing to Brixton, ringing the bell at the shop and getting fried out of my brain, but then I think "no, screw it. Screw Kip" and set my skittish feet in motion towards Brockwell Park: walking out of the station, up Denmark Hill and down the other side to the entrance at Herne Hill, my thoughts still circling around the fox... the little fox... the fox that the voice knew would be there.

I pass through the gates into the green and climb the hill to a spot between two huge oaks, accompanied now by an unmistakable presence. Warm zephyrs send patterns darting through the grass as I drop my bag and flop down.

Neither of us speaks for a while, but when he breaks the silence the haughty tone is gone.

"Do you know there was a river there once? The old Effra wound through the fields below us. Now it's trapped; hidden from the sun beneath the earth."

Leaves clatter above me in the breeze. They're browning at the edges, getting rigid; it's not long before summer goes. I look up at the sky and frustrated tears prick the side of my eyes, blurring the scudding clouds into blue-white mess.

"Why are you telling me this? Why is this happening to me?"

"You're just different." he says softy. "You tune in. I can't explain it more than that."

"Tune in to *what?*"

The question hangs for a moment.

"A long time ago people sensed my presence here, Finn, in the rivers and streams. They revered me; placated me with offerings. But those people died long ago and I must find new acolytes among the concrete and the bricks."

I bark a laugh.

"You are a very *specific* mental phenomenon, you know that? I'm sure the psychiatrists will be fascinated."

"Do you really believe that?" he says softly. "Really?"

And I think back to the fox sunning on the station roof; how he knew it was there. I struggle for a moment with the idea that maybe *I* saw it one time, but forgot, and then remembered... but the effort of convincing myself is too much. Despair blubs up as I shake my head.

"Do you begin to understand what I want from you? What sacrifice it is that *you* can make?"

Some of the warmth seems to go from the sun.

"What do you want?"

"You remember the story you told Kip that time? About Orpheus?"

"Oh you caught that conversation…"

For an invisible entity, he does a good shrug.

"You remember that Orpheus sang to the queen of the underworld? Reminded her of the world above? Think of it that way. I've been forgotten for such a long time Finn. The essence of London has been buried, and I want to remember life again. So make an offering to me: of your senses. Talk to me, tell me what you see, hear, think - that's all I want. And only for a short time, to help me wake up from this sleep."

I can feel my skin crawling.

"And why would I do that?'

"Because you need something in return." His voice grows colder. "I know what it is you want most in the world. But do you think you can be with her while I'm whispering in your ear?" His voice drops into insinuation. "Do you think you're *safe* to be around?"

"You leave her alone," I say thickly. "You hear me?"

"Let us make a deal then, you and I. The deal of Orpheus. Lend yourself to me; speak to me, listen to me - give me a window on your life for a few weeks. And in return I promise that when we're done you'll be free of me forever. You'll be free to get her back."

I look down at the slope below and try to imagine the peaceful reeds and river that he mentioned; purple points of iris on the banks - willows maybe. It seems a stretch.

"What if I say no?"

"Then others will say yes," he says mildly. "There are those who hear my call, even if they aren't aware of it the way you are. Your friend Kip, for one. Such a suggestible creature. What sacrifice do you think he would make to me, his living city?"

"I'm not afraid of Kip," I lie. But I remember the hunger in his eyes when he talked of Anne and a terrible thought grips me. She loved that poem - *Eurydice*. The girl who dies after running from the satyr. I didn't know what a satyr was before, but now I think I might.

"There *will* be a sacrifice, Finn, of one kind or another."

"You said you would let her be..."

"I said we should make a deal. Lend me your senses and you'll be free of me - free to be with her."

I shake my head, trying to get calm.

"I need to move," I tell him, and he doesn't object to that so we get up and walk down the hillside; the crazy guy with his disembodied voice following like an invisible dog.

At the gates we turn left and I stop at the shelter to wait for the next bus to Brixton. My head is spinning. The shops across the road - Georgiou's Haircuts, the Dulwich off-license, Caribbean Cuisine - all look like they could be scratched off like flakey paint, blow away, and not be missed.

I look back at the park, thinking of the last time I was in Herne Hill. It was at the start of this summer. The day the fox and her cubs looked at me on the station platform. I'd come to the park with a whole different set of problems then - Shelly and the screaming fit, my new flat. That was the day I met Anne;

the next day I would meet Yvonne and Miles in the Common. I think back to the fox and the way it fixed me with that burning, living stare.

"How long have you been watching me?"

A lady glances at me, then strolls out of the bus shelter with studied nonchalance.

"Long enough. Do we have a deal, Finn?"

"I could always damp you out you know. Go to Kip's and fry my brain with so much speed you'd never get through. I could do that if you don't keep your side."

"You won't need to," he says. But there's no river dancing in the sunlight now, and he can't keep the mud from his voice. Do I have a choice?

"We've got a deal."

***

For a guy with voices in his head and girlfriend issues - oh yeah, and a drug problem - I'm pretty chipper the next morning. I make my way north to Miles' office early, leave the tube at Edgware Rd and overdo it on two takeaway coffees for breakfast, just for the hell of it. It's sunny on the walk to his place.

By agreement with my imaginary fiend I'd had the previous evening off and used it to catch up on my life. A steaming goat roti from the Jamaican takeaway made for a decent early dinner, then I went to the Sainers to get fruit for breakfasts; bought shaving stuff, made plans.

We'd arranged to break radio silence again after my first day with Miles, and I already had some ideas about things to talk about that might pique his interest - and thereby get him off my back - but that was something to think about later. For now, for whatever his word was worth, I had the guarantee of silence for the whole day ahead and I resolved to put him out of my mind, to have a good first day with Miles and make a go of this job.

I might be early, but I'm not the first. The secretary's not in when I arrive -

I learned last time she's shared by the whole bunch of half-pie business types who rent these offices - but the front doors are unlocked, so I take the elevator up and I'm surprised to see lights on and what looks like Miles moving around in one of the glass-walled rooms. He hasn't seen me so I walk in, weaving around partitions and desks - the Miles shape becomes a distant green waver as more layers of glass paneling come between us - until I finally see him directly through the door. He looks up.

"Hello chum. Bright and early. I'm just sorting you out."

There's polystyrene on the floor and a mess of bubble wrap and a brand-new laptop on the desk. Miles looks confused - and downright haggard round the eyes.

"That's quick work. Will it be up to the task?"

"It'll do just... fine..." He's powered it up already and a dialogue box is prompting him to do something. "Insert...? Damn," he says softly and looks over at a sheet of printed A4. "They didn't say it would... insert disc..."

"Look, ahh" he booms - back at Miles volumes. "This is going to take a while. Why don't you go get yourself some breakfast. I'll be done when you're back."

"Well, sure - but why don't I do this and you go out? I used to do installations all the time."

His face looks pathetically hopeful. Anyway, I hate watching people muff things I can do better.

"Ah, look, better not old man." He holds up the A4 sheet and winces. "Passwords and instructions from building IT." But I just hold up my hands in a *come on*. He really looks tired.

"Ah, bugger their rules. I've got to trust my own people, don't I. And I need a coffee," he mutters. "You sure you'll be right?"

"It's got administrator passwords?"

"Everything."

"Then I can be done in ten."

Miles sighs, relieved. "Good man. Good man. You want me to get you anything then?"

I stick out my lip in indecision.

"Mmm. Coffee?"

"Good man..." and he shambles out.

When he's gone I sit down at the laptop and focus. Silly git was stuck at installing the mouse drivers - this *will* take more than ten minutes - but I work through methodically, click, click, clicking on okay, swapping out disks and cleaning the packaging off the floor as software loads up. It's while I'm picking up polystyrene that I notice that a sleeping bag, looking brand new in its stuff-sack, has been stashed behind the couch. The laptop bleeps.

I sit back down, click finish, and load up a web browser - connecting to the building's wireless internet the same way as last time - then open my personal web mail. I copy and paste all the administrator passwords into a draft email, delete the browsing history, delete cookies, delete private data, quit the browser - then scan over the IT cheat sheet.

It's quite interesting. There seem to be a few web-based start-ups using these offices - plus, at a guess, people doing media stuff or graphic design - and all sharing applications and servers. I snoop around as much as possible without being obvious and access a bunch of drives. I hide shortcuts to ones I probably shouldn't have opened out of casual sight, leave the rest on the desktop, and by the time Miles gets back I've found all the ConsumerU folders and started reading anything I can find.

They really need to change their name, though. We. We should change our name.

"Oh great," says Miles when he sees me up, running and working in a tidy room. "Jesus. You're going to be helpful round here," and he hands me my coffee. There are voices by the stairs. "That'll be Sav," says Miles. Come on over and meet the team. Bring that with you; we'll get you set up on a desk."

Sav is Savinder, a tall Indian lady with purpleish acne scars on dark skin. She doesn't smile much and barely acknowledges me when we're introduced. That's okay - she seems like a good person to be in business with. Lizzy, not so much. She gives me a too-personable hello and shakes my hand limply, everything about her saying 'undergraduate'. She's slim, but soft-looking. And not wearing office clothes - she's wearing an office clothes *outfit*.

"Savinder is our 2IC. Her background is in retail contract law, so she'll be shoring up our client relationships. But she's also going to be wooing prospective clients - aren't you Savinder? - and dirtying her hands on the sales side of things. She's up to her neck in this with us Finn - so send any questions her way that you like.

"Lizzy -" he flips his hand towards her. "Is at business school. Where is it Liz? She's helping out three days a week."

"Cass," says Lizzy as she gives me the clammy handshake. I don't bother to ask what that means. Jesus - maybe they're fucking?

"Finn, why don't you finish your set-up out here. Just pick a spot - the red chairs are hot-desked with some of the other tenants. Then in, say, forty minutes? We'll have a whip meeting where we can update you on where we're at, after which I suggest we one-on-one."

A whip meeting? What the? Clearly I'm behind on my buzzwords and jargon. I picture Miles bent over a table, trousers round knees while an impassive Savinder spanks him, but then I think whip... WIP... work in progress and Savinder's already gone, stalking across the office to be effective somewhere and Lizzy's offering to show me round the building.

"Okay," I say. "But I'll get my desk sorted first." And once I'm done fiddling with that, getting things how I like with pencils and plain paper and the phone out of sight Lizzy shows me the bathrooms and the water cooler and the plant that she's rescued - by which point it's time for the meeting.

We go to the room where Miles was this morning. It has one door into the main meeting area and another that leads to Miles' office. There's a healthy-looking rubber plant in the corner, a long table with new chairs and a red couch against the back wall. I look and the sleeping bag's gone.

We settle around the table, the two or three empty chairs between each of us making it feel wrong somehow - like a pretend meeting, not a real one - and Miles sits lasts, dropping his folder on the table-top with a loud, casual slap.

"So. Finn," he begins in his officious tone. "Welcome to the next year of your life. Finn is a friend of a friend of my wife..."

Really? They're married?

"...but don't hold that against him. You've both seen the work he put into our technical specs and I have high hopes for his future. Though if you haven't got what we want, then you can just bugger off and we'll be none the worse, right?"

"Ah... sure."

"Of course we're expecting great things. And if we get them, then in four years from now when you're comfortably retired you'll be explaining to people how you started in a shared office off Edgware Road with just three of you running everything. No offense Lizzy, but you don't count.

"That's down the track though. There are a hell of a lot of hours to put in before we get there - and you can stop rubbing your hands at that, because we're getting you off contract rate and on to a salary just as soon as Lars commits. So let's get going. Liz?"

Lizzy open her own laptop and prepares to take minutes. Crikey.

"Good," says Miles. "Now, for Finn's benefit, where are we at? Where we're at is the end of the first phase - documentation and proof of concept. We'll need you across both of those, sorry Finn. You were silly enough to demonstrate that you can string a sentence together as well talk to the machines, so we'll need you pitching in with the documentation as the technical work develops.

"Incidentally..." Miles fiddles with the cap on his pen before looking me in the eye. "I'm expecting that to be more than you can handle. There'll come a point, not so far from now, where stretching you across those two things will seriously cut into your productivity. So what I want is for you to work out when that's going to happen, and *two weeks* before - not as it's all coming to a head, or two weeks after, but a good two weeks *before* - I need you in here telling me exactly what's required for you to maintain your work rate and we'll find a way to spread the load. That goes for you too Sav."

She doesn't look ecstatic about being called Sav.

"I want the lines of communication here open, so we add resources as they're needed, as opposed to choking our growth by trying to do too much with too little. So Finn, once again: there'll come a time when the hands-on writing of binary bloody code, or whatever it is you do, will need to be lumped on someone else, no matter how much you enjoy hiding in the numbers. And I expect you to recognise that moment when it comes and talk to me. Got it?"

"Sure. Got it."

"Good. Now: documentation. Liz, you're getting this?"

Lizzy mmms, but keeps typing furiously as she gets the last of Miles' speech.

"I speak quickly. You're going to need to keep up."

She finishes.

"I'm with you Mr Charmers."

"Good, because we're on documentation. Make that a heading. Savinder, how are your power merchants?"

"They're okay. They know we want due diligence and that, pending an acceptable result, we want them written into our model."

"How did they take it?"

"They think it's kooky." Savinder looks uncomfortable. "But the power companies are on to them now, strategizing around squeezing them out. They know the writing's on the wall. I think they see no harm in a possible life-line from us. Plus, to be honest, Lars' involvement seemed to clinch it for them."

"Good. So make sure it is involvement with these people, okay Sav? I know you're not in love with the idea, but at this stage using honest language about 'potential' investment from Lars will do no one any favours - least of all them. We need to be clear on that, okay?"

Savinder brushes it away with an "I'm clear".

"Could you explain this part to me? I thought we were still preparing documentation, but you're chasing clients already?"

Miles looks at me like he's realised it's my first day and I know nothing.

"Yes of course. Why don't we take this offline this afternoon, and I'll explain it properly. But briefly? Power brokers: electricity, gas - have set up an online auction house where Joe Consumer can bid on power over set periods and potentially save themselves a bargain. The auction aspect is a gimmick, but beyond that, they're using essentially the same model as us - except that it's one-dimensional, because it focuses solely on power. And they're going to be muscled out within two years.

"So we're bringing them on board. We're looking to set them up as a test case for our entire business. They'll be part of the proof of concept that gets all the other companies we need signing up. Unfortunately we're half a year away from being able to demonstrate our business functions technically, physically. So what we're doing in the meantime is - very quietly - buying rights to include their intellectual property within our documentation, pending a decision to purchase outright. Are you with me?"

I think I am.

"I think so."

"Elizabeth?"

"No... hang on... technical, physical..."

"You're going to need to keep up."

"Sorry."

"I speak quickly. So: documentation."

And it goes on like this. I try to follow everything - I'm capable of it - but I keep getting distracted by the social play in here - particularly the cool detachment Savinder displays in the face of Miles' bluster. As the meeting spirals into greater and more baffling detail her interjections are like tent pegs that pin down the flapping canvas of Miles' voluminous waffle, giving it some semblance of shape. She's obviously very capable and that makes me think maybe there's more credibility to Miles' grand schemes than I thought.

Also, something about this makes me think of the voice. There's a general tone to all this talk of assimilation, liquidity, growth that reminds me of the hunger that lurks beneath his words and I'm glad when Miles finally wraps up.

"Lizzy," he says brightly. "How about that morning tea?" And she hurries out to return with shrink-wrap covered plates of fruit and cakes. We stand around, munching self-consciously; I get the feeling this isn't the usual way of things. Savinder, upright in her black blouse and pencil skirt, holds a scone awkwardly, trying to keep the butter off her fingers; Lizzy drops crumbs on her shoes.

"What time are you seeing their lawyers, Savinder?"

"2pm."

"You need me before then?"

She shakes her head.

"What do you say I take you to lunch then Finn?"

I nod with a mouth full of lamington - the first actual food of the day going down dry - and Miles says "grab you at twelve." I brush my hands clean of coconut as Lizzy stretches the cling-film back over the plates; there's a glimpse of soft breast as she leans over, gathering them up. Savinder clops off to her office and I take my laptop to my desk and plug it in.

All around now is the bustle of the building's other tenants; all young, all busy, all easy to ignore. I sit with my chin in my hands and stare into the middle distance - drifting off into the quiet sigh of the computer's fan, visualising my days ahead: going over the tasks I'll need to do, the gear I'll need to do them with, and occasionally scratching down notes.

When I come to, Miles is standing in front of me tapping his watch and there's a page of A4 on the desk covered in dense writing.

"Ready to go old boy?"

Uh.

I look at the notes.

"Yes. Let's go."

***

Miles leads the way outside, walking briskly down Edgware Road. Traffic is noisy - London at full steam - and Miles limits conversation as we walk to pointing out good kebab shops "for when you work late". There's a dingy looking pub by the tube. The sign says The Green Man, but the letters are gold on red. Miles makes straight for the corner entrance, a bell jingles as we go in, and when the doors whumph closed behind us the traffic roar drops to a sigh. Miles looks instantly more relaxed.

"What do you want to drink?" He lobs his jacket across a chair at an empty table and rolls up his sleeves.

"I dunno - what you're having" and I de-jacket as well and sit. The pub's only half full, despite it being Friday lunchtime, and Miles is back in two minutes.

"I ordered you ham steak."

"Sure," I say. "Thanks." And he slides my pint over.

"Cheers."

"*Cin cin.*" And we slop a little on the table chinking glasses. The light from the frosted-glass windows makes the bags under his eyes look puffy.

"So. How do you like it?"

"Well the set-up's good. How long have you got it?"

"We're three months committed."

"Are you're fronting the cash?"

Miles shrugs.

"Plenty to negotiate there with Lars. I figure if he comes in, he can come in from the start."

"And back-pay rent?" I say skeptically.

He shrugs again and sips at his pint.

"As for computing..." I venture.

"Here we go."

"...well the architecture's okay, so long as we're doing this documentation stuff, but you know we're going to need more servers when we get going? I'll need a testing environment, proper software..."

"Make me a list." He looks a bit harassed.

"I started. Listen, does that mean you want me in charge of procurement? And if so, who pays?"

"I'll deal with that when we get there."

I guess the man just wants his ham steak. His sips his beer; jiggles his leg, looks out the window pulling a face.

"Yvonne left me."

"Oh."

"Did you know that?"

"No."

That was out of the blue.

"So Anne didn't say anything?"

"Nothing. I thought... Well, I think she would have said. If she knew, I mean. She talks about you guys all the time."

I think back to the last conversation we had: me blabbering to the ceiling after telling her I want a break. I barely let her get a word in edgewise.

"I mean I guess she'd tell me..."

Miles *huhs* and sips again, trying not to look miserable. What am I supposed to say?

"Do you know *why* she left?"

"Nah," he shoots back, staccato; tension showing through. "I've got no idea. She just regurgitates that magazine stuff... you know, 'growing as a person' - all that crap. What the fuck am I supposed to do with that?

Anyway…" And sips his pint in a deliberate sort of way, recapturing composure.

"…I just thought you might have heard."

"No. Sorry."

"Well. Bloody women eh. They choose their moments." And at that moment the bar lady chooses her moment to bring over the ham steaks (which seems too soon; will these have been microwaved?) and that saves me replying. I sneak a couple of big gulps as the plates are set down.

"Enough of that. What about you? How did work take it when you quit?"

"Oh, it was great," I snigger, "I stuffed it to them."

"You only just told them yesterday?"

"Yeah. Resigned and walked out on the spot."

"Seriously? Man, that's great." Miles shakes his head. "You're a dark horse, you know that," and he munches a mouthful of ham. I do the same; it's actually pretty good.

"You know, I know what you think of me Finn."

"How do you mean?"

"There's no need to be coy about it. I know what I'm like. I'm a belligerent, bullying, big-mouth," he says mildly. "I'm domineering. I know what it does to people round me - and you know what? I don't care. I got over the insecurities that hold most people back a long time ago."

He leans back with his feet under the table, taking a break from his meal while I munch away.

"Frankly, I think the way I act is just the way most people wish they could be. It felt good stuffing it to your old bosses yesterday, right? Not being meek for once. Well that's how I like to live. And that's what this business is about, if you haven't already worked it out. I'm going to stuff it to the lot of them. I'll steam-roller Lars until he does what I want, then I'm going to drive this business forward through nothing but bloody, shit-headed stubbornness." He wipes his face and tosses the napkin on the plate.

"What do you think about that?"

I take the opportunity of finishing my mouthful to consider.

"Honest truth? I'll handle it. You can be a dick sometimes Miles, but right now that's the least of my worries. I'm glad to be working with you."

"Good." He seems satisfied. "I need to know sooner or later if people handle me. You're a hard read, is all."

"Am I?"

"Seriously?" He laughs genuinely. "Fella, I haven't got the faintest what's going on in there most of the time. You're just lucky you've got a mind reader like Anne on your side.

"How's that going, by the way?"

"It's fine."

"Not a bit rocky at the moment?"

"No, it's good."

"Okay. That's good."

He sips his beer in silence, and I finish off my meal. I'm still feeling vaguely cheerful.

"You want another drink?" says Miles.

"Sure. But shouldn't we get back?"

"I can't be arsed. Anyway, it's your first day - and Sav's out all afternoon. Plus we've got things to discuss; your pay for starters - we haven't agreed a rate."

"Oh yeah. Alright: what then?"

"What do you mean what then? What do you want to be paid?"

I shrug. "Suggest a number."

"Sixty-five" shoots out Miles.

"Okay."

"Alright - deal." Miles look like he needs to shake hands or something.

"You know," he says. "As a boss, it's not reassuring when someone doesn't care what they're paid. You realise that don't you? Frankly, it's weird."

It probably is. So much of my life at the moment is weird I'm losing track of what's considered normal. I shrug. "So is leaving a sleeping bag in a meeting room."

"Fair call."

That one got him by surprise. Normally this is where Miles would twitch his lashes furiously, but he doesn't. Perhaps being in the pub's loosened him up.

"It's temporary. I only moved out last week."

"It smells like BO by the couch."

"Alright, alright, you prick. I'll sort it out."

I laugh and get up for the bar.

"I'll get these. What are we drinking?"

"Stella."

A snort escapes my nose.

"Wife beater, huh?"

"Piss off," he says. "And get my beer."

So I do. I lean on the bar and wait for service, smoothing out a soft five pound note. He can be alright, Miles. I sneak a look back at the table, and for once he looks like a decent human being - elbows on the table, head hunched under his problems.

When I get back he's staring into the middle distance, lost in thought. I take my seat and slide him his pint, and he takes it, but he's still somewhere else. I don't mind - I prop myself in the corner and sip my drink.

The light is cold and diffuse coming through the frosted glass. It's like being inside a painting somehow. I once heard that epileptics report an overwhelming sense of oneness and understanding before a massive seizure and I've often wondered if I have a lick of that: right now, everything in front of me seems... I don't know. *Complete*. I look at Miles' skin, papery and dry, and his unfocused blue eyes. I look at the wet rings on the table's worn wood.

"I hear voices," blurts my voice.

Oh God, where did that come from? The spell breaks and Miles' eyes flick up, boring into mine. He frowns and his leg starts jiggling under the table; I stay frozen. Then he looks away, brow still wrinkled, before speaking.

"You think she'll take me back?"

What? *What?*

"Do you?"

Take a deep breath.

"I don't know Miles. You said you don't know why she's left you?"

"I don't have a clue. Seriously. And I know what you're thinking. I asked her if she thought I'd cheated, because I really hoped that was it, you know? It would have been an easy answer. I've played away before and she's found out. But this time there's been nothing. You can tell her that, if you speak to her. I'm not screwing anyone - alright?"

"Alright."

"It probably makes no difference anyway." He sighs. "She said that wasn't it. Says it's different this time."

He's shaking his head, starting to look properly miserable now - and confused.

"She said, if I'd cheated on her, she wouldn't care. What am I supposed to make of that?"

"That's rough..."

"I've always known what to do when we've broken up before. There was always something to say, things to work out, arguments to have - but now I don't understand. I just. Don't. Get it. What am I supposed to do?"

"You could always kill her."

Miles looks up, unamused.

"You're a weird guy, Finn. You know that?"

"Yip."

His brow creases as he takes a sip. He stabs a finger at me.

"You better not mess up my business."

"Miles - I'll try my best."

I'm feeling quite jolly all of a sudden. He actually just didn't hear me.

"Perhaps we should talk about work. Wouldn't that make you feel better?"

"...*christ*..."

"You could tell me some of the things I need to know to actually do my job. You know: the job which right now is costing you sixty-five pounds an hour."

"Jesus, you can be a dick sometimes."

"But you're glad to be working with me, right?"

He sighs, fiddling with the beer mat.

"Where to begin?"

"Well, for starters, how about filling me in on some long-term strategy. I've put some thought into how to build this magic app of yours, and I'm starting to realise you don't just need buy-in from consumers, you need to sell it to the big companies too. As in, they'll need to come up with whole new customer contracts. That's tricky. Have you really thought this through?"

Miles nods, looking at his pint. "Yeah, we've thought it through." The bar lady arrives to see if the limp landscape of lettuce on our plates is something we're saving for later, or if we're done, but he ignores her so I wave at the plates and she clears them away. Miles is warming up for a sermon.

He starts off small, then piece by piece walks me through it. His strategy is a kind of elegant puzzle that begins with a plucky, and lucky company that leverages and inveigles itself, phase by phase, into the way people manage their affairs - and changes their expectations along the way. I'm genuinely impressed at the way he's thought through the various piggy-backs and safety nets he's worked out for himself - and more than that, I'm impressed at the pitch that he delivers. Convincing people's going to be his job. Though one thing I note is the plucky, lucky company he describes is one with capital - which ain't us yet.

"Wow," I tell him. "You sure don't lack vision. You're not starting a new business; you're inventing a whole new *market*."

"You're finally catching on," he says with a grin. "And yeah - it's audacious, but let's be clear: our kind of business is going to happen one way or another. Access to data is growing at exponential rates. There's an entire new economy based on information - and the laurels will go to those who can shape that economy as they see fit."

"You really think you can pull this off?"

"Do I think I can pull this off?" Miles' eyes have gone blank and hungry - no fluttering eyelids now; there's nothing in his face that's not appetite or will. "Believe me, the facts on the ground support us. If I hadn't got *that* right, we wouldn't have attracted the backing of the most forward-thinking investment consortium in Europe. Lars knows we've read the signs right. So whether we can pull this off? That comes down to one thing: how hard are you willing to push?"

He leans back; I sip my beer. I guess that got his mind off Yvonne.

***

Back at the office I mull over Miles' speech. It's going to take some crazy work to get his ideas off the ground. Crazy work. Maybe he feels in his marrow that 'pulling this off' comes down to talking the talk, but what I know is that underneath the talk he still needs a technical construct that will be dazzlingly complex. I try to approach the concept from different angles, look for natural starting points, easy ways in, but it's overwhelming every way I look at it - plus a belly full of beer makes it hard to think. I spin a pencil around my finger and pull the A4 sheet of notes I made earlier towards me to re-examine them, trying to fit them into the bigger picture - then give up. I slump in the chair and resign myself to watching Lizzy work, the satiny cloth of her top shifting across her body as she moves. The phone rings.

Who even knows that I'm here?

I watch it for a while, wondering if it's for the desk's previous owner - then pick up.

"Hello?"

There's a busy hubbub of voices in the background, then:

"Oh hello. Could I speak to Mr Finnegan please - the head of research, grand schemes and great plans?"

Someone giggles.

"Anne?"

"Oh hello. It *is* you Mr Finnegan. I'm terribly glad to be through. I'm not interrupting anything am I?"

"No...I... where are you?"

"We are in a bar. A very good bar. And it's not far... from where you are - shush!"

"Hello?"

There's more giggling, someone says 'stop it!' then Anne says "We've finished work for the afternoon, finished early - that's what we do in this industry of ours, this fascinating industry of which you'll learn nothing, we've finished early and I and a couple of colleagues - namely Danni and Sarah - Danni and Sarah who have been properly -"

"She's a stripper!" shouts somebody.

"-properly briefed," continues Anne louder, "to reveal nothing - *nothing* - of what we do. We have gone to a bar, and we've been here quite some time, and we would like you to come down and join us."

I look over to Miles' office and can see him through the glass: standing up, on the phone, looking angry.

"It's 3 o'clock, I've still got lots to do."

"I know," coos Anne. "I know, but when it gets to five, you tell that young man Miles that I called and that you're not to work late, and that you're coming out to celebrate with us. Besides," and her voice goes louder for the benefit of an audience, "Danni here is *desperate* to meet you - frankly, I think she's hinting at a threesome - and she's got *great* tits."

Someone - presumably Danni - shrieks and yells out "bitch!" and there's more laughter until Anne comes back on the phone, sounding less theatrical - but still slurring.

"Seriously honey, it would be lovely to see you and I'd love to hear all about your first day. And we're not far from you - we're at a bar on the Haymarket - you'll come and join us when you're done?"

The phone goes quiet for a moment as she waits for an answer. My leg starts jiggling.

"It hasn't been a week..."

"Oh for fuck's sake Finn." Her voice sounds hurt and angry and needy all at once - all amplified by the booze. "It's Friday. I want to see you. Just come down."

Miles is still on the phone, Lizzy's somewhere across the office and Savinder's nowhere to be seen. But I still feel like someone's listening.

"Sorry Anne."

She hangs up. A deal's a deal.

***

"Well will you look at that," I tell nobody.

Between my feet, set into the pavers on Edgware Road at the intersection with Bayswater is a plaque. There's a cross and metal letters. The Site Of The Tyburn Tree. I think of how many people have died on this spot. It's kind of creepy.

"What are we looking at?"

"*Ughh*. Can you not warn me somehow?"

That's definitely creepy. There's no getting used to a disembodied voice shaping itself out of the traffic noise.

"We agreed that we'd talk. You'd forgotten our deal?"

"No, no... I didn't forget."

"So what were you looking at?"

"Can I tell you in the park?"

I look up nervously - half expecting to see Miles or Savinder walking by. It's rush hour after work, close to Hyde Park Corner, and standing still on the pavement is like being a rock in a river - a relentless stream of people buffet up around me and tangle themselves in eddies on the other side. I've clipped a hands-free mic on to my lapel to make me look less odd while I'm talking, but I'm still at risk of being knocked over.

"Alright," I hear the voice grumble - a nice match for the roar of a passing bus - so I turn downstream and cross at the intersection. It doesn't take long to get into Hyde Park and step off the main paths away from people. Immediately that I'm in the traffic noise drops away, baffled by the barrier of oak trees and London Planes that line the fringe. I walk across trampled grass gone yellow from some tent or event or summer concert, find a place that feels removed, and drop down. A police van blares an emergency path around the perimeter like an angry blowfly.

"So how was your first day, darling?"

"Oh wonderful," I say brightly against the dread in my guts. "My girlfriend has no idea why I'm avoiding her so she slips away by degrees, and my new boss is a megalomaniac."

"Ah yes. Miles."

"Yeah. As far as I understand it his business plan is to throttle the market into shape, regardless of consequences."

"It's funny how people who need control can create so much chaos."

"Well put, bodiless voice."

"Thank you. So what were you looking at before?"

I fold my hands behind my head and draw in breath. The golden mess of straws prick the back of my hands and smell like hay. It's too beautiful a day to be nuts.

"I wanted to see if it was there. I thought, well… it was something I read about once. About the Tyburn river. After our last conversation I thought it might be something you'd find… interesting."

"Do go on."

"Well… I read up about this area and it turns out this intersection was the site of the Tyburn Tree. You know what I mean? It was where London hangings were held."

Is this really what he wanted from me? Just talking like this? It feels like he's pretending to listen when all this is for some other purpose.

"You see, Tyburn… well, it means two rivers - there were two rivers that met here. And at the junction was London's hanging tree. There'd been killings here since time forgotten, but by the time written history starts the tree was gone and replaced by a triangular gallows. They'd do loads of them at a time - but sorry, is this what you... is this the kind of thing you wanted?"

"I'm interested that you're interested Finn. Go on."

"Okay..."

Faltering. Come on - get this done with.

"Well... like most people know, that was London's execution spot, although the two rivers have long gone underground. It's where lots of famous people met their end. But the story that stuck out when I was reading was about the guy who lit the Great Fire."

Invisible ears seem to prick up.

"Or said he did. You see, after 1666 when the Great Fire destroyed most of London, people went crazy looking for someone to blame. There was a general idea it might have been Catholics - some sort of agents of the Pope - so everyone was ready to believe him when a French guy confessed.

"He went straight to the authorities and said he'd done it. Except he hadn't. They strung him up on Tyburn Tree and they thought that was it, but after they'd hung him and ripped him up and all the rest, someone - a ship's captain - proved that he'd been out of the country before the fire. He couldn't have done it - he was at sea all the time. So all along the guy was just a crazy loner. Someone who wanted to commit suicide before a crowd. Isn't that sad?"

My friend falls silent. The truth is I wanted to talk about this rural rivers stuff because of the way he'd been in Brockwell Park. He seemed gentler somehow when we talked about things green, yet somehow I've managed to move into the kind of darker territory I wanted to avoid.

"Would you like to hear my story about the Fire?" he says, and by his tone I think maybe I wouldn't.

"The Great Fire burned away old London and cauterized the past. Before the Fire London was beautiful. It twisted and turned and for all that it was a man-made thing it followed natural law. It had grown slowly into its shape. It was still a place where the ancient world was recognised - worshipped even. But the Great Fire ended all that.

"The people thought that the flames were a punishment from God - a new Sodom and Gomorrah - so when they rebuilt London they Christianised it. Rationalised it. They killed everything that it was. Everything old was burned away and Wren, their bastard champion of the new, built roads straight and wide. But I still remember.

"I remember that when the city burned, rivers of rats ran down the streets chased by snakes of molten lead wriggling through the dust. My streams leapt up in steam and though the death of my city was hidden by a great fog and smoke, I remember its last great sights.

"The Fire's final light came from a huge house made from solid oak. In the way that a match glows orange when the flame is blown out, it shone out amongst the smoke and the steam for days after the other flames had gone. Day and night, the frame shone out orange, like a terrible symbol drawn in light. And on the third day, when it finally died, the last ember of the ancient world winked out with it."

My skin is crawling with goose-flesh. Oh please, I want my mind back. I so want to trust that this is temporary, but it's so very hard.

"Finn, do you understand what I'm telling you?"

And has he given up now on listening to me? Does he just worm the thoughts from my head?

"Sometimes a great loss changes you."

But I know what that means.

"I think I'm losing Anne," I say thickly.

"So you begin to understand loss. But think of this.

"The old London, it would have passed away eventually; it was already happening. The fire was simply a great sacrificial burning - my hail to this modern winter and a farewell to growing things.

"Because you see, Finn, sometimes it's better not to hold on. Sometimes you ruin what you love simply by gripping too tight. Sometimes, rather than lose something by degrees, it's better to make a sacrifice of what you most cherish.

"To burn it to the ground."

***

Come Saturday morning I sleep straight through til 10am. A breeze in the tree outside my window sends dappled light dancing across my eyelids and the soft flashes - plus clanks from the kitchen - wake me. I pad to the toilet in my socks and drain a very full bladder - then slink back to bed. Somewhere outside there's a lawnmower. I close my eyes again and listen to the distant percussive purr, realising faintly as I doze again that the sound cutting in and out isn't the mower stopping then starting - but part of my brain shutting down as I slip in and out of sleep.

Half an hour later the clank of the door closing wakes me properly and I get up, feeling groggier for the snooze, and venture to the lounge. How homely this feels.

Jane and Phil are there. Phil's obviously been allowed to smoke inside this morning, because the window's open, but instead of letting fumes out, the breeze - a breeze with just a crisp hint of winter in it - is scattering his blue rollie smoke into the house. Jane's reading the paper.

"Eh-up Rip," Phil says - or something like it. I rub my eyes.

"Mor-ning," chimes Jane. It sounds like they've just been bickering.

"Where's Henry?" I ask.

"You just missed him," says Phil. "Left ten minutes ago, dragging his poncy wheelie luggage, heading for Luton. Weekend in Amsterdam," he adds with a twinkle in his eye. Jane looks disapproving.

"When are you making my breakfast?" she demands.

"When I'm good and ready," says unflappable Phil. He seems in an immensely good mood, possibly because Jane's in a bad one. "You'll have some too, won't ya mate? That way I can cook real man food for the both of us, and insipid, pale muck for princess over here."

"*You're* going to have a heart attack."

"No I'm not. I'm going to have fried eggs and spuds." He stubs out his rollie and stands. "You want some?"

"Only if it's no trouble."

"Finn mate, I'd consider it a favour."

He stumps out to go clatter in the kitchen. I take his place on the couch, shivering a bit in the breeze.

"Do you want some paper?"

"I'm alright thanks."

"Close that window if you like - he's finished with his stink."

"Cheers." I haul the window down and instantly feel warmer with the sunlight on my back.

"How have you been? We haven't seen you for a while."

I suspect I haven't been the best flatmate lately.

"Not too bad," I manage convincingly. And: "I started a new job yesterday."

"Oh, right." She looks surprised. "You kept that quiet. How's it going?"

"Yeah..." I mumble. "It's okay." When people who aren't technical ask about your job, you know they hope you won't go into too much detail. It's just one of the things with my kind of work. The upside is you can avoid talking about it without sounding rude.

"I've just... you know... had to pull a lot of late nights lately. To get it all arranged."

"Oh well that's good," she says brightly. "Good for you" - with a smile. "Hey is Anne still in bed? Would she want breakfast?"

"No, no - she's not here. Thanks though."

"That's a shame. I've mentioned I approve of your girlfriend, haven't I?"

"I'm sure you have. Once or twice..."

"You should bring her round more. We haven't seen her for a while."

"Makes two of us," I chuckle and man, that sleep has really done me wonders - I'm feeling positively resilient. Phil bellows from the kitchen.

"You! You want coffee?"

"Yes thanks" I yell back and realise - damn - that is some good smelling stuff down the corridor.

Jane goes back to her paper; I recline in the sun trying to ignore an increasingly noisy rumbling tummy until, with a final crescendo of bangs and thumps, Phil reemerges from the kitchen with three plates stacked high - well, two and then a little one for Jane - dumps them on the coffee table and goes back for the drinks.

Turns out the jammy northern git can actually cook. That's how he puts it at least - but it's not far wrong: Jane's two delicate poached eggs wobble atop fancy toast, next to a proper-looking salad, while the two of us have huge plates of fried goodness: fried eggs, fried sausages and fried potatoes mixed into a sort of impromptu bubble and squeak - plus a super-strong coffee to wash it down. I try a first forkful and... "*oh my God.*"

"You know what the secret is?" says Phil. "Real lard. There's nothing like proper animal fat."

Gross. I have to mumble through a mouthful because damn it's delicious: "I think I'd rather not know."

We wolf ours down in silence after that - even Jane seems impressed - and when we're finished the bickery mood between them has vanished. Phil rubs his belly.

"I think... another fag."

"Do you have to? Why don't we go outside so you can smoke?"

Phil waggles his brows and looks at me

"Friz?"

"Give me five minutes for the shower?"

He rubs his belly and nods.

"I won't be long."

I hurry to the bathroom. Jane gathers up the dishes and I'm just stepping out of the shower when I hear a disapproving "Finn!"

"What?"

I turn the water off and listen.

"God you're a mess sometimes!"

What? I wrap a towel round me and lean out the door.

"What is it?"

Jane's in the corridor tsking at something on the floor. I go over and see muddy footprints on the carpet by the front door.

"What a mess," she says again.

I feel my forehead crease up.

"I don't think that was me."

Jane gives me a look that's normally reserved for Phil. Behind her dried scuffs and footprints lead straight to my door.

"You must have missed it this morning."

I don't get it. But I'm hardly about to argue - especially standing here dripping water on the rug.

"Sorry Jane. I'll clean it up now."

"Don't worry - do it when we're back. Let's head out."

"Okay," and I hurry to my room to get changed.

My trainers are caked with mud too - a smelly, greenish, mud going crusted at the edges - so I throw them in the corner and get my other shoes. For a moment, I sit on the edge of the bed trying to think what got them so shitty, but Phil and Jane are waiting so I biff the question into a mental What The Heck? basket and just go.

We walk our full bellies to the Common. And yeah it's warm enough, but it's not T-shirt warm - not like it was a month ago - and when we get to the grass, leaves crunch underfoot. Phil and I find a spot away from the crowds where we can fly the frisbee and Jane decides she'll walk to Northcote Road for a look at the shops. We flip the disc back and forth lazily - the light exercise making me realise what appalling physical shape I'm in - and by the time Jane's back with a bunch of red flowers on long fleshy stalks we're flopped on the ground, talking idly.

She prods Phil with a toe to get him going until she realises he's immovable, gives up, and sits on the grass with us.

"What are you doing today, Finn?"

She's hugging her knees. She's got long legs, Jane. I shrug.

"Just studying I think."

"You're kidding? It's the weekend. Life's not all work you know."

"All work, and no play," drones Phil, "makes Jack a dull boy..."

"There's just work stuff I've got to catch up on," I say, and stutter over the lie. "For the new job."

"Oh come on. We're meeting a bunch of girlfriends after this. Call Anne and we'll make a night out of it."

"She's got plans tonight, too, sorry Jane."

It's easier to fib about real human beings.

"Well just come along yourself. It's been like living with a ghost with you lately."

"Woo woo..." hoots Phil to no-one - then he throws the frisbee up vertically, misses the catch, and it boings into the turf. Exercise on a full stomach's turned him stupid. I'm stuck for an excuse, but Phil solves it by hauling himself to his feet, grabbing the frisbee and jabbing me in the ribs with it.

"You're coming" he says. "End of story. Come on. I'm getting bored. You going back to the flat, Jane?"

"I want to get changed first."

Phil looks at his watch and shrugs.

"Finn and I will go straight there. Take this back for me, darling princess?" And hands her the frisbee. "We'll see you soon."

He watches her walk away until she's out of earshot, then claps his hands together and rubs them with a noise like sandpaper. "Right!" he exclaims. "Let's get a drink into you!" and he puts a paw around the back my neck and shakes my skinny frame. "You look like you need it."

So I just give up. It's easier to follow for the time-being. And I figure I can put off reading until tonight.

Phil leads us towards Battersea Rise and a place called the Duck, "the finest non wine bar in the immediate vicinity" - which I suspect is not where Jane's arranged to meet her girlfriends - and we settle down to what turns into one of those afternoons: the first pint going down slowly, seeming far too early, and the second tasting pretty rough. But the third and fourth I don't notice at all and by the time Jane's joined us, and the girls start turning up, and they all argue for a move to a fancier bar so that we upheave ourselves and move to a place down the street - we're well in our cups. Everything seems funny and the people on the street seem absurdly sober - why would they do that to themselves? They should be celebrating, not grey and dull - and without time seeming to pass at all it's become evening and the Saturday night drinkers arrive to try and catch us up.

We've had a good head start on them though. And Jane's friends all seem okay. Mostly they're those usual kind of girls - satiny tops, boring jeans, baps more or less on display - except one whose name I don't even catch, but she's got dark narrow eyes and a fringe and wears sleeves that come down over her wrists and she doesn't even look like Anne - she's more like the opposite of Anne, a brooding thoughtful version - but it still makes me think of her so I get out my phone to check if she's called. But of course she hasn't. And then I think about calling her - but I don't. And then when I catch the dark-haired girl glancing across the table of empty glasses at me once again I think *screw this* and say a general "see you later", not directing it to anyone in particular - walk out - and head home.

It's not a long walk, but it clears my head a little and that's lucky 'cause when I open the front door I see the muddy mess still there, waiting to be cleaned. Jesus. But at least it's dry, so I get the hearth-brush and shovel and loosen it up and then I get the vacuum cleaner and do my best and then - even though I'm still weaving a little - I get a bucket and some hot soapy water and sponge up the remains.

I'm pretty tired when I'm done. There's no question of doing work. I fix peanut butter toast and go to bed and - damn my phone, damn this absence from the only person I care about - I can't help checking to see if she called, though I know that she hasn't.

***

"I think that girl was after you," Jane says in the morning.

"Lucky I'm taken" I mumble, still half asleep. I'm way too tired. My head hurts.

"Know who else will be after you?" Jane shoots back.

"Mmm?"

"Me - if you don't clean up your mess!"

Baffled, I say nothing. Just walk to the front door - and see a fresh trail of mud.

It's worse than last time. It's still wet in places. It's smeared on the doorstep and rubbed right into the grain of the carpet. I can even see the paler patches on the sides where I scrubbed it out last night.

I waste no words - just get a bucket and a cloth and set to work. It takes ages - my mouth is *so* dry - and when I'm done I avoid saying anything to the flatties and leave the house.

I go straight to the park. There's a chill in the air, fewer people around, but I walk right to the middle to get as far away from anyone as I can be.

"Hey" I yell into the empty air. "Hey!" At the top of my voice.

"What the *hell's* going on?"

There's no answer.

Off in the distance a woman is walking her dog.

But I can tell he's here.

***

On Monday a flurry of excitement erupts at work. In the glass office Miles and Savinder have animated conversations. Something's happening. I don't care what.

I meet with the building IT manager. I outline some of my needs, for now and in the future. He hmmms and strokes his moustache, taking notes. He seems a sensible guy. I can tell he's not had much of this from Miles. I think:

From now, I will split my time between development and documentation. I will build the core processes of our model in a kind of miniature, recording all the steps, and from this our future team will create our live application.

I run this by Miles and he ticks it off immediately. I think that's worrying.

Tuesday, the drama escalates. I still don't care what it is. Miles bullies Lizzy into coming in on her day off, promising double pay, and wastes it ordering her around unproductively while she pulls a sour face. I think:

I need to build my testing environment. In it, I will create a machine, a digital entity that will become an extension of a customer's personality. It needs to be capable of processing huge amounts of dull information then making good decisions based on a customer's wants. More than that, it needs to be changeable according to their needs: to be risk averse, or risk-taking; short-term cash focussed or in it for the long game - all at the click of a button. This is only a part of what I must do.

I meet with the IT manager again. We arrange for a technician to come to my flat, setting me up so that I can login from home.

Wednesday the excitement disappears. It was a red herring: one of the power companies had the capital to get us up and running - but then not. Miles says they were sounding us out. I don't care. What's worth caring about is Lars wants to meet again. In the midst of all the disappointment over their failed drama, just when Savinder and Miles are hanging their heads looking glum, he calls to set a date.

We're due Friday week.

He says we need to present version three of our business plan. He wants it technical and complete. He tells us he won't get sign-off from his board until we have the rudiments of an app and proper specs - so this is it. Do or die. There's talk of external consultants checking our work; trade secrecy. I can tell that Miles is getting nervous. He has terse phone calls standing up in his office that I presume are with Lars and it's during one of these that Yvonne calls my line.

"Hello?"

"Finn? This is you? It's Yvonne. How *are* you?"

"Yvonne? Jeez, it's been a while. I'm okay - what about you?"

"I'm alright Finn. Thank you for asking. You know it's nice to hear your voice."

"You too," I surprise myself with. "Do you want to speak to Miles? I don't know how to put you through to him, to be honest, but he's on the phone anyway - shall I tell him you called?"

"No. No, that's okay. Don't say anything in fact. I really just wanted to speak to you - to ask a favour." She laughs a little sadly. "I've got an ulterior motive: I want to recruit you to be my spy. But for nothing nasty." Her voice is going wavery. "I just worry about him. I worry, but not enough to call him myself. How about that? He's okay though, isn't he? He's holding himself together? I'm sorry to do this to you Finn, I don't want to make you a go-between."

"That's okay. And I think he's alright. I mean, not perfect - I think he's shaken up. But he's coping I guess."

"Has he found somewhere to stay?"

"I think he's renting somewhere now. But he was sleeping in the office for a while."

"Was he really?" Her voice tinkles. "Isn't that just him." Then she wavers.

"He's not... he's not seeing anyone is he?"

I look over at Lizzy stacking folders.

"I don't think so. Not as far as I know. I mean - I'm sure he's not."

"I'm sorry I asked you that Finn..."

"No no - it's alright." I don't like hearing her upset. "But I thought - I thought that wasn't why you separated?"

"It wasn't. It's hard to explain..."

What? To Finn, the emotional cripple? I wait while she hesitates.

"I actually... I wish he was seeing someone, if that makes sense? If he was seeing someone it would tear me up, but at least it would be something. But he isn't. So there's nothing. And it's just him."

She sounds resigned.

"Look, it's good to talk to you Finn. Don't tell him I called. And... you do know she's worried about you, don't you?"

I pull the phone into my neck, surprised at the emotion; it feels like I've swallowed vinegar. When I can trust my voice again I tell Yvonne thanks. Thanks for letting me know - then I tell her I promise I won't mention anything to Miles, and good luck. I hang up the receiver.

Goddamned girls. They make it hard to work. I stare into the middle distance thinking of Anne's face.

It's a strange thing not to trust yourself. And I know I'm not myself right now, but it's also hard being without her. It's not just that I miss her, it's her blind acceptance of me, the unjudging support that I've come to depend on and that's so hard to give up.

Could I test that acceptance to its limits? Will I throw myself open to her understanding? No. I won't. For me the instinct for concealment is a strong one. And there's too much to risk. I can't tell her everything, but I can't go without her either. I'll stick to the rules - and she'll help me without knowing how, or how much.

I pick up the phone again and punch the numbers. It rings once and then she answers.

"Is that you?"

"Hi Anne."

"I thought it might be. You've got good timing you know. You caught me between two, um..."

"What?"

"...periods of being unavailable," she says with a laugh - still playing the old game - then seems to remember she's supposed to be angry; changing tone.

"To what do I owe the pleasure?"

"Well... it's been a week. I wondered, do you want to hang out?"

"Oh, so you're ready now are you? According to your schedule?"

"Any time," I say weakly. "Any time you were free..."

"I think I'm busy."

Jesus.

"Some time that you're not?"

I sense, rather than hear her softening up. Amazing things phones.

"Oh, look," she says softly - resigned. "My diary's cleared. You around tonight?"

Briefly, briefly - in the little lift of elation I get from her saying yes - I consider playing it for laughs and saying I'm busy, but think better of it.

"Definitely" - emphatically - "Come to mine. Come round whenever you like."

"Well I finish earlier than you - nature of the job. Give me a time."

"Seven?"

"I'll see you then."

She pauses, weighing something up. I wait - but there's nothing.

"I'd better go," she says. "See you tonight."

***

As is the nature of these things, seven o'clock transforms from being an easy target for getting home and getting organised, to being a close-run thing. Miles dreams up a whole new class of things to worry about now that our deadline for Lars is looming, but I rush through my work at the end of the day, get home at ten to seven, and find Henry there.

He's in the living room wiring up a brand-new looking stereo. There's packaging strewn over the floor and a couple of expensive-looking speakers with blonde wooden panelling in the corner.

"Hey flatmate," he says - sounding more German somehow with a screwdriver in hand and the manual laid out. "Sorry about the mess - I'll be done soon."

"That's okay - that's okay - new stereo?" No time to make chit-chat. "Can I ask a favour?"

"Sure," he says, oozing calm as always and only making me feel more rushed and frantic. "What is it?"

"My girlfriend's coming round in ten minutes, and I've got nothing in the house and need to go to the supermarket. Her name's Anne. Would you let her in and explain where I am?"

"No problem. What are you making?"

"I don't know. What I normally eat I guess..."

"Peanut butter toast?"

I wince.

"Maybe something heat and eat?"

Henry pulls a skeptical face.

"Sounds like you need to take her out to dinner."

The door opens with a clang and Phil - carrying his work belt and tools - and Jane - with a fresh bunch of flowers - tumble in.

"Hey guys. What do you think - should Finn take his girlfriend out to dinner, or cook here at home?"

"Come out with us," says Phil immediately, not taken aback by the sudden quiz. "You can't cook for shite. We're off in thirty minutes." He hurls his tools into their bedroom with a tremendous thump which gets a sharp *Philip!* from Jane. "Have you got any wine?"

I shake my head, mute. Jane pokes her head round the door while Phil rolls his eyes at my crapness. "Would you like to offer her some of ours?" she says kindly.

"Yes thanks..." I stutter - and the buzzer rings.

"And *would* you like to come out with us?" she adds. "We're going to an Indian restaurant, it's very good."

"I think maybe that's a good idea. Can I see what Anne says?"

"Sounds great. You better get the door."

I hurry downstairs, feeling grotty in my work clothes, and open up.

"Do you know you have gouge marks from a crowbar on the frame?"

"They come free with the neighbourhood. Come in."

As always in my first few minutes with Anne I forget how to move and speak properly, so that my footsteps going up are clumsy and deliberate compared with the unthinking dance I did coming down. And normally this fades as her affection warms me up, but it feels different today. She seems distant - and I keep my awkward edge.

"Would you like wine?"

"If you have any. Did you just get in?"

"Yeah. We're stealing Jane's."

"Hey babe!" calls Jane from the lounge. "How are ya?"

"*Hiiiii*" throws out Anne, animating more for Jane than for me.

"Would you like a glass of wine?"

"Finn's just getting me one."

"It's in the fridge already Finn. With the white label. Pour us one too. You want one Henry?"

I note that's Henry's making no great effort to clear his stuff out of the lounge. Anne goes in cooing and helloing so I slink to the kitchen to get glasses - Henry calls out a "yes thanks, one for me too Finn" and stands to give Anne his best charming blonde greeting. I can't believe they've never met before. I hear her say "so you're the mystery flatmate". Great, Anne. Really subtle.

I'm still clumsy. I find some glasses: it takes ages to get them together and when I've poured them out and made sure the levels are the same there are more than I can take at one time. I start putting them on a chopping board to carry out like a waiter but it looks stupid so I pick two up - try for three, give in, resign myself to two - and make three trips.

Anne takes hers without saying anything and Phil's getting changed, so I set his on the table next to the stereo manual and some screws.

Jane's explaining the plan to Anne - she seems keen - when Henry's phone chirps. His face - bright and animated from the chit chat in the room - goes blank when he checks the number. He turns the phone off and his smile back on as Phil walks in, fresh from the shower.

"Shall we go?"

"Finish your wine first" says Jane - then "oh pig!" when he downs it in one.

"Fancy stereo. You coming Herr Heinrich?"

"I won't. I'll get this done - then I've got to see a man about a dog."

"Nice idiom."

"Thank you. Nice vocabulary."

"What, for a brickie?"

"For a Northerner."

Anne and Jane cackle.

"Come on Finn," says Jane. "Let's go."

Anne looks at my clothes.

"You're not getting changed?"

"I'll be alright."

***

The waiter places four banana leaves in front of us, spills a little water over each and polishes them into bright green plates. We sit at attention until he's done, Phil cocking his brow at me as if to say *how about that?*

"We found this place a month ago," says Jane conspiratorially. "It's South Indian - the food's *amazing.*"

Anne looks chuffed. I still can't shake the feeling that I'm tagging along with people who like each other, but are indifferent to me. I sit, sulking, as they talk.

"So what's your news Anne? We don't see you enough. Tell us something new."

"Well!" She says brightly. "I do have news. It seems I have a stalker. I'm very excited."

"Oh that's great!" Phil smacks his paws together in satisfaction. "Anyone we know?"

"Well, maybe." She turns to me. "Your tall, skinny, weird friend. What's his name? Kip?"

"What?"

"Ohhhh yes. So last week some of the girls and I finished work early and naturally popped out for a drink. Sadly Finn chose not to join us for some reason, but that's okay - we went on and had a smashing night. Well, more an afternoon because I left early, being" - she smiles sweetly - "'a little drunk. So I took the train home, and guess what? As soon as I'm out of the station - wham! - I'm pounced on by this creep."

"Ooh, how exciting. I haven't been pounced on in ages," simpers Jane as Phil rolls his eyes.

"Well it wasn't really that exciting. All he did was try to talk to me all the way home, which was almost flattering. I mean, he was quite charming - for a total junkie *freak*."

I've got my hands round my face. I think I'm supposed to say sorry, but I'm too angry. Phil's shaking his head.

"Oh Finn you spacker - it wasn't *him*? Did you know we met that squatter nut months back? And get this - Finn invited him back to ours. It was an open-ended invite, as I recall. You haven't been hanging around with *him* have you?"

"Oh, but wait - it gets better," beams Anne. "After that these flyers start turning up in the mail. Hand delivered I suspect?" Jane shudders. "They're invites to all sorts of wacky meetings and then tonight -"

I shoot her a look, incredulous.

"*Tonight*, as I'm walking to your place, who do you think was loitering by your door? He was standing by the hedge when I turned on to your street. When he saw me walking towards him he made like he was picking something up that he'd dropped - then walked off. But you know what he said as we passed?

"*Beautiful* evening, Anne' - and I'd made a point about not telling him my name!"

"Finn, you bloody knob-head," Phil starts emphatically then cuts out, I suspect, as Jane boots him in the leg. I know Anne's playing it for laughs, but I still feel awful. I'm too furious to say anything. I'm saved from the awkwardness of silence by the waiter coming back.

Jane steers the talk onto ordering, which keeps them happy and when the food arrives they all tuck in. I hardly taste it and spend most of the time waiting to leave.

They seem to genuinely enjoy themselves though and when the bill arrives we pay and leave for the flat; Phil, Jane and Anne matching their strides naturally - me stepping alongside self-consciously in work shoes.

Back home, Henry's gone and Jane finally seems to realise that she should leave me alone with Anne - but the night's beyond rescue. We go to my room and I expect her to berate me about Kip, or at least talk about it, but she seems not bothered. Instead she strips off - contemptuous, unerotic with her nakedness - and gets into bed. So I kick off my shoes, go to the shower and spend a long time there just standing and thinking. The water pours down my neck. The bathroom fan roars angrily, but it's blocked and the steam ignores it, curling seductively instead; lacing beads across my lashes and settling on the walls to feed the mould.

I think I was supposed to do something tonight. I think she expected me to grab this evening and shape it by sheer force of personality, but she's more and more like a ghost to me. Someone insubstantial who I clutch at but can't hold. How prophetic, I laugh bitterly: Eurydice chased away by the satyr, forever lost.

When I get back to the room, Anne's snoring already. I towel down, slide carefully in next to her and lie still, but instead of finding sleep I slip into a fidgeting, nervy state.

What the hell was Kip doing? Have I really messed things up with Anne? It must be past ten because the heavy cargo trains are running. They send a low rumble through the plaster walls as they pass outside, the sound seeming to shake a deep loneliness into me. Lying there - worried about waking someone who's sick of the sight of me - a kind of midnight horror steals inside. In spite of the warm body close by I begin to feel isolated; hyper-aware of myself and in terror of the outside world. Parts of me feel wrong. My fingers seem thick and huge; my legs are tree trunks beneath the sheets. Touch becomes unbearable - the sensation on my skin compounding the illusion of my sudden monstrous size - and now, just at the edge of my hearing, I can make it out: the sound of water.

I realise I'm only half awake. I try to control my thoughts, steer them on to happier pathways, but by now it's too late: I've fallen into the swimming hole and the only way is down. For a time there's a sensation of floundering in a black pool with sides too steep to climb and nothing but slimed tree roots to grab - then my mind kaleidoscopes and the last thing I recall is the roar of sucking water and somewhere else - somewhere distant - the sound of my own whimpering.

I come to fully dressed.

I'm sitting on the corner of the bed with dirty scrapes all over my trousers. I look at my hands: the heels of my palms are scratched. Inside there's horror, but there's resignation too - and a great well of tiredness. I put my head in my hands and sob quietly. It's how Anne finds me at dawn.

"Finn?" she says gently. "Finn?" and I think I'd been sleeping a little, sitting up. There's a rustle behind me as she gathers the sheets.

"Honey? What's the matter?" Her hand touching my back is unbearable.

I haven't got any strength for this. I've got nothing. I sit in my head and listen as my own voice, hard and ugly, growls "just get out."

"Get. *Out*" says the voice again and she says nothing after that. I hear her gather her things, hurry into her clothes without a word, and leave. When the downstairs door clanks closed I feel a little better and look up.

The morning light is grey.

I go to the bathroom, strip off my jeans and take a shower, then fill a bucket with water and scrub the muddy footprints from the hallway. Then, while everyone else is still sleeping, I go to my room and wait for Henry.

***

He's up first. I hear the quiet chirrup of his alarm, then him shuffling to the kitchen in his socks. He's slicing tomatoes for his toast when I walk in.

"I want to buy some speed."

"What's that?"

"You heard. The speed you offered when I moved in. I need three bags. Tonight."

Awkwardness crystallizes. He stops slicing.

"I'm not sure that's a great idea man."

He's still in his boxer shorts, only half awake.

"You *promised* Henry. As a thank you for keeping quiet. Remember?"

He frowns at the implication; shifts tack: "...dude, it's very short notice..." but I need this. Stay insistent Finn.

"You could bring it after work."

He looks uncomfortable.

"You said it was thirty pounds each? That's three for ninety. If it's still the same price I'll leave the money in your room today."

He sighs and looks resigned, though I see his knuckle white where it grips the knife.

"Look, alright. Leave the cash under my door. I can bring it home tonight."

***

There's an order to do this in, so get it right: booze, cash, sleeping pills - then call the boss. Don't walk into the pharmacy with a bottle of vodka; don't ring Miles so early that it's weird.

I walk to Boots and ask for sleeping pills. They shouldn't be selling me these the way I look but she pulls me down a packet with moons on it and tells me things I barely hear about not driving or mixing with alcohol. I walk over to Sainsbury's, but the wine aisles are shut so I go to the off-licence, buy the biggest, cheapest bottle of vodka I can get, then visit the cash machine and withdraw a hundred quid. With the cash stuffed into my pocket I put in a call to Miles.

He sounds bleary. I tell him I'll be working from home today, because *look*, I'm not going to get this presentation done for Lars with all the distractions in the office. I can tell he doesn't like it, but the threat of that big deadline looming over us is the clincher. Today's Thursday: tomorrow week we'll be in Lars' office at the prestigious number 30 St Mary Axe finding out whether we get the cash to make Miles' ambitions a reality - or whether they dribble away through lack of funding, because you know what? I'm starting to realise that Miles can't float this thing much longer.

And by the tension in his voice, he knows it too. I talk a bit of turkey about what, precisely, I'll be doing today which seems to set his mind at ease, and we agree to sit down with Savinder first thing tomorrow to start our battle plan. Job done: I might be a wreck right now, but I'm a wreck who's sorting things out. I walk back to the flat - which has emptied in the course of my little sojourn; everyone's gone to work - and plonk the vodka on the coffee table. I balance the packet of pills on top, fix myself toast and coffee, set up my laptop at the table and begin to work.

Two hours in, everything's fine. Four hours in, everything's fine. By 2pm my awful night's sleep is taking a serious toll on my concentration, but the work's starting to get interesting - I'm making real headway - so I fix more toast, more coffee and soldier on until the first signs start showing around quarter to four.

I was so engrossed in my task I didn't notice it begin; I look up to mull over a line of code and realise there's a new edge to reality - a sense of something in the air - and when I pause to listen there's the unmistakable... not sound... more a *feeling* of breathing in the room. No time to lose: I save my work in a hurry, snap the laptop shut and twist the cap off the vodka.

The cheap spirit fumes as I half-fill a glass then top it up with tap water. Fingers fumble open the packet of pills and pop out two bright blue gel capsules: the standard dose. I pop another two from the foil - then one more for luck - look at the cluster in my hand for a moment - so pretty in the way they cast that little blue penumbra on my palm - then neck the lot in one mouthful with the vodka to wash them down.

I tidy away the laptop, tidy away the bottle and the pills, then - woozy already - head for bed. On the way I stuff cash under Henry's bedroom door.

***

When my eyes open it's on a London that can only be dreamscape. Gone are the ugly trappings of the modern metropolis - instead the streets have become Byzantine and twisting; full of hints and shimmers of places that I know.

And I'm pretty sure that this is Soho - even though the streets have become dirt lanes, and the cars are gone - and the fact that this is Soho means this is a dream I've had before: the dream where I'm looking for the pub.

It's not just any pub - it's the perfect pub, a place that I'm convinced I found once, and then forgot. It has grey glazed tiles and a low ceiling, dark ruby carpet and just a few old men sitting on stools. It's a sort of East End boozer, old and comfortable, and in the dream I know that if I can find it again I'll be filled with the deepest contentment. I've searched for it often enough in my sleep that part of me believes it really exists, and each time the dream ends I wake to a kind of half happy, half sad feeling that lingers all morning.

Of course knowing that you're asleep is no defence against dream logic: within moments of realising that the street I'm walking on only exists somewhere between my ears I'm swept away by the possibility that my lost and perfect pub could be just around the corner. How funny, I think, the way I forget to look for it in my waking life, and set off at a jog down the twisting lanes, excited as they become more and more familiar.

Though as I make my way closer to my goal, a nagging feeling starts growing. Wasn't there something I was supposed to do? I look down at my hand and clenched inside it, sweaty from the jog, is the hundred pounds I thought I'd stuffed beneath Henry's door. Damn it! That was it. My memory of the voice comes flooding back - my fear of him and my plan to block him out - and I realise that I still need to give the money to Henry, that I need to buy some speed. There's no way I can keep looking for my wistful, contented pub. I've got to find my flatmate before the voice finds its way back in.

That's where I notice the music. Faint at first, it starts growing louder and louder until I decide the party must be where Henry is. It sounds like the kind of place he'd be, dealing his little deals, and I set off again, pleased I'm on the right track.

Almost immediately, as though London's geography were shaping itself around my thoughts, Soho's tight alleys open on to the banks of the Thames - and I gasp.

The river looks as it might have done a thousand years back. A long meadow crisscrossed with paths slopes down to the water, where reeds and irises march into the mud. On the other side, great imperial buildings rise from a sheer embankment, entwined in ivy and stepped with high gardens like some Victorian Babylon - yet that's not what's strange.

The strangest sight is the loose group of dancers. It's morning, so I don't know why they're here. Maybe one of the clubs has closed and the party crowd have spilled out, unwilling to go home, but it's clear this is where the music came from. Here and there among the throng small groups of people are sitting to relax and smoke - and there's one knot that gives a different vibe. There's a sense of urgency to them that's at odds with the music, so I drift closer to look.

They're gathered around a figure on the ground. He's tense, as if convulsing, and a spot of blood on his trousers marks his anus. Also, there's someone standing next to me watching. I can see him from the corner of my eye, but I don't want to turn.

"What's happening?" I ask.

"It's alright. They know what to do," the figure at my elbow says.

The man's ribcage gives a final spasm and then relaxes. One of the dancers, all day-glo and celebratory, bends down to put something in his mouth. Someone else begins wrapping him in a cloth, then the whole group gathers round to lift up his body. We follow as they carry him to the river's edge and slip him gently in, his body arcing down elegantly; the white face shining as he disappears beneath the brown.

"They understand, my people. Years ago, when the waters were unburied they did the same for me; making offerings both alive and of the dead. They fed them oat-cakes and mistletoe and killed them thrice, the bodies slipped into the current. Do you see? Even now there are some who understand."

"I know what you are," I tell the presence without turning, a chill chasing away my torpor - shocking me into wakefulness inside this dream.

"Maybe you were something sacred once. But you're twisted by what this place has become. They've forgotten you and now you're nothing but a gnawing thought flickering through the city. London's broken Gaia, tied to its rhythms and petty ambitions - craving the worship you once had."

The presence at my shoulder seems to spread around me. I try to blink away my fright.

"And yet *you* still hear me. Some still understand. You know what I want Finn. We had a deal," he says forcefully. "It's the only way I'll let you be."

The deal! Jesus, how could I forget? I'm here to find Henry - to find the only stuff that keeps this madness out.

"You're trying to get under my skin," I tell him. "But I know how to stop you."

I cast my eye around urgently and see him straight away: Henry in a red hoody, passing something to another man. I move towards him and I'm there instantly, the dream-logic carrying me where I will.

There's something in Henry's hand. I fish in my pocket for the money and hand it over - but it's all going wrong. A knife appears. Henry steps up to grip a bunch of shirt at my neck and instead of the languid, clumsy fumbling that comes with physicality in my dreams (and this *is* a dream, oh please it is) I'm surprised by sudden violence. The knife comes hard up into me - once, twice, again - like a punch to the guts, but with a deep, horrid pain and I feel the violation of my insides. There's a twisting in my stomach and know that this is bad - and even as it's happening, even as my body is bucking up above the force of the blows, I know that if I looked into Henry's eyes they would be black pools - buried, forgotten waters - and really this isn't Henry at all. This is *him*. And I'm being punished.

I drop to the ground, trembling like a shot rabbit as the crowd gathers. They drag me to the water, wrapping bed-sheets around me to pin my arms, and flop me in.

The current carries me away, sliding the crowd into the distance until I'm bobbing alone down the dark river within my own darker, spreading pool. I pass by houses and under bridges; the heron fishing at Vauxhall cocks an eye as I drift by. And then I see Anne's apartment block sliding past. There's a yellow light on in one of the windows with a figure there and I watch it until it's gone.

The water tastes salt now. It feels peaceful giving in. I glimpse the Isle of Dogs ahead - will they take my head and keep it there? I'm so confused - and then all begins to dim. Everything spins and is diminished: vision, solidity, the world - it all begins to curdle away, dissolving into the ether inside my head; everything growing faint except the knife pain in my belly, which is getting worse. I want to drift on, but the pain won't let me. It builds into a crescendo until I'm in agony - until I can't stand this - and I heave my eyes open with a mammoth effort and I'm not in the river, I'm in my bed, and I twist over the edge and heave vomit - blue, thin looking vomit - into my bin.

That makes me feel better, though my belly's still sore. I spit again into the rubbish and from there, draped over the edge of the bed I spy the three bags of powder pushed under my door.

Good boy Henry, good man. I sit up blinking, trying to rub the dream from my eyes, and as my knuckles press into my eyeballs, distorting them, I see him in the room: a looming man-shape that swims through the air towards me and oh my God I leap out of bed, grab a baggie and upend it on to a book; drag the white powder into my sinuses and *oh it burns* - the powder sears the inside of my skull, but the figure disappears - just drops out of my mind like sand through a sieve, leaving just a rush of excitement in my belly and white clarity in my head.

***

God it's good to be free of him.

I sit on the bed for a while, observing my insides. The speed seems to be moving through me like bleach in a blocked drain. Forgotten corners, bad thoughts, the accumulated problems of the past month - they all seem to slough off and flush away. I even feel like I can breathe better - though with a faint corona of anxiety when I fill my lungs. I try not to think about the shape that I saw, the voice's transgression from my dream into reality, because you know what? I think it's time to go to work. I think I'm ready.

I hurry through my shower, rinsing the wastepaper bin free of vom while I'm at it, and put on my suit. I tuck the opened bag of powder into my pocket, stash the others in my room, grab my laptop and step out as the flat is waking up.

I'm feeling good.

Looking sharp too. When Savinder and Miles get into the office a while after me they seem distinctly scruffier than I am. They look tired, yet keen for work; there's expectation in the air.

For twenty minutes we all fluff about - checking emails, downing coffees - and then, with no further fuss or preamble we gather in the meeting room. Miles has his head down and hands clasped; he seems reluctant to start.

"Well," he says, looking at the desk. We wait patiently for him to look up at us.

"Well. Here we are. One week out."

That seems to galvanise him and he looks at both of us.

"Friday week we're meeting Lars. Can we do it?" And for once it's not a rhetorical question.

"Of course we can," I say with confidence. "What needs to be done?"

Miles takes a deep breath.

"We need an application: a working micro-version of what we plan to make. We need to spec it up. And we need a final business plan." His forehead creases.

"Well that's all do-able," I say breezily. It's two hours now since my first line, so I'll need to top up soon - but at least for now my voice is steady and unrushed.

"Totally doable. Between the two of you, you could probably finish the business plan by tomorrow - am I right? - which only leaves the app. My plan next week is to spend all my time at home programming - so if I work through the weekend I'll have it done Tuesday, leaving two days for the specs. Basically, if you're happy to have me working out of the office - and away from distractions - I'll have no problem getting it done on time."

"I don't believe you."

Savinder's face is impassive; the acne marks on her high cheekbones stand out red.

"I appreciate that we're under pressure," I tell her - and I think, *and you must be too, to look like that.* "But you might not realise how much work I'm getting done."

I click open the laptop and swing it round. Any other time her criticism would have crushed me, but for now white filing cabinets are rolling open inside me, with answers to every question swishing out unbidden: my voice runs on.

"Look, to demonstrate ourselves properly to Lars we only need to frame two or three core functions within our database - then skin it, so it looks nice. I've already knocked off two thirds of the hard stuff - plus take a look at this..."

Savinder leans in, frowning, and Miles gets out of his seat to see better while I talk them through. Basically I've done the simple stuff of making our data talk amongst itself, but most importantly I've given it a skin, a basic interface, so that it can be demonstrated and explained.

Miles hums and hars. Savinder's anxious still.

"You can get this up and running in a week?" says Miles - and the answers come tripping off my tongue.

"Less than that if you like - if I get time and space to work. I won't lie to you guys, there's a lot to be done - all this needs to be meshed with data that's fed in live, not parked there static - but if I put the hours in next week" - I pause and eyeball them both - "you'll have your app."

Miles exhales and kicks back.

"What do you think Sav?"

Her face looks softer - unsure of herself - and I know I've got her.

"You're hooked into email when you work from home?"

Bitch, after this I'm going to the bathroom to honk powder up my nose.

"Sav, I plan to be back home and working before lunch today. Once I'm there I can live stream myself if you really want."

***

Turns out I don't get high in the bathroom after. I get talking with Lizzy when the meeting's finished - she keeps asking questions about Miles - and then when I start to think about a trip to the gents it's suddenly full of office workers and seems like a too obvious place to do lines. I pack up my laptop and head for home instead - and that turns into a close-run thing. Somewhere past Embankment a kind of snicker-snacker develops in the rails as I ride the Bakerloo. It takes on a rhythmic clatter - the ping and squeal of tortured metal - and in the noise I can just make out a ranting, chanting voice. I switch to the Northern Line, make it to Clapham North and run for it from the station. The chanting's become distinct now, leaping out of bus engines, from traffic noise and the clatter of startled birds, and he's angry - Jesus, he's *furious* - but I make it to Effra mansions, sprint up the stairs, dash into my room and catapult myself to safety with another scorching, heady line.

Which buys me time.

But how much, I wonder? I'm going to have to think about this in real terms at some point. Yes, it's occurred to me that this isn't a sustainable life, but in the trite, perfect logic of my fresh buzz a simple answer comes to me: I'll just vary my usage. Chop and change between stimulants and downers, experiment with what works at keeping the voice at bay, and once I've sorted things out job-wise - once I've proved myself to Miles and Sav and we've gotten through this first gate with Lars - then sometime after that, sometime I'll need to get some proper medical help - real psych stuff - and if I've got the guts to journey down that dark and scary road, maybe into the bargain I'll get Anne back.

I try not to think about her though. Those feelings live somewhere down below, in a level where the presence lurks, so I keep myself up, keep myself high in the white landscape of my work, losing myself for hours in my laptop - the architect of my perfect digital world.

Some time around Saturday I rub my eyes and decide to take a break. I've been working through the night and frankly some food would be sensible - even if I don't feel like it - and so would some fresh air, so I force myself to eat and then I track down Phil and convince him to walk to the park for some friz.

He doesn't say much on the way down - I don't mind - and when we get to the green I concentrate on my throwing, focussing on bettering my technique and catching the blue disc with snap and verve, trying not to jump and startle at the birds.

"You're strung out Finn. How long you been awake?"

He flings the disc at me, but it wobbles and flutters and drops on the grass.

"I'm on top of it," I tell him as I walk to pick it up - and as I bend down I see two familiar figures passing through the trees.

"You seem tense," he says. "Wound up - that's all" trying to keep the conversation open, doing his duty by Jane who'll have put him up to this, but I'm watching the figures as they walk, heading on their way to the Frog and Forget-me-not, kicking leaves as they go like children: my own personal satyr and his curly-haired lieutenant: Kip and Debs.

"Hold this."

"Aw come on fella," moans Phil as he follows my gaze. "Not him"

"I'll see you back at home," I tell him flatly and stride off on their trail.

By the time I reach the Frog, they've settled into seats with drinks. Debs sees me and looks up. I lean over their table, palms on the wood, until Kip looks too.

"Hello old bean," he says with a knowing grin. No mention that he's not seen me in three weeks. No surprise that I'm here. Just a "how's your back-end?" Debs smirks.

"You know why I'm here..."

But I'm choking on what I have to say; the anger rises from my stomach - literally rises; the food in my belly leaps at my throat and I have to swallow before I speak.

"Why you're here? Well I imagine you're..."

"... leave my girlfriend be," I spit out.

His face stays bright and smiling. He turns to Debs; playing to the crowd.

"Hah-hah-hah-hah-hah!" He says it more than laughs. "Your girlfriend? Oh Finn, boy. You're on the woolly rugs! You're in quite the state, aren't you?"

"I said. *Stay the fuck away from Anne!*"

Rage is building in my brain like feedback from a PA. My palms find the edge of the table and my world tilts with it as I heave it over. Beer flies everywhere as my view reels. Faces, finger nails, skin, smashed glass; someone has me by the collar, then someone's being thrown on to the floor - and it must be me because I'm on the pavement outside the pub, a burly barman mouthing as he turns: *now go fuck off.*

I wheel across the road. I'm in the Common, stumbling further into the green, fierce breathing through gritted teeth; walking to let the rage die down.

***

Jane tries to talk to me when I get back to the flat, but I'm too wired from the run-in with Kip; his manic eyes still fresh in my mind. He's a malignant force, I see that now; some modern-day Fagan, and my brush with him has left me with a full-body wobble, so I retreat to my room and close the door on my flatmates, close the door on my life; sniffing thin lines of speed off a book cover one after another until the shakes have gone and Saturday night becomes Sunday morning. All that day I push it to a whole new level, throwing myself into my project, blotting out Anne from my head, burying that lump of sorrow within my chest until the entire week dissolves in a white fury of work and logic and ideas and not once do I wake to find my shoes caked from some nocturnal mud-splashed outing, because I just don't sleep, and my phone says I missed a call from Yvonne at some point and Jane tries knocking but I ignore them all; staying in my room, pacing, pissing in a jar, sneaking out at night for the kitchen and the toilet and when my days start to break apart; when they flicker and jump like a time-lapse film from the Arctic; when I've perfected Miles' application so that it seems more like a work of art than a project - this white fire I'm feeling written into every line of code; when I've reached the limits of what you can do with no sleep and I struggle to remember what I did last night, or last year, or at all: just then the week is up and it's time for our meeting.

"Hmm? What was that?"

The ding of the elevator distracted me.

"I was saying we need to let Lars do most of the talking."

Savinder's never so communicative. She sounds nervous.

"Are you alright?" she says.

"Of course I'm alright," I snap.
"I was up all night finishing this thing, is all."

Which isn't true. I was in Anne's flat.

"I just hope it's up to scratch," she says, tense, and in the stiffness of Miles' neck, in the faint spermy whiff that hangs round them both and the minute transgression they make into each other's personal space as we stand here waiting for the lifts - Jesus, oh. I see.

"Sav's right," says Miles *sotto voce*. Other suits - looking less rough and tired - are waiting with us. "We need to sit tight and play it cool. Let the work speak for itself. God knows we've talked this through with Lars enough already."

"Will there be anyone else there?" I ask - regaining cool. I forced myself to eat this morning and took six codeine-based tablets from Jane's cupboard, which mulled my edge a little.

"Probably at least two from the board. One's likely to be a guy called Bashir - he's the tech enthusiast - but the others could be anyone."

Our lifts arrive. When the doors close I start to sweat. Just in time they open again and Miles takes the lead. We're ushered by a receptionist into an empty meeting room where Miles takes my laptop and busies himself plugging it into the projector with the receptionist's guidance; I wander to the windows for the view.

To the south the Thames is peeking between buildings like a strip of dull foil smoothed by someone's fingernail. Thunderheads are building in the distance and contrasted against their dark mass I can see a pale finger that must be Lambeth clock tower. That means Clapham is to the right - and somewhere in it Anne's place, where I sat and waited for her last night.

"It's quite something, isn't it?"

I jump. Lars has sidled in while I've been lost in the view, followed by a bear of a man with a dark, trimmed beard.

"Good to see you all," says Lars. "Miles, have you met..."

"Bashir!" says Miles too loudly, stepping forward to shake his hand.

"That's right," says Bashir - a little baffled, because they haven't exchanged names yet - and Lars says "You've done your homework."

Savinder looks embarrassed. We finish the intros properly, then take our seats. Bashir and Lars swap a look.

"Thank you for the preview of your technical specs," begins Bashir. Lars starts pouring himself a water, seeming engrossed in the task. "I must say that on an initial view your work is, frankly... fruity." He looks around at each of us, beard bristling on jutting chin. "Of course I'm hoping that today's presentation will prove that first perception wrong."

Miles's face looks suddenly set in gelatine. What was he doing sending them specs before this meeting? More to the point, what the hell did he send?

"I..." says gelatine-face. "I think... you'll find much of our work has been polished in the meantime. Finn has been putting in a lot of work..."

Miles has never understood what I do. I can see now he's wishing that he did. Muppet must have forwarded them my preliminary files - the load of crap I threw together days ago just to keep the two of them off my back.

All eyes on me.

"Perhaps Finn could talk us through his completed designs," says Lars evenly, though I hear his undertone. *I see right through you*, goes his softly softly voice - though his lips don't move.

"Finn?" says Miles. The blood seems to have drained from his face. Savinder slides me the laptop.

"Sure," I tell them - and tap the space bar. The projector comes to life and I talk them through it.

I show them how Miles' vision is for a database that's shared online among competitors. I show them how the data becomes mingled at the customer interface so that the streams of information flow together. I show them how ripples of financial advantage - and the eddies and whirlpools of loss - can be singled out; how the greater sum of many different parts comes to life as the customer's avatar. How it grows into an entity that interprets the consumer world for them. A surrogate for their financial life.

I finish and close the laptop. Savinder's face looks grey.

"I... I have some excellent market research that underpins some of... which is to say... much of the broader picture that Finn has painted has a basis in..."

"I've read your research," interrupts Lars. "And it was... intriguing." He rubs his fingertips hard into his eyes. "But from what we've seen today."

He stops to consider.

"I think it's clear to me now that you're not in a position to act on what you've learned."

Miles's eyes are twitching - I hear his lashes beat in papery flutters like a moth trapped in my hand.

"But we spent..." and his eyes tic *one, two, three.*

"Yes, it was intriguing," Lars carries on. "Intriguing as a view of how these sectors may some day develop - and I encourage you to share your findings with the marketplace in general, but" - he eyeballs Miles, making sure that his point is clear - "for the moment, I hesitate to waste more of your time."

How strange. I can't seem to catch the whole of this. I'm trying to look at Lars and work out if he's saying that we're screwed and this was all in vain, but I can't drag my eyes off his fingers as they straighten his pen perpendicular to him, twisting it in sluggish slow-mo.

"It's all true," I tell him, my voice coming out thick and heavy. "Everything fits together."

"It doesn't matter if it's true," he says gently and I look up, managing to catch his eyes now. "It's about whether you could make us money."

"Thank you for your work," says Bashir grimly as he stands and presents his hand. Savinder takes it on Miles' behalf as he gapes and blusters.

"Thank you and all the best," says Lars and then he's stepping out of the room, buttoning his suit jacket with one hand, and as they leave and the door closes I hear Bashir begin to laugh.

"Christ!" says Miles. "Jesus Christ!" to the empty table. "What the hell do you call all that?"

Savinder's face is pinched and angry; Miles turns his fury onto me.

"What the fuck, Finn! Honestly what the fuck was all that... *shit*?"

It's all gone vague and swirly. I look into myself, trying to find a snappy answer, but nothing I could say would make sense to Miles. So I just let go.

"That shit was yours Miles," comes my voice sounding crisp and contemptuous and a long, long way away. "They were your ideas made real. Maybe if you weren't screwing half your staff you might have picked up what was wrong."

"You fucking *prick*!" he yells at the top of his voice. "My fucking life!" and he hauls the laptop from its plugs and throws it crashing across the room. Heads turn in the corridor outside; Miles stands and kicks a chair, and finally from the roiling strangeness of what's inside me comes welling up my fear.

I hear laughter outside the room, but not Bashir's. It's the laughter that echoes from the underpasses where the foxes yowl and *oh please not this*. Outside rain clouds are looming in the south, while inside looms something darker: my week's worth of buried terror. I push my seat back and it falls with a clang. I blunder from the room and with my last sight of Miles ranting and Savinder cowed I get a flash of me in my old flat - screaming at poor Shelley, her crying with the towel wrapped round her - and the last little sane part of me wonders *where the hell did that come from*? Then I'm pushing through the bathroom doors head hunched under and irrespective of the suits pissing next to their briefcases I shoulder into a cubicle, fumble a line on to the cistern and try desperately to calm myself as I snort it - but the panic doesn't stop. It just gets worse. It's taken on a sharper edge now and I need to be out of this building - I've *got* to get out of here, away from Miles and Savinder and this crushing place - so I run for the lifts, hurry out into the sunlight and run towards the river, but who can help me?

Things begin to fracture. I'm pushing people out of the way, suit jacket flying - who will help? Panic flapping round me like pigeons. No one can. There's nobody here for me, so I run and run and run. There's a tunnel where words come floating off the tiles, blurred by tears so that I don't know if they're real - *the hurt sky is weeping* say the walls; *soaked nightingales have ceased to sing* - and a memory from last night that hits me like the stab from a knife: I will never see Anne again.

It all grows vague. There's a station and angry strangers - and others that try to help - but it's not until hours later that the panic drops away from me like the tide on the Thames and I find myself wandering down the street towards Effra Mansions with no idea how I got there.

I'm exhausted. I stop for a moment to close my eyes and drag my clammy hands across my face. Then I take a breath, fish my keys from my pocket, walk to my front door and spot Kip sitting in the passenger seat of a van.

He's parked outside my house, waiting. Trader Dave's on the driver's side, immaculate as usual, hanging an elbow out the window.

Kip cocks his head at me.

"Hello mate. Come for a ride."

I stand there stupid, keys in hand.

"Going where?"

"Just get in."

Dark rain clouds are massing above the houses. Trade leans across and looks me over.

"Not in his suit!" he says. "He'll ruin it."

"Alright," laughs Kip with an expression that's humourless. You've got five. Go get changed and if you're not down by then I'm coming up to get you."

"Go on," says Trade coldly. So I unlock the flat while they eyeball me, hurry to my room and slam the door.

What the hell is going on? Where are we going? I fish the baggie from my pocket on reflex and find it empty. That was the last one of the three.

I go to the window, sizing up the drop into the garden, considering clambering out and running for it, but what for? The ebbing panic has left a no-man's land behind where fear or love or sorrow have no purchase, so I shrug, take off my work clothes, pull on jeans and the crusted muddy trainers that I'd abandoned in the corner and two minutes later I'm walking slowly back down the stairs to the street. Kip slides the van's side door open for me, helps me up - then slams it shut behind me - leaving me in the dark as the engine starts, thinking about last night at Anne's.

**

In the end I broke in through her window.

It had been a warm, windless night; me working in my room. The mania had been on me and I'd spent hour after hour hunched over my laptop without really seeing it, turning columns of numbers over in my head - solving problems - coming closer and closer to completing my perfect app, but the fidgety jumpiness had been increasing. I'd get up - pace, work, think, work some more - lose track of where I was - until eventually I left it alone, satisfied that with one more session, with just a little finessing, I'd be done.

I realised I hadn't stopped since early morning. It was dark now, our street gone quiet and the night soft and warm. My window looks away from the street, out into the garden that joins with all the neighbours' gardens to form a long unkempt green corridor, running parallel with the train tracks that wall it off at the other end. I looked out the window and realised that as I'd paced with the light on, I'd been watched.

A fox was sitting on the fence. Just a little one, barely the size of a cat, and as I looked at him looking at me he got up casually and walked the narrow fence-top for a few paces before dropping off the other side. I listened for the sound of his landing, but there was nothing.

It made me wonder what else was out there. I'd been in my room for most of a week without having the faintest desire to leave, but now the wanderlust hit me. I was calmer too - softened by the sultry heat - and the thought of what lay out there grew into desire - desire for the cool underpasses, the back gardens, the promise of London's night. And it was a long time since I'd seen Anne.

Would she want to see me? Maybe not. But things had changed since I woke that morning, I thought. I'd changed. The terrors that had been stalking me had gone and the pressures of holding my life together - they'd backed off too. Maybe it was time to see her? To explain. By the next day it would be a week.

I looked at my watch: 10pm. I leaned out the open window and that decided it for me: the night air just smelled too good.

I took the back roads to Anne's - sneaking out of the flat without anyone hearing. A guy I knew used to walk home from work in dodgy neighbourhoods very late and I asked if it made him scared. I remember he said no. The way not to be scared of dangerous people, he said, was to be one of them. If you imagine yourself as the scariest thing in all that dark, then you become it - and the night belongs to you.

That's a good way to move through London. I took the quietest lanes and narrowest alleys all the way to Anne's and when I got there walked straight past the front door and round the corner to where all the back ends of the houses meet the road. I vaulted the high brick fence into someone's garden and then came a languid alive-time where I slipped from garden to garden, counting the houses back to Anne's and sitting still in the bushes when the security lights went on, waiting for the dark again, breathing in the smells among the leaves.

It took a while. But when I got to Anne's back garden - or at least the stamp of turf that belongs to the people who live below her; Anne's place has no outdoors - I recognised the wooden slat blinds on the second storey window and settled in to watch her room.

There was no light. But I sat and watched, content to be there beneath her window in the dark. At one point I heard a hedgehog and some other pattering in the leaves and then when I was sure that she was out - out somewhere with friends I guess, though surely home in some small while, I climbed in her window to wait inside.

Though that bit was hard. I went up the drainpipe, scraping my knees and getting lichen stains all over my hands and my trousers, but when I reached her window and got a finger to its edge it came away free like I knew it would - Anne always forgets her windows - and I managed to swing it open.

By wedging a foot between the pipe and the bricks behind it I managed to get my knee across to the sill. When my free hand found a good grip inside the window I committed to a haul over empty air, bruised my ribs slithering over the sill and plopped on to her bedroom floor. It was dark and quiet.

I sat for a while to be sure that the house was empty and to let my breathing slow. Then I got up and flicked the lights.

All her things were there. No surprise in that, but I'd never been in her room without her. It all seemed like a still-life, composed, waiting for her to come home and animate it. I walked about, touching her things. Smelled the pillow for the cool scent where her head had been - the bed where we'd laid so many times - and that gave me a lurch: the happy night feeling of power and lightness I'd had in the garden giving way to something muddier. A regret and hurt and anger.

I took down her book. The one that she'd read to me the night after we went clubbing - and though I knew the verses by heart I sat at her desk and read our poem again, losing myself in the memory of that night and all the others; feeling sorrow well up in me for how wrong it had gone until it closed my throat and my eyes were stinging.

I read:

Deep in hidden rooms filled with dust
and sour night-breath the lost city is sleeping.

Above the hurt sky is weeping,
soaked nightingales have ceased to sing.

And I must have read it aloud because a voice answered back - and by then I wasn't surprised. He is the lost city and those verses go with him.

"You understand what you have to do now, don't you Finn?"

"There's just no way."

"Look at you. Your mind's falling apart. You've crawled into the underworld - into *my* world - and you know that I can keep you here forever. You know that now, don't you? That there's no escaping me. Not without giving me what I want."

"I said *no*."

"Every change requires sacrifice Finn. There's no rebirth without death. What do you think brought you here tonight? What impulse?" My hands had started shaking. "You see? Every part of you understands this now - every part beyond this last corner of your mind."

"*All I want* is to explain things to her. That's why I came here."

"*All you want* is to be free of me. And you will be soon."

My head was so twisted I could barely see, but somehow I managed to get my hands under enough control to pull out the last bag of speed and sprinkle white crystals on Anne's desk.

"I won't do it," I muttered thickly. "I won't do your bad things."

"Look at yourself," he'd said, softer than ever - and I caught sight of my mud-stained palms as they shaped the crude line.

"You already have."

Could I be lower than this? A frightened moan escaped me; a not-quite-convincing-myself cry of denial.

"You're going to do it," came the gutter voice inside my head - but there was only one thing I could think to do: I pulled the strings of snot from my nose with muddy fingers and snuffed the line up hard.

That stuff wasn't working like it used to though. As the familiar burn shot up my sinus the voice scattered and dispersed, but didn't quite leave. It simply climbed the register into white noise; incomprehensible, but still there. I put my head in my hands and gulped for air.

It's funny, but in the end it was the painting that calmed me down. It was the same one that made it seem okay to tell Anne about my weird mental history on that night we took e. She has blonde hair, the lady in the painting - it stands out bright against a faded orange background - and she's looking over her shoulder, which is bare, and the whole thing's very kitschy. But ever since that one magic night I've always liked that picture.

"I should just go," I told her. But her pretty painted eyes kept giving their warm look, making me think it would be alright to stay. Then I heard the door downstairs - and then footsteps coming up.

Someone put a bag down in the kitchen; the taps ran - a guilty impulse made me want to dash for the window - and then the bedroom door opened. Anne stepped in, saw me, and stopped dead.

"Jesus you gave me a fright."

She stayed standing in the doorway.

"How did you get in?"

"I... you left the key out. Under the flowerpot."

"No I didn't."

"No I mean, last time." I was confused. "That was last time. I came in the window. I wanted to see you so I climbed in here."

She glanced at the window, and then the desk, taking in the faint dust of white and the open book.

"You weren't so keen to see me last time. When you kicked me out."

"I... I wanted to tell you something."

"Okay."

She stayed where she was.

"I'm finishing Miles' application tonight. It's almost perfect. We present it tomorrow afternoon. That's not what I wanted to tell you though."

I wished I couldn't hear that whispering on the fringes. It was so hard to think.

"What I wanted to say was sorry. About kicking you out. And being weird. I haven't been..."

So hard to say it.

"...I haven't been right lately."

"Oh Finn. What's wrong?"

"It was never work that made me stay away from you..." I pinched tears away from the bridge of my nose. "I don't think I'm safe."

She'd stepped forward to comfort me.

"Don't. *Don't*. I need to go. I just wanted to explain." I flicked a glance up at the painting's eyes. It calmed me a little and I sighed, resigned to telling all.

"You remember the poem you read me that night? I don't know why,

Anne, but it meant a lot to me. That night meant a lot and I wanted to understand, so I read the story - about Eurydice and Orpheus. And I guess... it's so hard to put into words. But it all just kind of got mixed up in my head. Does that make sense?"

Her mouth was an upside-down u.

"I had this idea that I was going to lose you. That how it was in the poem was how it would be with us. I think... I think I thought that someone like me was always going to lose someone like you."

"Someone like you?" She said gently, bending her head to catch my lowered eyes. "Someone like you - the gentlest man? Someone who makes me feel so calm?"

And I bent my head, ashamed.

"It all got so mixed up Anne. I think..." and the next words came out thickly. "...that I got crazy."

Say it, Finn. If she understands, you can make her safe.

"I got so crazy that I thought the only way I could get better was if I lost you. Lost you forever."

I couldn't look at her eyes. But I knew the meaning of my words was sinking in.

"I think you should go."

"I think I should."

I stepped around her with my head down. She couldn't help flinching as I passed, and that broke my heart, but my head felt a little clearer - as if the lurking presence had somehow relaxed its grip on my brain. I paused at the door from her room.

"I'm just not safe Anne. I'm *so* sorry. I need to get right and I can't be around you. But I still need to know. Would there ever be a chance for us?"

She made a tiny hurt sound.

"I mean," I went on hurriedly, "if I were well. It's just... Well, even if there is no chance, it's good to hope."

"Hope?"

I glanced up and was surprised to see her face scrunched with grief.

"For you Finn, *always*.

"But just right now?"

And she looked me in the eye and shook her head. I nodded and though there was a ball of hurt inside my chest I did feel myself lighten; breathe easier. Perhaps, I thought, I'd found a way to keep Anne safe and escape the voice as well - to forestall his revenge. Could I be blamed if in the moment I forgot all about Kip?

I nodded at her, stole a last glance at the painting, and walked out. I was halfway down the stairs when Anne called out "hey."

"Hey, you guessed right by the way," she said from the top step. There was a kind of resignation in her voice.

"I'm an art teacher. I teach rich kids how to paint."

And so the game ends.

"You know I thought you might be. But there was never any paint on your hands?"

"You heard of this thing called soap?"

I smiled back despite myself.

"Goodbye Anne."

***

The van comes to a stop. I hear Trade graunch the handbrake on and get out, then the van's side door is hauled open. I blink in the light.

"Here we are sunshine. Hop out."

"There's a bag behind him. Pass it over," says Kip.

I get out and Trade fishes around behind me for the backpack.

Over the road is an imposing church, the spitting image of St Matthews in Brixton; it's even set on a narrow wedge of garden at the meeting of two roads like the Brixton Peace Gardens. The dark clouds are closer - a few drops of rain begin a *pink pink punk* on the van roof.

"Where are we?" I venture.

"Norwood, you muppet. Call yourself a South Londoner? That's St Lukes." Kip shoulders his backpack.

"You sure this is a good idea?" says Trade, wiping a raindrop from his lashes.

"We won't be down there long. It's only two miles to the shop as the crow flies. A bit more as the turd floats." Trade grins. "Come on. Over the road," snaps Kip - and Trade hustles me through the busy traffic, keeping a painful grip on my elbow. On the far side Kip leads us down a lane near the rear of the church, by a sign that says 'South London Theatre'.

There's no one around. An overgrown tree hides us from the main road. Kip walks past the theatre entrance - it's a motley looking place - and vaults the low fence into the back of the church grounds.

Trade and I follow - there's no need for the elbow-grip now, I get the picture - and we find Kip crouched over a square manhole cover in the shade of a tree. There's a padlock, but he has a key, and the metal cap levers off with no trouble. Kip puts on a headlamp, grinning like a Cheshire cat and tells Trade to give me a torch.

Trade holds the manhole open and prods me with my light: a bulky flashlight sealed in a zip-lock plastic bag.

"See you at the shop" grins Kip and lowers himself into the blackness, feet ringing out on steel rungs.

"Down you go pal," says Trade. "Next stop, Brixton. And good luck with your swim," he adds conspiratorially.

Short of anything else to do, and still feeling stunned by this afternoon, I take the torch and lower myself clumsily into the hole. The cover booms shut above me. It's completely dark and I hang for a moment on the ladder, confused. I hear the padlock snick above me.

"Come on old bean," calls out Kip. "We're on a time budget. Can't wait for the rain to wash through here."

He clicks his headlamp on, and points it at the ladder so I can work my way down. Eventually my trainers splash into ankle-deep water running over pebbles.

"That's the lad. We're heading downstream."

I switch on my light through the plastic bag - it casts a fat yellow circle - and look around.

We're inside a large oval sewer. Well above my head is a perfect arch of mossy bricks, with the ladder ascending through a hole in the ceiling. The water around my feet is brownish - not murky brown; more tea coloured - and it smells cleaner than you'd think, though the odd bloated tampon and plastic bag gets picked out white in the light. Down the tunnel Kip's back is disappearing into the gloom, foam sloshing around his feet as he walks.

For a moment I watch the light from his much brighter headlamp wobble and shrink as he travels down the tunnel - then claustrophobia crowds around and I dash to catch up. When I reach him, he's lecturing; not caring whether I listen or not.

"...we're in the Norwood Branch Sewer. It was built in the mid 1850s - and it's nothing to write home about - the older stuff's all further down..."

And he chatters on, happy at the sound of his own voice.

I follow him, feeling disoriented by the dark, scatter-brained, and after a while of stumbling as I try to keep up, I begin to feel that something else is down here.

Definitely there's something's here. I keep swinging the flashlight to check behind me, but that makes it worse. Soon the water I'm wading in takes on a sinister feel in the way it wraps around my legs, and before long the whole conduit rings with his presence; with his watching and waiting. We pass narrow pipes and other tunnels that merge with our own and I have to hurry past their open mouths, latching on to Kip's voice to stop my fear going free-fall once again.

"Here we go," he says and he pulls up short. I step into the back of him.

"Easy tiger. Look at that."

We've come to a Y-junction. The tunnel splits in two with the right half going down a series of steps which spill into a further chamber done in modern yellow brick; while the left, carrying the majority of the water, turns into something that looks as much cave as sewer. There's brickwork up the walls, but the roof is raw rock.

"Guess which way we're going?" says Kip, and wades left. I hurry on his heels for another five minutes until the blackness beyond the torchlight is unbearable.

"Please Kip - where are we going? What's this about?"

He comes to another halt.

"It's all about the Effra," he says into a darkness thick with presence - and what I can see beyond him terrifies me.

About twenty feet ahead of us the roof drops down until it's barely three inches above the water. The current, meanwhile, grows suddenly deeper and faster in the narrow space. Peering down the gap between the water and the rock roof I can see that it bends to the right just at the limit of the light - but whether it opens into a breathing space or goes totally underground is anyone's guess. The only way to find out would be to let the current carry you down; and the only possible outcome if the roof didn't open again would be death.

"Tantalizing, huh? The right-hand branch, the one we passed back there, it's no good to us. That carries on under Dulwich, all the way to New Cross. But this..." Kip fishes a plastic-wrapped map from his jacket pocket "...this is the beginning of the Effra Sewer. What you're standing in now is the old Effra river, and if we can follow it from here it will take us right underneath the Shop."

I shiver. There's a tone in his voice I don't like.

"See, I came down here last week, but this is as far as I got. For a moment I even thought about testing my luck trying to float down, but Jesus! You'd have to be mental. That got me wondering though: who *would* be crazy enough to try?"

He looks at me and the head-torch makes me blink. The glare blots out most of his expression, but I can still see his open mouth and white teeth.

"Who," he carries on softly, "would be prepared to go down there on the end of a rope? Would Trade do it? *No*, I thought. Trade's too fussy about his clothes. Plus he's got that thing about drowning. And then I remembered my old pal Finn…"

"There's no way..."

"Think of it as a special treat," he says with slow menace. "For trying to make a fool of me in my favourite pub."

"No fucking way…"

My voice sounds weak. Kip just shrugs off his backpack to produce a coil of rope and a set of steel bolt-cutters.

"There's no *other* way."

He takes a step forward, hoisting the bolt-cutters menacingly, and throws the coil of rope into my chest.

"So be a good boy and tie this round you. Jump on in, let the current wash you round the corner, and if there's space to breathe then tug on the rope three times so I know to follow. But if you get to the end of the rope and there's still no air, tug on it frantically for a minute or two like you're drowning, then just lean on it with a dead weight.

"Got that old bean?"

We're facing each other at the mouth of the cavern, him with the bolt-cutters - me clutching the rope to my chest.

I make a burst back down the tunnel.

There's no thinking - just a sudden thrash of feet in water and the knowledge that it's the only chance, that to go down that sucking channel is my death. Light lurches behind me - my shadow leaps huge across the wall - then there's a crippling pain in the side of my knee and I'm down in the shallows, Kip's bolt-cutters wedged against my throat, shoving my head under.

His face is insane with fury. "You! Are going! Down -" he spits as he straddles me, spindly legs scrabbling for purchase in the gravel as he crushes the steel bar into my windpipe.

"You! Are going! Down!"

With every word he bounces the bolt cutters into my neck, shoving my face under the water. But I'm not afraid anymore.

From beneath the water I see Kip's wavering halo and feel a new calm steal into me. A kind of catatonia creeps inside - the end result of weeks of grief and insanity - as I accept that here, in the Effra's very veins, I'll make my own journey into the underworld.

Kip hauls my head above water.

He looks baffled at my sudden limp compliance. Around me a vast presence has crystalised. I give myself to it utterly.

Kip reaches over me to retrieve the sodden rope and offers the end silently. We lay there for a moment - he still straddling my chest, me staring dull-eyed - until I take the rope. Kip staggers off me and I knot it under my arms.

"Good boy," he whispers. "Good boy," and it sounds like what he's done frightens him a little. He reaches around me to check the knot and it's strangely comforting; like some echo of being dressed as a child.

"Yeah, that should hold you. So then," he says flatly, handing me back my torch from where I'd dropped it and wrapping the other end of the rope around his hand. "In your own time..."

I turn to look at the mouth of the cave.

It's sucking greedily at the bouncing water. Has the level risen since we arrived?

"Do it!" yells Kip above the sound of the current and I feel the presence around us hold its breath.

I take a step into the flow.

Instantly the water surges over my knees. It pushes and tugs at the same time, making it hard to balance, and Kip takes up the slack in the rope to give me something to lean against. I wade further in until the ceiling is low over my head and the water reaches my hips. My hand flails up trying to brace a palm against the roof, but it's slick with a white crust of fat and I slip off, stumbling up to my chest and gasping at the cold.

The rope's the only thing holding me up now, but Kip keeps laying it out, hand over hand, forcing me forward. The pressure wave behind me threatens to wobble me off my feet; the mouth is right in front of me now. Orpheus into the underworld. Oh God I'm going to die here. And I scrabble again for the ceiling just as Kip jerks out more slack. I lose my footing, and then I'm under and all resistance drops away as I'm swept down by the current.

The sensation is surreal. Traveling at the same speed as the water, it's like I've stopped moving. There's just a faint forward vertigo, almost like falling asleep, along with a sensation of bathing in a panic so complete that it's almost soothing. *So this is drowning* I think absently - until with a tremendous jolt the rope comes tight around my middle and all the air shoots from my lungs. The torch is flung out of my hand; I gag and kick and my feet hit something - stones - my arms thrash wildly and with a great sucking breath I manage to stand up in water that's waist high and moving slowly. I stagger to the side.

It's utterly dark. After a while I remember to tug on the rope three times and barely a minute later a faint light shimmers at the upstream end of the pool as Kip's head pops up like an otter.

"Fucking hell. This is huge!"

Kip wades up the pebbly beach and sits next to me, gazing around the cavern.

All semblance to a Victorian sewer is gone. We're in a wide chamber with a low rock roof - and all around me is a slow, rhythmic breathing. Kip might be in a London drainage system, but I know that I've come to a different place.

How many people ever see this, I marvel to myself. And how many ever make it out? I think back to his words in Anne's room last night. There's no rebirth without death, he'd told me. Every change requires sacrifice - and I wonder if our deal could still be satisfied. Now, with my feet on the path he has laid out for me, all things seem possible. Could I yet escape this place for good?

Kip starts shaking my shoulders vigorously, suddenly chummy.

"Gee old mucker! Ain't this great? But you can't do the thousand-yard stare all afternoon, you know. Water's rising. We've got to go. It would be a shame to meet a sticky end after you made it through that."

Looking about, his headlamp picks out a partly-bricked exit tunnel and he heaves up and slops towards it, beginning to lecture again. I watch him go, an idea taking shape in my head.

"You see, I discovered we had an entrance to the main Effra sewer under the shop quite some time back. For a while I got carried away in the romance of having a buried river under the house, but beyond that, I couldn't think of a practical use for the knowledge. I even tried exploring from the shop end, but it stunk the house out.

"Then a few months back, Timmy got busted. He was caught with half an ounce of weed down his pants - and luckily the silly prick kept mum about the shop - but now I'm sure they know where he was headed. It got me thinking..."

His voice is fading. I'm not afraid to be in here now, but I hurry to follow Kip as if pursuing a last glimmer of hope.

"...I found the outfall for the Effra at Thames embankment. Got right down on the mud flats - that's what gave me the idea for the party you know - but the entrance is locked up tight and what with being at Vauxhall bridge, right under M16 and all, the whole area's under heavy surveillance. What I'm after, see, is a way of getting into the shop without going through the front door, because after Timmy got busted and then the attention from the party I'm dead sure that we're being watched.

"Issue being, I've got a bit more than just weed and old veges coming in soon. That lovely meth you've been sampling? Pretty soon I'm having a big load brought in from Amsterdam - and I'll be fucked if I'm walking it through the front door to get busted.

We're wading waist deep now, the odd rat splashing away from the torch beam; turds and kitchen peel floating by.

"So I started looking for an upstream entrance. At first I stayed above ground, trying to follow the route of the old Effra - you can see it sometimes if you know where to look. There'll be a strip of moss up the side of some buildings. Or a smell. And it's always near cheap houses, because it makes them damp. Get this: the underground rivers trace lines where the plague struck hardest. And tuberculosis. Ghost sightings, even. But anyway, that all came to nothing - there was too much guesswork involved.

"But then you Finn, you little prick, you came along with your books and got me thinking about the library. So I went and signed up and bugger me if there aren't records for this whole area. I found sewer maps - old ones at least - plus that entrance to the Effra in the Norwood church yard."

The passage that we're moving down has narrowed again into formal brickwork, and we've reached a metal grill that blocks our path. There's no way past.

"So the upshot of what we're doing here today," continues Kip, "is we're working out a safe route for my supplies. And *you* - you're my mine canary. Now. How do we deal with this?"

The current rushes past us through the grill and drops about four feet into a broad pool with an arched ceiling. On the other side three tunnels lead away. Wedged against the grill is the plastic bag with my torch in it. Kip fishes it out and tests the switch - it's broken. He tosses it through.

"Hmm."

He begins probing with the bolt-cutters.

The ironwork must be 200 years old. He scrapes at the shroud of fat and hair around the bars to reveal a rusty section underneath. The cutters snip through with no trouble and he tosses one bar and then another through the growing gap. While he works I watch the flow coming towards us, mesmerized by the movement, feeling detached and dreamy. Though I do notice the mix of detritus is changing. There are leaves and twigs in it; rubbish that's been washed off the streets. It must be bucketing down above.

Kip tosses the last bar through and slips the bolt cutters back in the bag.

"Current's definitely stronger."

He checks his plastic-sealed map.

"We take the tunnel in the middle. It's not far now though. My guess is this runs a short way. After that we'll be under Effra Road, and from there it's the home straight to the Shop. We better get moving though - through you go!"

I lower myself into the pool, where the water is up to my chest. Kip follows nimbly and sets off, a white wake breaking before him. There's a fresh smell that wasn't there before.

"Look at me! I've found my own personal smuggling tunnels - perfect for bringing in all my goodies.

"Oh and about that, by the way." He loops an arm over my shoulder. "You might want to think about your consumption. At the rate you're using, you're going to fry that little brain. Cause you're a bit funny on the speed, aren't you? I think you got yourself hooked pretty bad. Probably it's about time you took a break. So you know what Finnegan? I'm going to make it easy for you and just cut your supply right off."

Kip stops and turns to face me.

"Consider it a bond on good behaviour. You play nice about what happened down here today and after a while... well." He shrugs. "The supply might come back on."

"Fuck you and your bargains," I shoot back angrily - jolted out of this trance by his threat. "I'm not getting it through you. I can get what I want, when I want."

"Hahaha! You mean from Henry? Oh you silly little man." Kip leans in smiling viciously.
"Who do you think brings it in for *me*?

"You never worked that part out, did you? No, our Henry - he likes to keep his hands clean on the sale side. But mine mate -" he holds them up, fingers wriggling " - they're *always* dirty."

Anger flares in me and I thrash the water in impotent rage. Kip sloshes on down the sewer, oblivious, back to being breezy.

"Don't worry old pal, I know all about your little arrangement with Henry. And if I feel like it," he glances back at me to snap his fingers. "Then your supply is -" but his face spasms and the word *gone* gets gargled into the water as he lurches forward. He flails, finds his footing and comes coughing upwards - clearly in pain.

"Fuck! Oh, Jesus. My goddamned ankle! *Shit.*"

I stop and watch him. One foot seems stuck in something, and with the current behind him and only one good leg to brace with, he's struggling to stay up.

"I'm fucking stuck."

I watch him mutely.

He pushes himself into a more stable stance with his free leg, then tries to run his hands down his thighs to reach his ankle. He can't get low enough, though, without putting his face under. He tries yanking on his trouser leg a couple of times, but all that does is mess up his balance. I see his eyes flick side-to-side as he thinks, then he sucks three deep breaths in quick succession and ducks himself under the water.

Gloom crowds round me, though I can see his red jacket through the murk and the eerie white of the headlamp. It's only moments before he comes up again, gasping.

"It's wedged proper," he explains, as if he hadn't been holding my life to ransom just moments ago. "My ankle's stuck in a grill."

He gulps and goes under again, this time for much longer. His back jerks and thrashes as he tries to pull himself free and when he comes to the surface he flails as he gasps for air, ragged and desperate. Eventually he manages to hold himself upright and waits there, pulling in oxygen and calming himself as he tries to think. His eyes flick to me.

"Get the bolt-cutters. They're in the bag."

Kip's facing downstream so, mutely obedient, I wade behind him and get the pack unzipped. Even moving that far in the current takes effort. I fish them out and step back in front. The water's breaking around my armpits.

Kip eyes me as I hand the bolt cutters over, studying my face. Then he draws a breath and goes under.

This time he seems calmer, his movements underwater more deliberate as he tries to wedge the cutters under his foot. It's quiet when he's down. I look up at the ceiling and in the pearly glow cast by the submerged lamp, well above our heads, I can just make out the high water line left by storms past. My idea takes final shape.

"Would this be enough?" I ask softly, and the words are swallowed up by the tunnel.

Kip heaves up again, gasps, then dives under. His movements are becoming frantic and in the white-lit murk I see a puff of red roil away. When he surfaces he's wide-eyed and desperate. Truly frightened now. It takes him a long time to be able to speak.

"Don't just fucking stand there," he pants, angry and scared. "Think of something. It won't budge! I can't get it out. *Think of something* you moon-eyed cunt!"

"Like what?"

I can tell he's struggling to avoid panic.

"The bars. The bars we cut out and dropped in the pool. Listen: my foot is wedged into a grill, I think the ankle's broken -" he wobbles forward and has to stop talking until he gets his balance or else swallow water "- and there's nothing to lever the bolt-cutters against. But if you find one of the bars from the pool - are you listening? If you get one of the bars and lay it across the grill, you'll be able to put the cutters over it, get them under my foot and pop it up. Do you understand? *Do you!?*"

"Of course. But you need to give me the lamp."

We stand there for a moment facing each other - me with my hand out, him watching my face; a mirror of ourselves at the tunnel mouth when we both thought I would drown.

He pulls the lamp off his head and passes it to me.

"And the cutters."

He hands them over. I take a step back. He watches me adjust the light over my head.

You can't look back, I think, as my hands run on auto-pilot, adjusting the straps. You can't look back.

"Finn?"

His face is white and frightened in the torchlight. He's blinking as he tries to see my eyes.

"Will this close the deal?" I call down the long cavern - and my voice comes echoing back from the sewer's curving roof.

"Is it enough!"

Enough, enough…

"Of course it is!" Kip brays desperately, as if answering for them both.

"Please. *Please* just do it!"

I swing the bolt-cutters.

The heavy hinge connects with his skull with a comic-book *clonk* and he makes a cry that splutters as his face goes under. He comes up and I hit him again - harder - and again until his head opens like a chrysanthemum. I hit him until he's limp and his torso rag-dolls in the current, then I toss the bolt-cutters into the water.

A great sigh seems to fall from the air. From up ahead comes a rushing sound - the unmistakable noise of water moving in a torrent down the tunnel. I take a last look at Kip - his mouth is making spasmodic gulps beneath the water - then I fall back into the water and let the current take me.

Soon I'm far down the tunnel. I twist upright and kick to find the floor. My feet bounce me off the bottom and I travel like that at great pace, the current hurrying me along as I make great moon-strides, feeling almost weightless suddenly. Free.

As the current draws me with it I notice another flow moving in the opposite direction - back upstream to where I left Kip lolling. Something seems to be drawing out of me, withdrawing from the world and leaving behind both a clarity and forgetfulness. Soon, I sense, the details of what happened here will fade from me, like a dream that gets harder to recall as the day goes on, and I give myself up to the current again.

Eventually the sight of a ladder dropping from a neatly bricked hole in the ceiling jolts me out of my reverie. I lunge for it and manage to haul myself on to the lower rungs, knocking off chunks of toilet-paper-mache as I pull my sodden bulk from the stream. I climb upwards, heading for the surface, and as I leave the Effra's tunnel I hear a voice, faint and weak, calling to me.

"Please," I hear. "Please don't leave me here Finn. Please come back."

Kip?

I pause on the ladder. The temptation to turn around is strong, but I close my eyes against it and grip tight.

Everything I have to live for is up above me. There's nothing for me down below. I call up a picture of the future and see me in it, clear and sane, and let myself imagine the faint possibility of *her* again - that warm room; the wry smile - until my limbs find their motion. They pull me up out of the underworld as the voice follows behind; plucking and pulling at me like a phantom as I clamber into the first faint hints of light.

Even when I shoulder open a manhole cover, slithering out into the cold rain in some marshy corner of Brockwell Park, I can still hear the tiny sound behind me - a desperate ghost begging me to save him.

Please, I hear it faintly. *Please...*

But I know this story now. I know what I want.

I don't look back.

ABOUT THE AUTHOR

A fiction writer, journalist and editor, Greg Roughan's notable articles range from an investigation of the quirky-yet-true history of occultism in New Zealand, to an account of a first-time hunter's kill.

He is currently writing a young adult series about a British girl kidnapped in the Far East. The first two books, *The Valley Apart* and *A Subtle Way* are out now, and the third – titled *Kushan Empire* – is under way.

Greg lives in Auckland with his wife and their two lovely daughters. He has a passion for the outdoors, which these days mostly means hunting red deer or free-diving (and spearfishing) in the waters around New Zealand.

Visit www.gregroughan.com or follow GregRoughan.com on Facebook to stay up to date.